THE VIEW FROM A RUSTY TRAIN CAR

DeeJay Arens

The View From A Rusty Train Car
By DeeJay Arens

The View From A Rusty Train Car is a work of fiction. Names, characters, places, and incidents are either the product of the author's imagination or are used fictitiously. Any resemblance to actual persons, living or dead, business establishments, events or locales is entirely coincidental.

Published by Writers AMuse Me Publishing, August 2012 (British Columbia/Boston/Los Angeles)

© Copyright 2012 by DeeJay Arens
Cover © Kurkul/Dreamstime.com, Leciaphinney/ Dreamstime.com

All rights reserved. No part of this book may be used or reproduced in any manner whatsoever without written permission except in the case of brief quotations embodied in critical articles or reviews. Visit and/or contact us through our website at www.WritersAMuseMe.com.

ISBN-13:978-1-927044-34-6
ISBN-10:1927044340

DEDICATION

Anything I've accomplished is only because I've been lucky enough to be surrounded by amazing, incredible people. This book is no exception. I would like to thank the remarkable people I am proud to call family and friends for their love, support, and encouragement.

As always there are certain people that deserve a special note of thanks.
Paula: Thank you for loving this story and pushing for it to be shared.
Dave: Thank you for being the master who's surrounded himself with the best and for being an all-around amazing person.
June: My inspiration. Thank you for giving me hope, encouragement, and pointing me to the wonderful people that are WAMM.
Jax, Bettina, Jules, and Heidi: Your love and knowledge kept me constantly striving to become a writer. Thank you for loving the story as much as I do.
Mary: My muse in human form. Thank you for holding me up, pushing me, teaching me the craft and for being there as my editor, friend, and sister.
To my parents, sisters, brothers, nieces and nephews: Thank you for your unconditional love and for being a source of inspiration.

Finally, thank you Steve, for "every day". You've given me more than anyone could promise. Thank you for making life an adventure.

.

I AM WHAT I AM

"No one talks about what happens when you fall in love with the boy next door -- not when you're the boy living beside the boy next door. You just know that you can't even ask. You can't talk about it. Even though Mom says to forget about girls and focus on studying, you know she can't wait for you to bring a girl home. She wants to plan the proms and think about what the grandchildren will look like. Parents don't plan for their son to bring home the 'man' he loves. I don't understand why people get so angry about it. Why does it bother them? It has nothing to do with them." Luke caressed Jared's arm and took a deep breath. "I don't care what they think. I know what I want." He ran his fingers through Jared's hair. "It's just that simple. I love you!"

Jared pulled away. "But it's not that simple, is it? None of this has ever been simple. It should be. Everybody else gets to fall in love with who they want and go on double dates with their friends. What do we get? We get to hide in here -- a rusty old train car. We steal moments when no one's looking. We constantly have to look over our shoulders to see if anyone's watching. God forbid someone should see us or figure us out. What if they do? Then what?" He pointed to his bruised eye. "This. Or worse. We'd be hated by everyone, including our own families." He grasped Luke's hand, looked him in the eyes. "He could have killed me, Luke. And they know we hang out; I'm sure you're on their list." Lying back down on the blanket, he put his hands to his head. "I want this so bad, but I don't know how it will work out. I don't know if it's worth getting us killed."

Luke leaned over him, holding Jared's face. "I don't know either. We can try to figure it out, right? Maybe we just do what we can to survive until we can leave here. Leave everything behind us. There are other places... places where it will be easier for us to be together. We've only got one more year of school left then we're free. It'll go by fast."

"Maybe. I just don't want you to have to go through all of this when you're not sure about it. I couldn't stand if something happened to you. I'd feel responsible. Maybe you should just try... you know... to find a girl."

"No! I can take care of myself. I don't want that. What can I do to prove to you that it's just you? All I want is you."

Jared smiled, leaning his head against Luke's chest. "I just don't know."

Luke thought for a moment, his heart racing. Without thinking, the words came out of his mouth. "Let me make love to you."

Jared jumped away. "What? No! We can't!"

Luke ran his hand down Jared's arm. "Why not? I love you. I always have."

"I just don't know if it's..."

Luke held his finger against Jared's lips. "We're adults now. I can't promise when we'll figure this whole mess out, but I need this. I want this." Kneeling in front of Jared, he gave a reassuring, but nervous smile and kissed him. He started to unbutton Jared's shirt.

Jared laid back, his arms around Luke's neck.

Luke could feel Jared's body trembling, assuring him that Jared was just as nervous. It felt right. It was the right time.

#

THE VIEW FROM A RUSTY TRAIN CAR

What the hell am I doing here? Who cares what Jared Montgomery has to say about anything? The phrase repeated in my mind. I tried reaching for a mint from my pants pocket, inadvertently jamming my finger against the skirt of the oak desk in front of me. Hoping no one noticed, I reached in, unwrapped one, and finally got it into my mouth. There was no moisture left.

I looked toward the front of the room. Everything went out of focus so I looked down at the desk and took a deep breath. Making eye contact with the people in front of me was not an option. One would think I'd be used to it, but it was disconcerting not knowing who was friend or foe.

I got the signal to begin. I sat, pulling my chair in, making sure I was close to the microphone. When I opened my mouth, nothing came out so I reached for my glass of water. Taking a drink, I closed my eyes, and forced another deep breath.

"I want to be clear that I'm not here for the pleasure of reliving this story. I suspect many of you are already uncomfortable and I've just begun. The fact is I've spent a lot of time trying to put these memories to rest, but I can't. Not to say there weren't some wonderful memories; there were many incredible memories, but they are quickly overtaken by the sad ones. Thinking back, I know that neither of us was really aware of how prophetic Luke's words were that evening. We were both eighteen years old. We should've been worrying about what movie to see, or whose party we should go to, not thinking about how to survive. Why am I here? I'm here because I need people to understand that their words and their actions have consequences whether they realize it or not. I need people to understand that my love for Luke was not some perversion, nor was it something evil. It was real and true, just like many relationships that are happening every day between two people who love each other who happen to be members of the same sex." I cleared my throat in an effort to maintain control of my emotions. "Loving him wasn't difficult. It was trying to create a life together that proved complicated."

NEW BEGINNING

March, 1987

Jared watched the trees and power lines go by from the window of his family's white Chevrolet Caprice. He became more eager as they got closer to their new house, which was located on the edge of town. His parents had finally been able to afford to build the house they'd always wanted. He was excited to get his own room. He got to choose the carpet and the color of the walls. He'd no longer have to sleep in the cold drafty upstairs room in the old farm house they'd been living in.

As the car pulled into the driveway, he shifted in his seat in the back of the car. He looked over to his sister Megan, who was thirteen, to see her reaction. She smiled back at him and looked through her window.

The car came to a stop. Jared wiggled out of his seat and ran to the front door. Megan followed.

"Megan! Open the door!" He stood on his toes, trying to look over her shoulder to see through the window.

"I can't! It's locked! Stop pushing!" She shoved Jared backwards to get some space.

Jared turned, running toward the car. "Mom! Dad! The door is locked!"

Their dad, Michael, took boxes from the trunk. "Jared! Settle down. Help your mom and I get these things in the house."

"Megan, you too." Candace, their mom, motioned for them. "We have to get things arranged before Aunty Grace and Uncle Rick get here with the truck."

Jared ran to the trunk of the car and loaded his arms with small boxes. Megan had followed him, picking up some small items that had fallen out of the boxes into the trunk. He arrived at the door just as his dad unlocked it.

He'd come with his parents a few times to see the house while it was being built, but now the walls had been painted and the carpet and new appliances had been installed.

He watched Megan run down the stairs to the basement. Since she was the older of the two, her bedroom was downstairs while Jared's was upstairs by his parent's bedroom. When he got older he'd be able to take the other bedroom downstairs.

Jared ran up the stairs to his bedroom, wondering if it would look like he'd been dreaming it would. He was filled with excitement as he looked around the empty room. It was perfect, just the way he had wanted it to look. He thought about how he was going to set it up.

Jared and Megan laughed as they ran around their new house. They raced up and down the stairs, checking out every room. When they entered the kitchen, they knocked a box out of Candace's hands.

"That's it!" Candace pointed to the door. "If you're not going to help, then go somewhere and stay out of the way!"

They ran over to pick up the contents that had fallen to the floor.

Candace looked out the window. "Jared, go outside and play. There's a little boy across the street. Go introduce yourself. Megan, you go too."

Jared studied the boy staring toward his house. He appeared to be around Jared's age. Once outside, Jared met his gaze. He was now standing at the road. Jared looked down, but gave him a shy smile.

Megan nudged Jared. "Go say 'hi'."

"No. I don't want to." He looked down at the stones he was unconsciously kicking around. Jared wanted to meet new kids in the neighborhood. That was half of the excitement of moving to a new place. He cursed his shy nature. He wasn't use to meeting new people.

"Go! Don't be such a big baby." Megan grabbed his shoulders and pushed him toward the road. "Mom said!"

"Come with me," Jared mumbled, staring down at the stones he was unconsciously kicking around. He glanced at the boy whose wide eyes were focused on him. *Does he even want to meet me?*

As the standoff continued, four girls came around the corner and walk toward them. They all appeared to be around Megan's age.

"Hi, Luke," one of them called, waving to the boy standing in front of them.

Luke held his hand above his eyes to shield them from the sun. "Hey, Jenny. Hey, Carrie."

The girls stopped in front of Jared and Megan. One of them took the initiative, offering her hand. "Hi, I'm Jenny. Are you moving in here?"

Jared looked to Megan who answered her. "Yes, we are. My name's Megan."

Jared struggled as Megan took his hand and offered it to the girls. "This is my little brother, Jared."

"Hi." Jenny shook his hand. She pointed at each girl in the group, introducing them. "This is Carrie, Bonnie, and Shannon."

Carrie pointed across the street to the boy who had been the cause of debate a few minutes earlier. "That's my cousin, Luke."

Luke waved and smiled.

"Hey, Megan! Do you want to come with us? We're going to Bonnie's house to listen to the radio and play some games." Shannon looked at Jared. "We'd ask you, but it's just going to be us girls."

Megan's face dropped. "Maybe some other time. I should stay with my little brother."

"No!" Jared's head popped up. "Go ahead. I'm okay."

Megan smiled. She touched his arm and headed to the door. "Okay, but I have to go tell my parents. Do you guys wanna come in and see our house?"

The group followed her into the house. Jared and Luke kept their posts facing each other in their respective driveways. Neither said a word.

After a few minutes the door opened again; Megan and the girls came out of the house. Their chatter continued as they walked down the driveway. Megan stopped in front of Jared. "I'll be back in a little while. Go play with Luke!"

Luke was sitting on the curb, looking down the road. Jared couldn't muster the courage to walk over to talk to him. He paced in front of his driveway, sneaking peeks to see if Luke had moved. When he noticed Luke was gone, he was momentarily disappointed, but mostly he was relieved. "What would I have said to him anyway?" He turned to go back inside and almost ran head-on into Luke.

Jared felt the blood rush to his face as they made eye contact. Unable to say anything he looked down at his feet.

"Hi! I'm Luke. So this is your new house?"

Jared froze with nervousness. He managed a quick, "Yep."

"Cool! So what do you like to do?"

Jared met his gaze and smiled. "I don't know. Anything."

"Do you play baseball?"

"Not really. I'm not very good at sports."

Luke looked puzzled then broke into a smile. "What do you do?"

THE VIEW FROM A RUSTY TRAIN CAR

"I like to read... and play Nintendo." Jared put his hands in his pockets.

Luke's face lit up. "I love Nintendo. I have about twenty games, but mine isn't working right now."

"Wanna go see if mine's here yet?"

"Sure!" Luke smiled, standing in front of Jared. "Do you wanna see something cool first?

"Sure."

"Come on." Luke led Jared through some tall grass in his back yard, along a row of aspen trees, across a gravel road, and into a junkyard. It looked like a cemetery. Jared saw the remains of a few large machines, the bones of old farm equipment, a semi that lay in pieces, and a large truck that was smashed on all sides. It felt like they had run into another world.

Luke stopped at a large tree and pointed down to an old rusty train car. "Look at that! Isn't it cool? Come on!"

Jared followed Luke as he ran toward the faded brown, time-worn train car. He wondered what its purpose had been when it was being used. It didn't appear to be meant for passengers. It must have hauled something like grain, water, or other farm supplies. Its sides were filled with pin-sized rust holes. It looked like it had been there so long that the back end had sunk into the ground.

Jared stared at it. "Wow!"

"Isn't it great?" Luke grabbed onto the ladder that was bolted on the side of the car and started to climb up.

"Are you sure we can do this?" Jared looked around. *We are going to be in so much trouble!*

"My mom says I'm not supposed to, but no one's ever caught me. I've never seen anyone else here. Come on! It's cool in here!"

"Inside?" There was no way he could go inside it. He took his hands off the ladder and stepped back, looking around to see if anyone was watching them. He was ready to run at the first sign of trouble. He jumped when he heard a noise.

"Jared? Where'd you go?"

"Down here. On the ground." He looked up at Luke who'd crawled to the edge, looking down at him.

"What's the matter?"

"I don't think we should be in there."

"Come on! It's all right. Just trust me."

Jared thought it over one more time. It was against his better judgment, but he decided it was worth a try. He'd never been this close to a train car. He just had to see what it was like on the inside. If Luke said it was okay then it must be. He somehow felt like he could trust him.

Jared gave Luke a nervous smile, starting up the ladder. When he reached the top he lost his footing, nearly falling off the rounded side. His new friend caught his arm, pulling him back.

Jared shook as he lay on the top of the car. The panic subsided and he stood. His legs felt like rubber from the near fall and he almost lost his balance again. He caught himself by grabbing the hatch cover. His heart was beating fast. He looked over at Luke and noticed he had turned white as a ghost. He laughed once he realized he was secure. "That was a close one!"

Luke laughed, the color returning to his face.

Jared looked over the edge into the train car. "Sure is dark in there."

"You'll get used to it. You go first." Luke grinned.

Jared was puzzled as to how to maneuver his way inside.

"There's another ladder on the front of the hole." Luke took Jared's hand, helping him get situated. "Be careful!"

Jared held on to Luke, searching for something to grab onto with his other hand. He found his footing, caught the rail, and made it to the bottom. He looked up, seeing Luke smiling down at him. "I hope it's a lot easier to get out of here." Jared laughed, waiting as Luke made his way down.

"You worry too much." Luke jumped off the ladder, landing in front of him.

THE VIEW FROM A RUSTY TRAIN CAR

"I know. I'm scared of everything... sort of."

"You're safe with me." Luke reached around Jared's neck, pulling him toward the inner part of the car. "Come on! I'll show you around."

He led Jared around and pointed out each little 'room'. There were four smaller areas with a hallway running through the middle that led to a larger room that made-up the back of the train car.

Jared had a hard time making out all the parts of it because of the dark. "You need to get a light in here."

"I know!" Luke scratched his head. "I haven't figured that out yet."

"My dad has about a hundred flashlights. I can ask him if we could use one."

"Good idea." Luke held on to Jared's hand and fumbled around in front of him to make sure there was nothing in the way.

After the tour was concluded Jared led the way back up the ladder to the top of the train car. Emerging through the hatch, he realized he could see the whole neighborhood from this vantage point. He spied a tree fort just a short distance away. "Is that your fort?"

Luke suddenly became serious. "No! That's Devin's. He lives over there." He pointed to a house in the distance. "His dad is the wrestling coach. They act like they own the world. He's really mean. Don't even go near it, and stay away from him."

Jared's heart raced. "Mean?"

"He likes to beat people up. He's a big jerk! He beat me up a couple times, but I'm not scared of him anymore. I can take him. Don't worry. I won't let him hurt you."

Jared smiled, somehow knowing Luke meant it.

"Look over there!" Luke pointed to a row of trees in the other direction. "See that big tree with the gnarly branch going out over the dirt road by the baseball diamond?"

Jared stood next to Luke, looking toward where he was pointing. "Yeah." His foot slipped a bit.

"You're going to fall one of these times. Hold on to me." Luke reached backwards, taking Jared's hands and putting them on his shoulders.

Jared held on for fear of falling to the ground. His shyness gave way to practicality for safety's sake.

Luke pointed to a tree in the distance. "That's where we're going to build our fort."

Jared stared at the tree as excitement filled him. "I've always wanted a fort!" He put his chin on Luke's shoulder, making sure he was situated so as not to fall. "It's perfect." He was content, thinking about their tree fort, taking in his new surroundings.

Luke broke the silence. "Do you want to see my Nintendo games?"

"Sure." Jared got on his knees with Luke still holding on to him. He crawled to the ladder and climbed down to the ground. Luke followed then they ran toward home. When they reached Luke's driveway, Jared saw Megan and her friends walking down the road.

Megan was motioning and calling to him. "Mom and Dad have been looking for you. It's time to eat." She and her friends headed toward the house.

"We'll be right there. We're just going to look at something." He followed Luke into the garage. They walked up the steps and went into the house. A woman was in the kitchen, unpacking groceries.

"Hi, Mom. I'm showing Jared my Nintendo games. He just moved in the new house. Jared, this is my mom, Ellen. Mom, this is Jared." Luke walked through the kitchen, disappearing into the next room.

Jared wondered if he should follow or stay by the door. He was taught never to go into a house unless invited. However, not knowing Luke's mom, he felt uncomfortable standing in the silence. He decided to go find Luke.

"So..." Ellen stopped him, not looking up from her task. "You just moved in, huh?" She sounded agitated.

"Yes, Ma'am."

"How old are you?"

"Eleven."

"Your family new to the area?"

Jared got more nervous as the inquisition continued. She was angry about something. "No Ma'am, but we did just move into town. We used to live on a farm a couple miles out."

Ellen finally looked at him. "I've never seen you at the school before."

"I go to St. Joseph's, Ma'am. I don't go to Luke's school."

Ellen laughed. "Oh! You're one of *them*. That figures."

Jared was unsure how to respond. He had no idea what she meant. He swallowed hard, reached for the door behind him, preparing to bolt out of the house.

Luke burst back into the room from around the corner carrying a large storage container. "Here they are. I told you I had a lot."

"Luke! For God's sake, don't make a mess. I just got home." She grabbed his arm, stopping him.

"I'm not." He jerked his arm away, nudging Jared toward the door. "I'm just going to give these to Jared until my Nintendo is fixed. God!"

Ellen followed them into the garage. "Where are you going?"

"I'm going over to Jared's." Luke didn't look back at her.

"Fine. Then they can feed you, too." She slammed the door behind them.

Jared was uneasy at what had just happened. He was glad to be heading home. He followed Luke who seemed to be on a mission and who appeared unphased by it all.

"You can eat with us if you want. My parents won't mind," Jared offered as he caught up to him.

"Thanks." Luke smiled. "Then maybe we can play some games."

"Yeah."

Jared led Luke into the house. He was about to introduce Luke to his parents, but Luke marched up to Jared's mom and dad and held out his hand.

"Hi! I'm Luke; Jared's friend."

Candace walked to Luke and shook his hand. "It's nice to meet you. I'm Candace and this is Jared's dad, Mike." She motioned to the container Luke was still holding. "What have you got here?"

"Nintendo games. We want to play them if Jared's Nintendo is unpacked. Mine's broken, so I brought them here."

"Well, I just finished hooking up the TV and Nintendo downstairs in the family room." Mike smiled, patting each of them on the shoulder.

Jared and Luke ran to the stairs. Candace stopped them. "Not until you have some supper! Both of you!"

Jared pulled Luke into the kitchen.

"Wash your hands first." Candace put plates on the counter for them.

After they finished their supper, they ran down to the family room. They laughed and played games for hours.

Luke went to the stack of games then flipped through them. "Now which one?"

"Doesn't matter to me." Jared reached for one, stopping when his mother called down the stairs.

"Luke! I think your mom is calling for you. You'd better get going."

Luke and Jared groaned.

Luke went to the window and waved to his mother who motioned for him to come home. "I guess I better go." He frowned and nodded back at his mother.

Candace shook her head at them. "Boys, for heaven's sake, you can play again tomorrow. It's not the end of the world!"

Jared smiled at Luke. She was right. Tomorrow was Sunday; they could play all day.

Luke said his goodbyes and made his way out the front door. He turned to Jared. "See you tomorrow, Jed!"

"Jed?"

"That's my new name for you." He smiled as he ran for home.

Jared watched him disappear into the garage. He closed the door and went back to the kitchen where his mom was cleaning the supper dishes. Candace mussed his hair and pulled him close.

Jared was excited to think he had a new friend. Soon summer would arrive and they could play every day.

BEAUTIFUL THING

July, 1989

Luke looked towards the western sky. The sun was setting just beyond the trees. It filled the sky with hues of orange, red, and pink. The smile on Jared's face showed he appreciated the view as well. Luke chuckled as their fading shadows colliding into each other as they ran.

They had reached the field near where they'd started to build their tree fort. Luke had stopped Jared to point out the sunset over the hills.

"Last one to the train car has to be it for Freeze Tag tomorrow," Luke called out. He'd already run ahead before he finished the challenge. He looked back when he heard Jared protest, but saw him follow right behind.

As he neared the junkyard, he looked over his shoulder to check on Jared. When he saw that Jared had almost caught up to him, he made a sudden push and landed against the train car first. "I win!"

Jared arrived two seconds after him.

Luke grabbed the metal ladder and climbed to the top. Jared followed him, as he'd been doing all summer.

Luke looked again at the sunset. He put his hand above his eyes to block some of the light so he could have a better look. "What should we do tomorrow?"

"I have to be an altar boy at church in the morning." Jared scowled and shook his head.

"Again?" This had thrown a definite wrench into Luke's plans.

"I'll be home by ten. We'll have the whole day," Jared explained. "Do you want to work on the fort?"

Luke smiled and tucked his knees into his chest. "Sure. I'll get all the tools and stuff from your garage, and we'll meet there."

A familiar voice called out in the distance. "Jared. Get over here right now!"

Luke gave Jared a smirk and headed for the ladder. "See you in the morning."

"Night."

This time Luke followed Jared, who seemed to know the tone in the voice calling him was not very happy. They ran through the tall grass and into Jared's back yard.

Luke smiled at Jared as he ran past him. He walked into his house and sat down on the couch, reveling in his contentment. His mother worked late almost every day and his sister stayed with a friend who worked with his mom. He enjoyed his alone time.

As was his usual routine, he dragged a stool and brought down a box of cereal. He took his bowl into the living-room to settle in front of the TV. A light shone from the house across the street. In the window, he could see Jared and his mom at their table, talking. He smiled to himself as he settled in for the evening.

BOYS DON'T CRY

Jared pulled close to Luke. "I think we should turn around. We're too far from home. What if we get caught?" He checked to make sure he still had the money for the Gummi Worms in his pocket.

Luke kept peddling. He looked over his shoulder and smiled at Jared. "Stop worrying. It's fine." He took a sudden turn down the next road. "You go on ahead. I'm going to find Scotty. He owes me a dollar. I'll meet you there."

"Okay. I'll start picking out the worms." Jared took a deep breath and continued toward the gas station.

Jared parked his bike on the side of the building and walked to the door. He noticed a group of older boys staring at him through the window. *Holy crap! The Johnson boys.*

They pointed at him and whispered to each other.

Jared stopped in his tracks. He turned and ran for his bike, watching for Luke as he jumped on.

"Your mommy let you come all the way over here?"

Jared was surrounded. He lowered his head and stared at the ground.

Chuck pulled the bike away from Jared. "Look at this. A new bike. I think I'll take it for a ride."

"I'm not supposed to let anyone else ride it." Jared whispered, his voice shaking.

Chuck laughed. "We won't hurt it. We promise." He jumped on Jared's bike and headed toward the road. Once he got it to a high speed, he jumped off. Jared looked away as the bike flipped and landed on the highway. A truck swerved to avoid hitting it.

Jared ran toward his bike, but was pushed to the ground. The gravel scratched the skin on his belly as they dragged him back toward the side of building. He coughed and choked on the dirt he inhaled. Sharp pains ran up his fingers as he dug them into the ground, hoping to slow them down and buy some time. Once they let go, Jared tried to run. Chuck caught his arm and pinned him against the wall.

"Now look what you did. You ruined your new bike. What's your mommy going to say?"

Jared freed his hand to wipe his mouth and prayed someone would notice what was happening. Despite his efforts, tears ran down his cheek.

"The little baby girl is crying. Poor baby." Jared felt a tug on his collar then a push that sent him face-first into the gravel. A sharp rock cut his cheek. He rolled onto his back and saw them coming again with rocks in hand. Arms over his head and teeth gritted, he tried to protect himself, prepared for what was coming. He screamed as the first rocks hit him. The rocks would be first. He knew that fists and boots would soon follow. He took a deep breath and readied himself.

Instead he heard a spray of gravel from tires, followed by muffled grunts and groans. He lifted his head when he heard a thud close to him. One of his tormentors was getting back to his feet then ran away. Luke was kneeling on top of Chuck, punching him in the chest and face.

"What's going on? Stop that!" The old guy who worked the counter of the store came running over, pulled Luke up under the armpits, and shook him. "Juvenile delinquents! All of you! Get out of here!"

Chuck scrambled to his feet and ran toward the others.

Luke freed himself, pushed the old man away, and ran to the highway to get Jared's bike. He brought it to Jared and knelt down beside him. "Jed? Are you okay?" He helped Jared sit up.

"It only hurts a little bit." Jared wiped the dirt off his mouth. "Thanks."

Luke put his arm around him, brushing the dirt and small bits of gravel off of his face with his other hand. "You've got cuts on your face! You're bleeding! Maybe we should call your mom..."

"No. I'm okay. Let's just go." Jared limped to his bike. He felt Luke put his hand on his shoulder.

"Don't worry, Jed! I won't let anyone hurt you ever again."

Jared looked into Luke's eyes and saw an intensity he hadn't seen before. He gave an appreciative smile, got on his bike, and tried to peddle. The bike started to tip over. The front wheel was bent and the tire was off the rim. Jared sighed. He pushed his bike toward the road.

"Jed, stop!" Luke took the bike from him. "You ride my bike. I'll push yours home."

Jared wanted to argue, but he was thankful for Luke's help. He wasn't sure he could've walked the whole way home with the pain in his leg. He reached down, pulled up his pant leg and saw a large scrape and blood running down from it.

Luke waited for him up the road. "Are you okay?"

"I'm fine. I'm coming." Jared jumped on Luke's bike, ignoring the aches and pains.

CRAZY LITTLE THING CALLED LOVE

The following day, Luke sat at the counter eating his cereal as fast as he could. It was a warm summer afternoon and he and Jared had planned their whole day.

He caught a glimpse of Jared standing across the road waiting for him. He scarfed his food, threw his dirty dishes in the sink, and ran outside. "Let's go!" He stopped, noticing Jared wasn't right behind him. Jared limped along.

Luke ran to him. He put his hands on Jared's shoulders. "Are you okay? We don't have to go. We could just play games today."

"I'm fine. My leg is just a little sore. No big deal." Jared started to run.

Luke followed behind him, watching his every move to make sure he was all right. Jared stopped a few times to take a quick break. After the third time, Luke insisted they walk the rest of the way. He had Jared lean on him.

Luke let Jared rest and ran ahead to the fort, clearing the path for him. He froze. "What the hell?" He picked up a scrap piece of board and hurled it at a tree. "Every damn time!"

Jared limped toward him. He put a hand on his shoulder, smiling. "You'll figure it out. You figured out the steps. I know you'll figure out how to keep the walls up."

Luke began devising another plan. He knew he could do it. After all, he'd concocted a series of small boards of varying shapes and sizes that they used for steps. He had also come up with a wealth of materials to use for building. He found them in the junkyard near the train car. He knew he could figure this out. He had to. He'd promised Jared a fort.

Luke looked at the pulleys, took a deep breath and pulled the rope. The walls lifted and hung back where they were supposed to be.

Luke pointed to the steps leading up to the top. "Jed, you can work on those. I'll climb up and work on the walls."

"I want to help with the walls. We have to get them done."

Luke put his hand on Jared's shoulder. "I'll do the climbing today. You stay close to the ground. I don't want you falling and getting hurt worse." He could see by Jared's face that he wanted to argue. "Besides, the steps aren't solid yet. It's important to get them done."

Jared frowned at him, picked up a hammer from off the ground and went to work. Luke finished attaching one of the walls. He looked down at Jared working; his silence and demeanor told Luke that he was upset. Luke felt terrible; he didn't like to see Jared unhappy, but he needed to know his friend was safe.

Jared wiped his forehead, threw the hammer up into the fort, and went inside. Luke crawled down from the tree and met him. He stared at Jared as he lay on the floor of the fort. Jared took in some deep breaths as he looked up at the sky. He seemed lost in thought. Luke pulled at the hair on the back of his head. Something had been on his mind the last few days. He tried to speak, but the words wouldn't come out. Instead, he walked over to Jared and lay beside him on the floor. After a couple more minutes of silence he looked at him. "Jed? Am I your best friend?"

"Yeah. Am I yours?"

"Yeah." He smiled. "I was just wondering."

They lay in silence again. Luke rehearsed in his mind asking the real question. He looked at Jared again. This time he put his hand on Jared's arm and smiled. "Jed? Does that mean that we...you know?"

Jared stared back, his eyes wide, eyebrows furrowed.

"Love each other?" Luke's heart pounded as he waited for Jared to respond. He had to look away.

Jared rolled onto his side and leaned his head on his hand. "I think so. What do you think?"

Luke was able to breathe again. "Yeah! I think so, too." Jared's smile reassured him. "I love you!"

"I love you, too." Jared giggled as his face turned red.

Luke sat up. He tucked his knees into his chest and rocked back and forth. "I saw on this TV show, when you love someone, you're supposed to kiss them." Jared's smile evaporated; Luke's pulse raced. *Oh no! Did I go too far?*

Jared stared at the floor. "Should we? Do you want to?"

"Only if you want to." Luke couldn't look him in the eye. His heart raced as he waited for Jared to answer.

"Sure." Jared walked to Luke, leaned down and gave him a peck on the cheek.

Luke smiled. He was lost in thought for a moment then got up and stood in front of Jared.

"I think you're supposed to do it different. Not like kissing your mom."

"Oh! I'm sorry." Jared blushed and turned away from him. "Do you know how to do that?"

"You know that girl, Tracey? The one from my class who got mad at my birthday party because she didn't get the part of the cake she wanted? She showed me how to do it at school during recess." Luke walked up to Jared and turned him. "Just do what I do." With a hand on each cheek, Luke pulled Jared's face to his, tilted it, and kissed him. Something wasn't right. He thought back over what he'd been told. The mechanics of it didn't feel very easy to him. He tried again and put his lips on Jared's.

Jared followed his lead.

Luke looked into Jared's eyes. "Was that better?"

"Yeah. That was okay."

Luke panicked. "What? Did I do something wrong?"

"No. It's just... aren't you supposed to hug, too?"

Luke laughed with relief. "Oh, yeah!" He wasn't able to hide his excitement. He threw his arms around Jared and kissed him again. He smiled at Jared and lay down on the floor. Jared lay down next to him. Feeling more comfortable, he moved closer, putting his arm under his head. Jared snuggled in.

Luke looked up at the sky. He felt wonderful; he didn't understand it all, but it felt right. He sat up and looked at Jared. "I suppose we should get back to work." He picked up his hammer and climbed back up to where he'd been working.

As evening approached, Luke realized he was exhausted. He noticed Jared had stopped working a while ago. He saw him leaning against the tree staring off into the distance. "I think it's time to go home for the night."

Jared nodded and started to put things away.

Luke walked Jared to his backyard and watched him head for his back door. "See you tomorrow."

"Should we do some more work on the fort?" Jared called back.

"Sure!"

Jared smiled and started up the stairs.

"Wait." Luke ran up the stairs to Jared, turned his face to give him one more kiss, his thumb stroking his face several times before they broke apart. He then ran to his house and into the kitchen.

Ellen was leaning against the sink with her arms folded. "What in the hell was that?"

"What?" Luke was startled by the tone of her voice. "I was just playing with Jed."

"I saw you playing! That's disgusting! You don't do that to other boys! What's wrong with you?" She grabbed his arms and shook him. "You go to your room! Right now! That's horrible!"

Luke couldn't keep his feet under him as she dragged him down the hallway. She threw him into his room and slammed the door.

Luke picked himself up, stood looking at the door a moment then sat on the side of his bed shaking, fighting the urge to cry. *What was so wrong?* Through his bedroom window he saw Jared smiling and running around the dining room. Luke leaned his head against the window.

"How did such a wonderful day end so horribly?"

He crawled into bed and pulled the covers over his head. "I knew I could trust Jared. I knew it. It was everyone else that I should've worried about. I just don't understand why."

The next day, Luke was rushing to get ready. He was to meet Jared at the fort as they'd planned the night before.

Ellen walked in with a pile of folded laundry, dropping it on the bed. "Where do you think you're going?"

"Outside."

"You are going to stay away from that kid. He's a bad influence!"

"But, Mom!"

"No! You stay in here and be quiet." She closed the door and yelled at him from the other side. "Call one of your other friends to come play."

Luke walked to his window. He watched as Jared ran through his backyard toward the fort. Jared looked excited.

Luke wanted to run with him, be with him. Jared disappeared around the fence. "How am I going to tell Jared that Mom won't let us play together? He's my best friend. I do love him."

Luke sat on his bed. His stomach twisted in knots. Hitting his fists against the bed he jumped up and went to the window. "I'll figure it out, Jed. I promise. I'll see you soon. "

WICKED LITTLE TOWN

Jared waited at the fort for hours, keeping watch for Luke. Eventually, alone, he headed home. As he came through the row of aspen trees, he stopped when he heard a voice. *Luke!* Following the direction of the sound, he emerged from the tall grass. The tree house that Luke had warned him about came into view; Devin and his friends stood below it. He looked for an exit, his heart racing.

"Well, look who it is, guys." Devin stood tall, smirking at Jared. "It's that little queer who moved in down the road."

Jared backed away, readying himself to run at the first chance.

The boys dropped their tools and circled around Jared. "What's wrong? We just want to talk to you, little faggot-boy." Devin walked up to him. The others laughed, closing in around him.

Jared opened his mouth, but no words came out. Cornered and trapped against his neighbor's fence, he shook, seeing no way out.

"We don't allow fags around here. Come on. Let's teach him a lesson!" They rushed him, but stopped as a car drove by on the dirt road.

Taking advantage of the distraction, Jared climbed over the fence. One of them noticed his escape and yelled to the others.

Jared ran. Looking over his shoulder, he saw them catching up. He crawled over the fence on the other side of the yard, jumped from the top, landing hands first to the ground in his yard. Devin and the others landed just behind him. Jared struggled to his feet and ran toward his mom standing on the back deck. Candace waved to them, smiling as she shook out a mat.

Jared looked back, saw that Devin and the others had noticed her and headed the other way. He took a deep breath and leaned against the fence. It was then he noticed Ellen in her driveway. He walked to the road. "Is Luke home?"

Ellen disappeared into the garage, shooting him an angry look.

Devin and his thugs had turned around, walking back toward him, yelling and making rude gestures. Unsure of his safety, Jared ran home.

Candace was in the kitchen taking a pot out of the oven. "Hi, you. Where's Luke?"

"I don't know. I haven't seen him yet today." Jared crawled onto the stool, watching his mother work on their evening meal. "Mom?"

"Yes, Sweetheart?"

Jared took a deep breath. "I've been thinking. I know I'm too young, but I already know who I'm going to marry."

Candace looked up at him, smirking. "Really?"

"Yeah."

"Are you going to share who this lucky person is going to be?"

Jared jumped off the stool and leaned against the cupboard. "It's Luke. I love him so I'm going to marry him."

The smile disappeared from Candace's face. She went back to cooking. "Jared, don't be silly. Boys don't marry boys. That's a sin."

"But I love him!"

Candace turned to him, dropping her mixing spoon on the counter. "That's enough! Of course you love him. He's your friend, but you're not going to get married. That's gross."

"But..."

"You're too young to understand. Just stop thinking about it. You have plenty of time to worry about those things when you're older." Candace turned back to her cooking.

Jared wanted to talk about it more, but he sensed now was not the time. He went out to the patio, looked across the street to Luke's house, monitoring everything that was happening. *What happened to you, Luke? I need to talk to you. No one understands.*

The sound of a car door slamming shut made him jump. He watched Ellen pull out of her driveway and down the road. Once she was out of sight, he ran to Luke's house, looking back to the road, making sure Ellen wasn't coming back. Halfway there, the garage door swung open. Luke appeared, motioning for him to come into the garage.

Jared quickly closed the garage door behind him, taking one last look down the road in the process. "Are you okay? What's going on?"

Luke looked down at the floor. "I don't know what to do. My mom says we can't play together anymore."

A tear came to Jared's eye. "How come?"

"She said boys aren't supposed to... you know... kiss and hug."

Jared cringed, feeling the blood rush to his face. Candace's words replayed in his head. He turned to leave, but his heart raced at the thought of leaving Luke and not seeing him again. Looking back, he reached out and touched Luke's arm. "I'm sorry. If I promise not to do that stuff anymore, can we still be friends?"

Luke took a big breath. A smile grew across his face as he put his hand on Jared's. "Sure. Wanna come in and watch TV?"

"I don't think I should." He looked over his shoulder toward the driveway.

Luke grabbed him by the hand, pulling him inside the house. "She had to go to work. She won't be back for hours."

Jared sighed, leaning up against the counter.

Luke sat on the couch, motioning for Jared to sit by him. He grabbed the remote and flipped between channels. "Want something to eat?"

"Sure. What do you got?"

Luke walked into the kitchen and rummaged through the cupboards. "How about some popcorn?"

"Okay." Jared settled into the couch, laying his head back. He picked up the remote.

"What should we watch?"

"I don't know. Anything." Luke put the bag of popcorn in the microwave.

Jared flipped through the channels, stopping when he heard someone say a familiar word.

"Queer." A large man yelled from a podium, holding a Bible. Jared listened, trying to understand the meaning of the word. It was what one of Devin's friends yelled at him.

Luke sat beside him, offering him the bowl of popcorn. "What did you find?"

Jared looked up at him. "Do you know what 'queer' means?"

A frown formed on Luke's brow. "I've heard it before. It's not good. Why?"

"That's what Devin called me. I ran into him and his friends earlier..." Jared's attention was pulled back to the television as the man at the podium said the word again, along with another word that they'd yelled at him. "Fag."

"Men loving other men," the preacher screamed, "was why God destroyed Sodom and Gomorrah! It is why he continues to send hurricanes and floods and famine across the earth."

Jared felt sweat forming in his palms.

"God will eradicate the earth of homosexuals!" The pastor pounded his pulpit. "The Lord God will not rest until every one of them is punished. They will die a horrific, painful death."

Luke sat motionless, his gaze shifting between the television and the floor.

Jared sensed the tension, noticing Luke moving farther away from him. *He's talking about us.* Petrified, he awaited a reaction from Luke.

His attention turned back to the man on T.V. "Yes, my friends, God has sent a disease to wipe them out. Just as with Sodom and Gomorrah before, they will not be saved from God's wrath! None of them can hide from the Lord's fury. They will all die in pain equal to their horrendous sin." The crowd erupted in cheers and applause.

Luke jumped from the couch and ran to his room, the door slamming behind him.

Jared followed, but stopped in the hallway. "I can't." Running from the house, he felt nauseous. Tears filled his eyes.

He ran into his room, opened the closet door, and hid in the back. "I'm sorry, God. I didn't mean it. I don't want to die. Please. And please don't hurt Luke." He lay curled up on the floor, shaking for hours, afraid that any minute he'd start to feel the pain of the disease that would kill him.

Weeks went by, summer came to an end, and a new school year started.

Jared got out of the car, grabbing bags of groceries. Across the street Luke appeared from his garage and walked in his direction. Jared's heart raced. *Is he finally going to talk to me?* Luke got to the end of his driveway and headed down the road, never looking at Jared.

Jared helped his mom carry the groceries into the house then excused himself. From the family room in the basement he watched Luke disappear from view. *Why is this so hard? Why do I feel so desperate to want to be with him?* He leaned against the window and stared off into the distance. His only comfort was imagining what it would be like being with Luke again, hoping there was a chance.

BORN THIS WAY

The lump in my throat threatened to choke me. Eyes glared at me from over frameless half-lenses, harboring anger. Or was it hatred? A shiver twitched through my body. *What the hell am I doing here? Damn my Don Quixote complex!* The reprimand kicked around in my head repeatedly until I saw 'her'. There was something different in her eyes. She was who I needed to talk to, if for no other reason than to get through this ordeal. I was doing it for the sake of every 'Jared' and 'Luke' out there, hoping they might find strength to keep going and come to celebrate who they are instead of hiding in shame. *They all need to hear it.* I wished my body believed me. It would've made getting through it a lot easier. I took a deep breath. Seeing a loving face smiling at me just over my shoulder, I felt less afraid.

"There were a few incidents that made me aware of what we were up against. I didn't fully understand at the time what it all meant, but I understood fear. There are many people like me... your sons, daughters, brothers, sisters... who wake up and immediately start thinking about how to blend in so they won't be figured out, thinking through how to act or what to say to make sure no one finds out that they're different. I've felt the consequences of being different. At a young age, I knew it was dangerous. I couldn't understand why what I was feeling was wrong... or evil. The hardest part was that I tried... I honestly tried to act one way, but I couldn't stop the feelings. No matter how much you fight, they never go away. That one part of you continues to fight to be who you are even when you know the consequences."

IN & OUT

October, 1990

Jared walked past his sister's room as she was studying at her desk. He hesitated to bother her. With Megan now a freshman in high school, he felt like they had nothing in common. She didn't seem to have time for a kid brother.

His mind wandered, thinking about how tough it was adjusting to junior high. He hated that he had to leave his other school. It was a completely different world from the class sizes of four and five students. It also brought more of a challenge in avoiding Luke. They shared a school, walked the same hallways, and attended some of the same classes.

He stood just outside his sister's door, trying to build the courage to talk to her.

"Jared, I know you're there." Megan looked to the door. "Do you need something?"

He peered around the corner then slowly entered. "No." He looked around her room, taking a seat on the bed. "Just bored."

"Don't you have homework?"

"I did it already."

Megan threw her pencil down. "I'm never going to pass this test!" She stood up and rubbed her eyes. "Is Mom home?"

"Not yet."

Megan smiled at him. "I'm going over to Jenny's house. I'll be back in a little while. Will you tell her?" She left the room.

"Sure." He answered as the front door slammed.

Jared noticed the light on Megan's desk was still on; the sound of his dad's voice echoed in his head about not wasting electricity. Reaching to turn it off, he noticed the title written at the top of the page: 'AIDS'. His hand trembled as a lump formed in his throat. He sat down at her desk, reading through the notes she'd taken.

The first two pages caused tears to form in his eyes. He took a deep breath, reading through the rest of the paper. He looked up and stared at his reflection in the mirror over the desk. "You can't get AIDS from just kissing someone or touching them. There's nothing to be afraid of." He needed to find Luke.

He ran out the door, excited about the chance to make things right. Halfway down the driveway, he stopped, thinking about what might've changed over the months. "What if Luke has new friends? What if he still doesn't want anything to do with me?"

He headed back home, realizing that he had to think more about how to talk to Luke. He needed to take his time and do it correctly.

Jared veered off through the backyard. Without thought, he found himself at the train car. Tears came to his eyes. He hadn't been there since the last time he and Luke were there together.

He climbed the ladder, wiping the tears away with his arms, and sat on the top. Unable to think straight, he hit the top of the train car with his fist. "Why is this so hard?" He laid down, looking up at the sky. "Because I'm scared. I don't want to know that he hates me."

THE VIEW FROM A RUSTY TRAIN CAR

A noise came from inside the train car. Jared jumped. He opened the hatch and peered in.

"Who's there?" A voice echoed from inside the car.

Although deeper now, Jared thought he recognized it. "Luke? Is that you?" His voice broke, hands shook as he stared at the shadowy figure below him stepping into the light.

Luke met his gaze and smiled up at him. "Yeah. It's me, Jed."

Jared's stomach fluttered. He made his way down the ladder. Standing in front of Luke, he threw his arms around him then pulled away. Luke didn't seem as enthusiastic about the reunion. "I'm sorry. I was just excited to see you."

Luke took Jared's hand, smiling at him. "I'm happy to see you, too."

"It's been awhile." Jared tried to break the ice.

Luke looked down at the floor. "Yeah." He chuckled and met Jared's gaze. "So? What've you been up to?"

Jared leaned against the wall and crossed his arms. He looked away from him, still nervous. The reunion wasn't how he had imagined it would be, but at least they were talking and Luke didn't run or scream at him.

"Not much. Just school." He couldn't breathe, waiting for Luke to respond. Nothing came. "Luke, listen... I..." He stumbled over his words, still unsure how to bring up the subject. *Maybe I should just let it go.*

Luke walked down the hallway, into the back of the car. "I'm sorry I didn't come and see you. I wanted to, but I just didn't know what to say."

Jared sighed, following him. "I know. I didn't either." He sat by Luke on the blanket they'd put in there a few months ago.

"I'm really sorry I freaked out. It was just a lot. You know? I was scared." Luke shook his head, placing it into his hands.

Jared reached out, touching his shoulder. "I was too."

"I missed you." Luke took Jared's hand. His face flushed as he smiled.

Jared knew it was now or never. He pulled his hand away, looking him in the eye. "Luke, I read something on Megan's desk... about AIDS. That was the disease they were talking about on TV. You can't catch it from just touching. All we did was give each other a kiss and a hug..."

Luke jumped up. "I know! I know all that! We watched a movie about it in health class a few weeks ago. That still doesn't fix things."

Jared tensed. "What do you mean? What we did is fine. We aren't going to catch it."

"I don't care about what we did! I'm not worried about catching it. That's not the point!"

Jared put his hands on Luke's shoulders. "Then what's wrong?"

"It's... this." Luke turned to him. "How I feel when you touch me." He leaned his head against the wall. "The movie talked about guys who... well guys who did what we used to do. It's called 'gay'."

"I know." Jared sat down on the blanket. His mind raced. "So what if we are? It's okay, right?"

Luke shook his head. "No! It's not okay. It's wrong. That's what my mom was talking about." He sat down next to Jared. "I'm not gay! Not really."

"I think I am," Jared blurted out.

Luke stared at him. "You don't know that. We're not old enough. It could change. You're just curious."

"Sometimes I wish it would change." Jared choked up. He turned away. "I've spent so much time at church praying that it will just go away. Don't you think I want to be the same as all the other boys? But it doesn't work! It never happens. I just keep thinking about you and being with you." Moving to the other side of the room, he wiped tears away. "I miss being with you."

"I know. I thought if I stayed away from you that I would just forget about you. It didn't help. I watched out the window for any glimpse of you. When I did see you, I'd smile and get excited."

Jared felt Luke's breath on the back of his neck. He turned to him, reaching to take him into an embrace.

Luke stopped him. "Jed, I'm not gay. I don't feel like this about anyone else. It's just you. I don't know why. I don't know what to do about it. I don't want to be away from you, but I don't want to be this way either."

"So what do we do?"

Luke shook his head, taking Jared by the hand. "I don't know."

"Now what? Can we still hang out?"

"Of course. Jed, I love you."

Jared was about to respond, but Luke took him into an embrace and held onto him. He trembled. It felt more amazing than he imagined.

Luke kept hold of Jared's hands and looked him in the eye. "I don't know what's going to happen, but we'll figure it out. I promise."

Jared grasped onto Luke's shirt, snuggling his face into his neck. "Thank you."

RUNNING WITH SCISSORS

March 1991

Luke ran up the driveway. Track practice had lasted longer than he thought it would. He knew Jared would be waiting for him at the fort. He rushed into the house, grabbed some clothes from his room, and jumped in the shower.

Ellen called to him from the living room as he was about to run out the door. He hadn't noticed her car in the garage when he got home.

"Where are you going?" Ellen called from the living room.

Luke walked to her. "Just out."

"Who's going with you?" She leaned forward and turned on a lamp.

"No one. I was just going for a walk."

Ellen stared at him, her eyes studying his face. "I lost my job today, in case you're wondering why I'm here."

Luke sat on the arm of the couch, putting his hand on hers. "I'm sorry. What happened?"

"Stupid ass I worked for said I had an attitude problem. Stupid son-of-a-bitch! I showed him an attitude problem." She chuckled, taking a sip from her drink.

Luke grasped her hand. "What are you going to do? What should I do?"

"Nothing! It's fine. I'll find something. I have a call in to the bank. They're looking for help." Ellen looked up at him. "Just going for a walk, huh? Didn't you just get done with track practice?"

Luke swallowed hard, knowing from the tone in her voice where the conversation was heading. "Yes, but I need to clear my head."

"You're not hanging around with that weirdo from next door again are you?"

Luke pulled his hand away as her nails dug into his skin. "No! God! Do you have to ask that all the time?"

"I'm sorry. I just saw him smiling and running around like a little faggot in his backyard when I got home. I'm glad you've stayed away from him. They try to turn all of you guys, you know." She made her way to the kitchen and refilled her drink.

Luke glanced through the window before following her. "Do you mind if I go or can I help you with something?"

Ellen laughed. "What can you do about it?"

"Fine. Never mind." Luke brushed past her to the door.

"Wait!" Ellen marched up to him, sipping on her drink. "You can do something. Take your sister with you."

Luke panicked thinking about how he would see Jared with Susie tagging along. "Mom, no! I just want some time alone, and it's already dark outside."

"Well, I want some time alone, too, for once! You'll take her with you or you can go to your room. She was just saying she doesn't see you except in the mornings when you're getting ready for school." She crossed to the hallway and leaned against the doorway. "Susie! Come on out here! Your brother wants to go for a walk!"

"But, Mom!"

Susie came running from her room, a big smile across her face. "Really? You want to hang out with me?"

Luke took a deep breath and grabbed her hand. He forced a smile. "Yeah. Come on." He led her out of the house.

"Don't be too late." Ellen called out before slamming the door.

Luke sneered. Looking down at Susie, he couldn't help feeling guilty. They didn't spend much time together anymore. It was different now that he was in junior high. Susie smiled at him as she took his hand. She battered him with questions and told him all about what had happened at school since the year had started. His mind turned to Jared. With Susie in tow, he couldn't come up with a way for them to be together tonight.

Luke and Susie walked down the road near the junkyard. Luke was on constant vigil for any sign of Jared. They walked around the corner and neared the row of trees on the other side of the fort. Luke noticed movement from the tree line and saw Jared waving at him.

Susie pulled on his sleeve. "What's wrong, Luke?"

Luke looked to Jared then back to Susie. "Nothing. I thought I saw something over there. You wait here while I go check it out. Okay?"

"But Luke..."

"It'll be fine. I'll be right back. Just stay here." Luke gave her a quick smile then ran through the trees.

Jared ran to him, ready to throw his arms around Luke.

Luke took his arm, pushing him back into the trees. He looked back at the road.

"What is it? What's the matter?" Jared tried looking over his shoulder to the road.

"I'm sorry I'm late! I got held up at practice and now my mom made me take Susie for a walk." Luke touched Jared's face. "Can we meet tomorrow?"

"Sure." Jared smiled, finally throwing his arms around him and kissing him on the cheek. "See you tomorrow."

Luke gave him a quick embrace. Closing his eyes, he slid his hands down Jared's back. When he opened his eyes he saw Susie standing just behind Jared. He pushed Jared aside, standing in front of him. "What's wrong? I told you to wait for me on the road."

Susie craned her neck, trying to see who Luke was hiding. "Nothing. I'm cold. I want to go home!"

Luke gave her a smile and turned her around. "Go ahead. I'll be right behind you. Go on!"

Susie glared at him over her shoulder before disappearing through the trees.

Luke watched until he could see her heading down the gravel road. Turning back to Jared, he offered his hand. "Jed... look. I've got to go. I'll see you tomorrow."

Jared grabbed his arm as he turned to leave. "Do you think she saw anything?"

"I don't think so, but I have to make sure. Plus I promised I would hang out with her tonight." He glanced toward the road. "I'll see you tomorrow. Okay?" He winked at Jared then ran toward Susie, his heart beating rapidly as he wondered about what she had seen. *How the hell am I going to get out of this?*

"Susie, wait!" Running up beside her, he grabbed her arm. The muscles in her face tensed, her eyes darting around, unable to look at him. "What's wrong?"

Susie wiped a tear away, looking up at him. "Who was that in the trees?"

Luke put his arm around her, pushing her down the road. "No one. Just a friend of mine." He tried to change the subject, continuing to escort her home. "Let's go home. What do you want to do?"

"It was Jared. I saw him."

Luke took a deep breath. He turned to her, plotting his cover up until he saw the pain on her face. "Yes, it was."

Susie looked away and continued down the road. "I have to tell Mom."

"What?" Luke grabbed her shoulders. He shook her. "No! You can't! Susie, please!"

Susie cried. "I have to. Mom said if I ever saw you two together, I had to tell her right away!" She pulled away from him. "She said he'd kill you and she had to stop him!"

Luke ran ahead of her, grabbing her shoulders again. "Susie, please. You can't tell Mom. She doesn't know what she's talking about. Jared's a good guy. He's not going to hurt me."

Susie's face turned red with anger. She pushed his hands away. "Then why would Mom say that?" She put her hands on her head, tears streaming down her face. "I'm scared, Luke! I don't want anything to happen to you."

Luke put his arm around her, comforting her. "I don't know why Mom's acting like that, but you have to promise me that you won't tell her. Ever! Please? For me?"

Susie stopped. After a moment she looked him in the eyes. "I'm sorry. I have to. She made me promise." She wiped the tears from her cheeks. "I don't want to."

Luke's eyes welled up with tears watching the pain of his sister stuck in the middle of the situation. "Susie, you know I wouldn't ask you if it wasn't important. So please. Don't tell her. I'll get you anything you want. What do you want?"

Susie thought for a moment. Smiling, she wrapped her arms around his waist. "I want you to spend more time with me. We never do anything anymore."

Luke held her tightly. "I will. I promise!"

Susie pulled away, holding on to Luke's arm. The smile had vanished from her face. "And I want to hang out with you and Jared sometimes. I want to see if there's something wrong with him like Mom says."

Luke chuckled. He stood up straight and shook her hand. "Okay. It's a deal." Looking into her eyes, he wiped her tears away and smiled. "I think Jared would like that."

Susie smiled, took his arm, and pulled him down the road toward home.

THE VIEW FROM A RUSTY TRAIN CAR

ANGELS IN AMERICA

May 1991

Jared had waited with the rest of his classmates. The room was hot, uncomfortable, and he wanted school to be over.

The Sister admired him for his interest and knowledge of Catholicism. In kindergarten, the teachers pegged him to be the one who would surely become a priest. He knew it should be an honor, but there was always something about it that never sat well with him.

Sister Frances walked into the room and proceeded to pass out papers. "Good afternoon, class."

"Good afternoon, Sister Frances." The students answered her, sitting up at attention.

Jared picked up the paper from his desk and started to read it. His throat tightened. He broke into a cold sweat as he read the first line.

"Today we're discussing *Homosexuality and the Bible*," Sister announced, making her way to the front of the class. "Jared?"

"Yes, Sister?" Nearly jumping out of his seat, Jared felt his face turn bright red, and his hands start to shake. He couldn't breathe, sensing the judgmental looks directed toward him from certain individuals in the room.

"Could you open the windows please? It's awfully warm in here." Sister turned to the blackboard and began to write.

Jared took a deep breath and got out of his chair. He pulled open the windows, enjoying the breeze that blew through. He hoped the cooler air would help calm the redness he could feel on his face.

He took one last deep breath, beating himself up over his reaction, before heading back to his desk. *Here we go.* Knowing the discussion would be the same, Jared lowered his head, trying to disappear behind the student in front of him. It was getting hard for him to hide that he was the 'abomination' always referred to in the discussions.

As Sister read examples of text from the Bible about homosexuality being evil, Jared fought the urge to scream. *I'm not evil!* He wished he had the courage to challenge them, but outing himself was just not an option.

Looking at the clock, Jared realized he was kicking the leg of his desk. He leaned back and crossed his leg to hide his anxiety. He prayed for the bell to ring, to usher in relief from his misery.

When it did, the sound was more welcome than usual. He gathered his things, trying to make it out of the room as fast as he could.

Sister Frances put her hand on his shoulder. "Jared, I'd like to talk to you for a moment."

Jared backed into the room and put down his books on the nearest desk. "Yes, Sister?" Unable to bring himself to look at her, his gaze fixed on the desk in front of him. He whispered a prayer. "Please Lord. Not here. Not like this."

Waiting for the rest of the class to leave, Sister turned to him and sat on her desk. "Are you all right? You're usually so into discussion and we didn't hear a word from you today."

Jared raised his head, forcing a smile. "I'm fine, Sister. Thank you. I'm just not feeling well. I think it's the heat."

Wiping the sweat from his forehead, he hoped she'd buy the excuse. *What if she doesn't? What will I say to her? I can't talk to her about Luke!*

He'd imagined the scenario a million times. The priest would be called in, his parents would be told, and the news would spread through the small town like wildfire. He'd become a cipher.

The moments that went by without Sister saying anything made his heart race. His face tightened as he waited for her to ask him the question. From the corner of his eye, he could see her staring at him, studying his face.

Sister rose from the desk, putting her hand on his. "I thought that might be it. You don't look well. Will you be fine to get home or should I call your mother?"

Jared jumped to his feet. All the tension in his body released. "No! I'm fine, Sister. I think I just need some fresh air. The walk home will be good for me." He picked up his things and headed for the hallway. "Have a good night. See you tomorrow."

Sister followed him out the door and called to him. "I'm here if you need to talk."

Jared stopped. Wiping a tear from his eye, he wondered if she suspected. He remembered why he admired her. No matter what, she cared enough to make sure he was all right. "Thanks, Sister."

THE BROKEN HEARTS CLUB

May, 1993

Jared lay on his bed taking notes. He glanced at Luke, who sat on the floor, staring at the wall. They'd been sitting there for an hour, having only had a brief exchange over what the other wanted to eat while they studied. He put down his notes and crawled to the edge of the bed.

"You okay?" He nudged Luke with his foot.

"Fine." Luke continued to stare at the wall.

Jared put down his book and snuggled up beside him. "What do you want to do this weekend?" Luke got up, never responding to the question. Jared waited, watching as Luke stood staring at the floor. "All right. What is it? Something's on your mind."

Luke walked to the other side of the room. He placed his hand on his head, turned around, looking at Jared. "I'm taking Cassie out to a movie on Saturday."

Jared closed his eyes, feeling like the wind had just been knocked out of him. "Cassie Evenwoll? Are you kidding me?"

"No, I'm not. She asked me and I said yes."

THE VIEW FROM A RUSTY TRAIN CAR

Jared jumped up and paced around the room. He clenched his fists as his body shook. "I can't believe this!"

"Come on, Jed. I have to start this." Luke sat on the edge of the bed, massaging his temples. "We talked about this. You knew this would happen."

Jared sat at his desk, wiping the tears from his eyes. "Fine. That's great. Don't let me keep you from it."

Walking up behind him, Luke put his hand on Jared's shoulders. "Maybe we can do something on Sunday. Drive to the lake or something."

Jared pushed his hands away. "No. That's all right. I don't want to ruin your life."

"Come on, Jed."

"If you don't mind, I have to study. Just leave." Jared watched him pack his things, the anger growing inside him. He turned away from Luke when it looked like he was about to say something. His body tensed, feeling Luke walk up behind him.

"I'll talk to you later. Okay?"

Jared sat on the chair at his desk. "Wait." Luke stopped. Jared opened the top drawer of his desk, rummaged around, took out a wrapped box, and threw it at him. "Happy Birthday."

"Thank you. That's very..."

"Just leave."

"Jed, I..."

"Now!"

Luke tucked the present into his backpack and left. Jared followed him, watching through the window as Luke made his way down the driveway. Luke stopped, reaching inside his backpack. He took out the gift and opened it. Smiling at the cologne he held in his hand, he looked back at Jared's house. Hand trembling, Jared switched off the light on his driveway. Luke stood in the dark for a moment then left.

Jared continued to watch until Luke disappeared into his garage. He shook with anger, pacing back and forth in his room. Seeing one of Luke's notebooks on the floor, he picked it up and threw it across the room. He went to his desk. Unable to decide if he was more angry, sad, or jealous, he laid his head on his books and cried.

The dreaded Saturday arrived. Jared sat in the living room, getting up every few minutes to look if there was any activity at Luke's house.

Candace walked into the room. "Are you still sulking? What's the matter with you these last few days? You've been in a horrible mood!"

"Nothing. Just thinking."

She sat beside him. "Thinking about what?"

"I don't know! I don't want to talk about it." He gazed toward Luke's house, his arms crossed.

"Where's Luke? He hasn't been around for a couple days."

"He has a date tonight." The acidic tone of his voice surprised him.

"Really? With whom?"

"Cassie Evenwoll."

"That's great! Good for him! She's a nice girl."

Jared stared at her. "She's horrible! You don't even know her!"

Candace walked to the window. "I think he's nervous. He sure doesn't look very excited."

Jared ran to the window. He fought to control his urge to scream. He pushed himself away from the window, wanting to get away. "I don't want to talk about it."

"So that's what's wrong."

Jared stopped, turning to her. The mocking tone of her voice and the smile on her face made him cringe. "What?"

"You're jealous."

He could hardly breathe. "Excuse me?"

"He has a date and you don't!"

Jared threw his head back, taking a deep breath. Relieved at her response, he chuckled. "I'm not jealous. I don't want a date. Certainly not with her!"

"Well? What is it then?" Candace stood in front of him, searching his face.

Jared had no reply.

"You're mad because he's not hanging out with you? Sweetheart, it was bound to happen. You're getting to that age." She walked over to him and put her arm around him.

"You don't understand." Jared jumped away from her, trying to make his way down the stairs.

"I know what you're going through! It's part of growing up!"

Jared sighed, leaning his head forward against the staircase banister. He was in just the mood to finally tell someone else his secret. *Does she really want the truth?* He chuckled at the thought.

"Isn't there someone you want to ask out? There are a lot of cute girls in your class."

Jared pulled himself together. "I'm mad at Luke, not at her." He forced a smile at her. "Mom, I really don't want to talk about this with you!"

"Okay. I understand. You can always talk to your dad if you'd prefer." She stood, looking him in the eyes. "You really need to stop being so shy. Go out. Have some fun!" She kissed his forehead and left the room.

Walking down the steps to his room, Jared's mind raced. He couldn't help imagining what was happening on Luke and Cassie's date. The more he thought about it, the more upset he became. He started to feel nauseous.

It was 11:04 p.m. when car lights threw shadows on the wall of his room. Jared jumped out of bed, finally taking his eyes off the clock. Luke's car pulled into the driveway across the street. He got out and leaned against the car, staring up at the night sky before turning his gaze toward Jared's house.

"Shit!" Jared dropped below the window, hitting his elbow on the window sill. He stifled a scream. Moving cautiously, he peeked over the sill. The garage door was closing. He caught a glimpse of Luke's shadow in the hall. The light went out. Luke was gone. The knot in his stomach continued to twist.

Jared crawled into bed, emotionally exhausted, knowing the night would be spent tossing and turning. Thoughts of Luke would swirl in his head. Sleep would be elusive.

TAINTED LOVE

Luke slid open the side door of the Montgomery's house. He stepped in, looking around the quiet house. He walked to the stairway that led downstairs to Jared's room. Halfway down, a stair creaked. His heart beat rapidly, listening to see if anyone stirred. After a few moments, he continued.

He walked to Jared's door, put an ear to it, hearing nothing except for the occasional snore. There was something adorable about it.

He went inside, having to tiptoe over the books and papers scattered over the floor. The clock next to Jared read 6:30 a.m.

Luke sat down on the side of the bed, looked down at him, hoping his plan to smooth things over would work. "What am I going to do about you?" His hand found Jared's forehead, pushed back a stray lock of hair before sliding his finger down the cheek to caress it.

Jared turned over, kicking the blanket off and leaving his backside exposed. Luke's pulse and breathing increased, looking at the naked body. He needed to touch him. The attraction was exciting and terrifying.

Jared turned onto his back. He rubbed his eyes then opened them. "What time is it?" He felt around for the clock.

Luke leaned down, kissing him on the forehead. "Good morning, Baby."

"Wait. What are you doing here?" Jared grabbed the blanket to cover himself.

"I'm taking you to the lake. Everything's packed. Come on. Get up and get ready!" Luke pulled Jared's dresser drawers open and rummaged through his clothes. "Where are your swimming trunks?"

Jared wrapped himself in the blanket and jumped out of bed. "What do you think you're doing? I'm not going anywhere with you! Why don't you go and get your girlfriend and take her to the lake?" He tried pushing Luke out the door, but his foot got caught in the blanket and he fell to the floor.

"Would you knock it off?" Luke took his hand, helping him up. "She's not my girlfriend. We went to a movie. That's it."

"I'm sure there's another one tonight. Go get ready for that one!" Jared pulled away and lay on the bed, facing the wall.

Luke lay down next to him, putting an arm around him. "It was just a date."

Jared picked up his hand, throwing it off. "Not to me."

The hurt in Jared's voice made Luke uneasy. He leaned on his arm, looking down at him. "I'm sorry."

Jared sat up. He put his head in his hands. "You're sorry? That's it? You don't think I have a right to be mad?" Luke tried to pull him close, but he jumped out of the bed. "Okay! Maybe I don't. But, damn it, it hurts! I wasn't ready for this. I wasn't ready for you to love someone else. I know we talked about it. I just wasn't ready!"

Luke got off the bed, put his arms around him, and stared into his eyes. "Jed, come on. I don't love her. I love you. You know that, but I have to try. We agreed."

"Well, I don't! I don't have to try. I know what I want."

Luke touched his arm. "I wish I could tell you what's going to happen, but I don't know. I just... I have to try."

Jared pushed him away. "Then what do you expect me to do? I can't just turn it off and on like you can -- one day pretend it's all fine and dandy then the next day watch you take a girl out. What happens to me in all of this? Where do I fit into the picture? What happens when you find the one you decide to marry? Then what's left?"

Luke took a deep breath. "I don't know. I don't want to think about it right now. Let's just be together. We'll figure it out. Something will work out. I promise."

"I can't." Jared turned away, shaking his head. "It's not fair."

Luke put his arms around him and kissed his neck. "No, it's not. Just come spend the day at the lake with me. It'll be fun." He kissed his lips then grinned. "Please? You won't be disappointed."

Jared stared at him, raising an eyebrow. He sighed and lowered his head. "All right, fine. I'll get dressed."

Luke smirked, watching him walk across the room. "Do you have to? I kinda like you like this!" He ran to him, kissing his neck again.

Jared pushed him away, trying to put on some clothes. "Stop it. I've gotta find my trunks." He grabbed his swim trunks out of the bottom drawer of his dresser. "Oh, shit! I better leave my parents a note and let them know what we're doing. Mom's going to be pissed. I'm going to miss Mass!"

"Taken care of. I'll just tell them I forgot all about it and had something planned for my birthday. They'll be fine." Luke winked at him. "I'll leave them a note."

"You really don't know them very well, do you?"

"Come on! We'll worry about it later! I'll take all the blame. Let's go!" Luke grabbed the swim trunks from him, stuffing them in his back pack. He grabbed Jared's hand, dragging him out the door.

As he drove away from the house, Luke glanced over at Jared. Content with having his friend at his side, he tried to push the issue of their future from his mind. Jared was right. It wasn't fair. "We'll figure it out. I promise." His words of that morning echoed in his head. Jared stared out the window with a smile on his face. Luke picked up his hand and kissed it.

TRULY, MADLY, DEEPLY

April 1994

Jared waited for Luke to arrive. The announcement about the Junior Prom lay on his desk. *Luke's going to be here any minute. How am I going to get him to go?*

The front door slammed, waking him from his day dreams. He ran to his bedroom door.

Luke yelled a greeting to Candace and Mike then winked at Jared as he raced down the stairs. "Hey, you."

Jared smiled, closing the door behind them.

Luke gave him a kiss on the cheek then lay down on the bed. "What's the matter? You look nervous?"

Jared took a deep breath, forcing a smile. "Nothing's the matter. I'm just glad to see you." He walked to his desk and picked up the announcement. Luke was recounting his day. Jared tried to pay attention, but his thoughts were on the dance.

"How about you? How was your day?" Luke tossed a pillow at him.

"It was fine. The usual." Jared looked down at the paper again.

THE VIEW FROM A RUSTY TRAIN CAR

Luke hopped out of bed then wrapped his arms around Jared. "I can tell something's up. Just tell me what it is."

Jared looked him in the eyes, leaning back against the desk. "Well, I was wondering..."

"Yes?"

Jared took a deep breath, turning away from him. "Okay. Here it is." He stared at the floor. The words flew out of his mouth. "I want to go to the prom. I have it all figured out so that we can spend most of it together. You can ask Megan and I'll take your cousin, Carrie. We'll do whatever it is... the Grand March and take pictures... then you and I can leave to spend the rest of the night together. What do you think?" His pulse raced while silent moments went by.

Luke turned his gaze from the wall to Jared. "We can't." He sat on the edge of the bed, shaking his head.

"It's okay. I've thought of everything."

Luke grabbed his arm. "Jed, it wouldn't be fair to the girls. We can't just dump them at the dance. Even if we did, where would we say we're going? Not to mention our parents... like they're going to let us go out for the night. It won't work." He sat on the bed, head in his hands.

"We tell them we're going to an after-prom party. My parents have to let me go. They let Megan go to one."

"Jared... it's not going to work. Trust me." Luke walked to the bed and sat down.

Jared knew it was going to be a hard sell, but Luke not listening to him was proving to be more frustrating than he anticipated. He sat on the bed next to Luke, grabbing his hand. "I know I ask a lot and I knew you wouldn't be excited about this, but this is really important to me. There's no way in hell we can go together, but we can at least be there together. We don't get to do things like everyone else gets to do with their boyfriends and girlfriends. This is as close as we get."

Luke jerked his hand away. "Jed, I..."

Jared knelt down, holding Luke's hands. "Please. Just think about it. I promise I won't go over the top. We'll do it whatever way you want."

There was a knock at the door. Jared jumped to his feet, staring toward the door.

"Jared? Luke?" Candace called from the other side of the door.

Jared ran to his desk, pretending to be involved in homework. "Yeah, Mom. Come in."

Candace appeared, smiling at them. "Supper's ready. Come on upstairs."

"Thanks. I'm not quite hungry yet. I've got a lot of homework to get done." Jared glanced over his shoulder at Luke, wondering if his mom could feel the tension in the room as much as he did.

"All right. You'll know where to find it when you're hungry." She looked at Luke. "How about you? You hungry?"

Luke smiled. "No thanks. I'm not hungry yet either."

"Suit yourselves." About to close the door, she stopped to pick up the announcement in front of Jared. "How fun! Luke, you must be taking Cassie, huh?"

Jared stared down at his desk, wishing he could turn to see Luke's reaction.

"I'm not sure yet."

Candace mussed Jared's hair then put the announcement back on his desk. "What about you? There must be someone you want to take out."

"I don't know." Jared gripped the pencil in his hand. "We'll see."

"Luke, would you talk him into going? He needs to get out and do things, instead of hanging out around home all the time." Candace shook her head, closing the door.

Jared shifted uncomfortably in his chair as he stared at Luke.

"Fine." Luke ran his thumb down Jared's cheek. "We'll try, but if it looks like it's not going to work or things get too complicated, I'm not going."

Jared jumped out of his chair, throwing his arms around Luke. "Thank you! I promise I'll work it out!" He held on to Luke, repeatedly kissing him. "I love you!"

Luke laughed, holding Jared's face. "Me too." He kissed his forehead and smiled.

OUT OF THE GAME

Luke sat on a swing, watching for Jared. He'd insisted they meet to talk about plans where no one could hear them. Tugging at the collar of his shirt, he thought about how to start this discussion. *I can't do it. He's going to be so pissed!* Making Megan and Carrie pawns in some horrible game they were playing felt wrong. *He has to understand.*

Jared ran to him, a big smile on his face. He sat on the swing next to Luke. "Okay, so I talked to Megan. She wasn't excited about the idea, but she finally agreed."

"Oh... thanks."

"She wasn't hesitating because she would be going with you. She just wasn't thrilled about going back to high school for another prom. She said she went through hers and that was enough."

"I don't blame her." Luke stared at his feet, kicking up dirt.

"But when I told her that she would just need to show up for Grand March and that we would be headed off to a party, she agreed."

"What happens if I want to stay? You know? Dance for a little bit. That's what prom is for." Luke was aware that his voice had a harsh edge to it.

Jared's smile disappeared. "I thought you'd want to get out of there as fast as you could."

"Well, maybe I don't. Maybe I want to dance some." Luke jumped off the swing, turning away from Jared.

"Is something wrong?"

"No! I just thought since we're going to spend all this money on the tuxes and flowers that maybe we should stay a little longer." Luke picked up a rock, throwing it across the road.

Jared leaned against a pole of the swing set. "Who is it? Who's the one you're interested in?"

Luke turned, shocked at the lack of emotion in Jared's voice. "Well... no one in particular."

"Oh, really? If it's no one then why are you trying to get out of spending time alone with me?"

Luke grabbed the pole. The acidic tone to Jared's voice was more like what he was expecting. "I'm not! We have the whole night. I just thought it would be nice to..."

"I thought we already agreed to all of this!" Jared pushed the swing out of his way. It swung back, hitting Luke in the chest.

Luke marched up to him, putting his finger in Jared's face. "No, Jared! You agreed to it! I haven't said anything one way or another."

"Only because you've done nothing to help. You just sit and nod your head." Jared pushed his hand away.

Luke took a deep breath, knowing Jared was right. He put his hand on Jared's shoulder, turning him.

Jared threw his hand off and walked away. He stopped, turning back to him. "You know what? Fine. I get it. You don't want to go. You never wanted to go. Just don't worry about it anymore. You just do whatever the hell it is you want. I won't bother you about it."

"Jed, wait!" Luke started toward him.

Jared turned, looking him in the eye. "No! Just stop! I'm sick of this. This is obviously much more important to me than it is to you. If you don't think it's important then... This whole fucking situation is hard enough as it is. I don't need to keep going through this!"

Luke watched Jared disappear down the road. "Damn it! He's right. Why can't I do this one thing for him?" He had to stop him. "Jared! Come back here!"

Jared yelled over his shoulder. "Luke, no! I'm done with everything. Just leave me the hell alone."

Hearing those words was like a punch in the stomach. Luke quickly wiped away a tear, ready to run after him. He stopped, thoughts swirling around in his head. "Maybe it's all for the best. Life would be easier." He watched Jared disappear around the corner then made his way back to the swing. "Then why does it feel like life is over." Everything in him wanted to run to Jared. "What did I do?"

Luke got off the swing. Deciding he wasn't ready to go home yet, he headed toward town. He needed time to clear his head.

Memories of the two of them bombarded his mind as he looked at the familiar surroundings. A memory of Jared was attached to everything, reminders of how easily Jared could make him laugh and, most importantly, how Jared was the only one who made him feel loved.

Luke turned to the chain link fence around the basketball court and slammed his hands against it. "Why does it have to be so damned hard?" He laid his head against it, not noticing his classmate, Phillip, was just a few feet away on the other side.

"Luke? Are you okay?"

Luke jumped, trying to regain his composure. "Oh! Hey, Phillip. Yeah. I'm fine. How are you?"

Phillip walked up to him, standing just on the other side. "You look awful. Something's wrong."

Luke forced a smile, not realizing it was so evident. "It's nothing. I just had a fight with someone."

"Jared?" Phillip whispered.

Luke's heart raced and his throat tightened. "What?"

"Well I just thought..."

Luke could barely breathe, forcing a chuckle to cover. "Oh. So you've heard the rumors, huh?" He shook his head. "The guys can be such assholes!"

"I haven't heard any rumors." Phillip crossed his arms and grinned at Luke. "I can just tell. Jared's in love with you. It's pretty obvious."

Luke laughed again, walking away. "Whatever. You have no idea what you're talking about."

"Yes I do!" Phillip yelled, running up beside him. "I know exactly what you guys are going through. I can't say that I blame him."

Luke stopped, turning to see Phillip standing with his head down. "What do you mean?"

Phillip looked him in the eyes with a smile. "You know what I mean. It's difficult to be like us... especially in this town."

Luke was stunned. It was one thing for him and Jared to be going through this, but he'd never thought there might be others. A thousand questions raced through his mind as he walked back to Phillip. "How... what do...?" He took a deep breath. "It's so confusing. You know? The feelings... The..."

"Attraction?"

"Yeah. I guess." Luke looked away, folding his arms, uncomfortable admitting it. "Phillip, listen. I'm not gay! I'm not attracted to other guys. I just have all these confused feelings about him. I don't understand."

"Do you love him?"

"What?" Luke looked around, conscious about who might hear them. Realizing they were alone he leaned into Phillip.

"Jared? Do you love him?" Phillip lowered his voice.

Luke rubbed his face. "You mean...? I don't know. Maybe. I guess I love him. You know. Like that."

"Luke, come on. You either do or you don't."

Luke clutched the fence. "It's not that simple."

Phillip made his way around the fence. Standing in front of Luke, he put his hand on his shoulder. "I get it. I do. It's hard because Jared is sure, isn't he?"

Luke looked at him and nodded. Surprised by a tear that formed in his eye, he brushed it away quickly and stood up.

"Come on." Phillip tugged on Luke's arm. "Let's go to my house. We can talk about it."

Luke felt uneasy about the invitation. *Can I trust him?* Caution stilled his tongue. *What if Phillip isn't genuine about what he's saying? Is he setting me up?*

Phillip touched his arm. "I know we don't know each other that well, but you need to talk to someone about this – someone besides Jared. He's too close to what's happening."

Luke looked into his eyes and started to cry. "I don't know if I can. I spend all my time thinking about how to hide it, not talk about it."

Phillip smiled. "Then do it for me. I don't have anyone to talk to about it either. Maybe we'll figure something out."

Luke thought for a moment. It would be great to talk about things with someone that understood. "Sure. What the hell. I've got nothing to lose."

Phillip laughed. "And if you're interested, I stole a bottle of vodka from my dad. I've never opened it. I think tonight's the night."

Luke was unsure again. "Are you sure? What about your parents?"

"Don't worry. They're out of town on some sort of business meeting. It'll be just us – no interruptions, no one to overhear us." Phillip winked.

Luke took a deep breath. He needed to do something. He didn't want to spend the night at home with his mom hovering around him. "Okay. Let's do it!" He put his arm around Phillip's neck and playfully punched him in the arm.

SOMEBODY TO LOVE

Luke lay in bed thinking, already awake for two hours. He hadn't seen Jared in almost a week. He couldn't help worrying about him. "I am such a jerk! This isn't Jared's fault. This is my problem."

He sat up, staring through his window, thinking about what he had decided to do.

There was a light knock on his door.

Luke grabbed his blankets to cover himself. "Who is it?"

A small voice called through the door. "Luke. Can I come in?"

"Sure. Come in, Susie." He was relieved it wasn't his mother. They'd been fighting constantly the last few weeks.

Susie entered, looking down the hall before she closed the door behind her. She hurried over to Luke, handing him a small box.

"What's this?"

"It's from Jared. He asked me to give this to you," she whispered.

"When did you see, Jared?"

"Just now." She looked down at Luke. "He looked really sad."

Luke opened the box, shuffling through its contents. It was everything he'd ever given Jared over the years. "Did he say anything else?"

"No, just to give that to you."

"Thanks." Luke lay back down, staring at the ceiling as Susie left the room. "Maybe I'm too late. Why would Jared ever want to talk to me again, let alone give me another chance?"

He jumped out of bed and threw on some clothes. "No!" Grabbing the box, he ran out the house. He rehearsed his speech to make it convincing. It would be a heated discussion, but he was determined. He was not going down without a fight.

He knocked on the front door of the Montgomery house, bolting inside when he heard Candace tell him to come in.

Standing in the entryway, he called up to her. "Hi, Candace. Jared around?"

"Hi, you! I was wondering where you were. We haven't seen you in a while." She leaned over the railing, giving him a smile. "He should be in his room. I heard him come in a little while ago."

"Thanks!" He ran down the stairs to Jared's door. He was about to knock, but thought better of it. That would give Jared the chance to refuse to talk to him. The conversation was going to happen. He had to act while he still had the nerve.

Luke burst into the room. He let the door slam behind him.

Jared jumped up, grabbing his chest. "Holy shit! You scared the hell out of me!"

Before Jared could protest, Luke marched up to him. "You're going to sit there and listen to me."

Jared got up off the bed. "Get the hell..."

"No." Luke pushed him back down. "I know I was an asshole and I'm sorry. You have every right to be mad, but I am not taking these back." He threw the box down on Jared's bed.

Jared picked it up, trying to hand it back to him. "Luke, I'm not..."

"And another thing," Luke interrupted him. "I've been thinking a lot this last week. I've figured very little out, but I know one thing. I love you, Jared Montgomery, and that's all that seems to matter to me right now."

Luke sat on the edge of Jared's bed. He leaned forward, putting his head in his hands. "I've put you through a lot. I know that. It's really unfair. None of it was your fault. I've decided that, if you'll take me back, I want to try. I want this... us... to work!" He looked to Jared. "What do you say? Can you forgive me?"

Jared stared up at him. "I don't know. Are you sure? I mean, are you really sure about what it is you want?"

Luke stood in front of him. "I'm sure about wanting to try. How and if it's going to work, I'm not so sure. It's worth a try, isn't it?"

Jared got off the bed, pushing past Luke. He sat at his desk.

Luke's heart raced waiting for him to say something. Jared didn't move. "I'll give you some time to think about it. It's a lot to take in." He went to leave, but stopped at the door when he heard Jared chuckle.

Jared turned to him. "Why are you doing this? Can't you leave well enough alone?"

Luke looked down at the floor. "I'm sorry." His heart sank.

Jared pulled him back in the room, slamming the door shut. "I did some thinking this last week, too." He motioned for Luke to sit on the bed. "I decided that I was asking too much."

"Jared, no..." Luke reached for him, but Jared walked away.

"Yes! You made it clear you didn't think you were gay and that you didn't see it working out. How can I do this to you? Or to me, for that matter? If you tried to smooth it all over I was going to say no, no matter how much it hurt." Jared wiped the tears away with his arm. "I've never made it a secret that I'm in love with you, that being with you is what I want. It's all I think about. I'm gay. I can say it, but you have doubts so I think you need to stay away from me. You have to do what you have to do. I've got to figure out what it is I have to do."

Tears rolled down Luke's cheek. "What are you saying?"

"I'm saying you can stop. I know you care for me in some way, but this needs to stop. I don't need your pity. It's not doing either of us any good. So, please, just go!" Jared walked over to the window, staring out toward the hills.

Luke turned to leave. Taking one last look at Jared, he watched as Jared buried his face into his hands. "No!"

"Go!" Jared yelled.

Luke ran to him. He grabbed his shoulder and turned him so they were facing. "No! I won't." Unsure of what else to say, he pulled Jared into a kiss.

Jared tried to pull away, but couldn't break the hold. He cried, putting his forehead against Luke's lips. "Please don't do this, not if you don't really mean it."

Luke grabbed his hand, led him to the bed. Sitting beside him, he laid his head on Jared's shoulder. "I know it's hard to trust me after everything I've done. I don't blame you." Lifting his head, he held Jared's face in his hands, staring into his eyes. "I'm begging you to believe me right now. I do love you. I do want this to work. Can you give me just one more chance? Please?"

Jared took a deep breath, bowing his head. "I don't know."

Luke stroked Jared's cheek before walking to the door. "Just promise me you'll think about it. Okay?" Jared stared off as tears rolled down his face.

Walking up the stairs to leave, Luke felt numb. He was saddened by what had just happened, but it was beyond that. It was as if he had nothing left in the world. Nothing mattered. He took one more look down the stairs, sure this was the last chance he'd have, then left.

Luke needed to clear his head. He didn't know what else to do. It was time to walk... and think. He hadn't thought much about what the future might hold. It surprised him that in all his dreams he and Jared were together. "God I'm stupid!" He knew he was in love with Jared, but he had blown it. He was in love and now it was over. The longer he walked, imagining what life would be like without Jared, the sicker he felt.

He walked a bit faster towards home. He was cold, miserable, wanting only to be alone in his room. What he would do after that, he had no idea.

He was too tired to deal with walking past the fort or the train car. He changed his route home.

He realized he was more tired than he thought. He massaged his chest. It felt tight. "Come on, Luke. Don't let it get to you. Not again." He took a deep breath, hoping it would go away like before. "Coach said it was because you're out of shape and holding on to stress. Stress? Really?" He chuckled.

Wanting to get home as quickly as possible, he turned down the gravel road that ran by the old fort. "Just don't look at it. You'll be fine."

A noise approached from behind. He glanced back to see a figure running toward him. Not giving it any thought, he continued, stopping only when he heard his name. It was Jared. He looked as if he'd run a marathon; his hair was wet from sweat and he was breathing heavily.

"What are you doing?" Luke called to him.

Jared caught up to him, throwing his arms around him and collapsing into his arms.

Luke didn't know what to say. He reached around and held him. The embrace felt more amazing than any before. He wanted it to last for as long as possible.

Jared pulled back, keeping a hold of Luke's arm to keep steady. "No wonder I'm not in any sports. This sucks." He looked up at Luke, panting. "You really like this running shit?"

Luke chuckled, caressing his arm. "Jed, what are you doing?"

"Trying to catch you, you jerk. I almost had you twice, but you'd speed up again." He let go of Luke, standing in front of him. "Didn't you hear me calling you?"

"No. I'm sorry. I guess I was thinking." Luke caught Jared, who almost lost his balance. He helped Jared sit on the curb, smiling as he caught a glimpse of their fort standing behind them.

Luke sat close to him. His mind raced, wanting to say the right thing to make everything better. "Jed, I'm so sorry for everything."

Jared put his finger to Luke's mouth. "Luke, I just have one question for you."

Luke waited for him to continue, trying to read Jared's face. "Well? What is it?"

"Will you go to the prom with me?" Jared laughed as a smile stretched from ear to ear.

Luke jumped up, grabbing Jared's hands, pulling him into an embrace. "Really? You're giving me another chance?"

"I'm probably going to regret it, but... I had to. I can't help it! There's obviously something mentally wrong with me. For some reason, I believe you. We've got to try. I've got nothing else. I don't want anything else." Jared smiled then kissed him.

Luke looked Jared in the eye. "I promise you, I'll make you happy. I will. It might take me some time to get it all right, but I'll work on it! I swear."

"I know you will." Jared winked at him. "Walk me to the fence?"

"I'd love to." Luke held Jared's hand, leading him toward home. As always, he let go before reaching the corner, before anyone might see them.

Jared started for home, smiling over his shoulder. "See you later."

Luke looked around. Seeing no one, he took Jared's arm, pulling him back around the fence, and kissed him. "Goodnight, Baby."

Jared smiled, touching his cheek. "Goodnight."

Luke walked home, thinking about all that had happened. "God, Jared is amazing!" He shook his head. "Now you know what it's like feeling like you've lost him. Don't screw this up. You do want this."

Luke readied himself for bed, laughing as he looked in the mirror, seeing the silly grin on his face. "You are one lucky guy."

He lay on his bed, turned onto his side he reached down between the wall and his mattress. Pulling out a photo, he smiled as he stared at Jared's school picture. He caressed it with his thumb then held it close. "Sleep tight, Jed. See you tomorrow." After one last look, he returned it to its hiding spot.

Looking through the window, he stared up at stars filling the clear night sky. "I love you, Baby."

IT'S MY PARTY

Jared looked at the clock again. He shifted, tapping his foot on the floor as he tucked up the cuff of his sleeve to check the time on his watch. "God, Luke. I wish I could believe you. I know you'll try." He shook his head to clear his mind of any doubt, trying to focus on the positive.

There was soft tap at the door. Luke peered in, a big smile on his face. "Excuse me, Sir. May I come in?"

Jared grabbed Luke's arm, pulling him into the room. "Get in here, you goofball." He laughed, closing the door. Sitting back at his desk, he shuffled some papers around.

"Whatcha working on?" Jared felt Luke behind him. Arms wrapped around him. A kiss landed on the top of his head.

"I was... um..." Jared hesitated, still uncertain about Luke's real commitment to the relationship. "Just making plans. You know... prom."

"Oh, God!"

Jared grimaced, turning to him. "What? What's the matter?"

"I forgot all about it! It's the weekend after next, isn't it? What can I help with?" Luke knelt down beside him, looking at the notes.

THE VIEW FROM A RUSTY TRAIN CAR

Jared studied Luke. "It's fine. I think I've got it all figured out."

Luke lay down on the bed, patting the spot beside him. "Come here. Bring the notes. I want to hear the plans."

Jared grabbed the notes and ran to him. Jumping into the bed, he landed beside Luke, snuggling into him. Luke put his arm under Jared's head and kissed him.

"Okay. Now, let me know what you think. If you want to do something different, we'll change it!"

Luke's eyes were closed, a broad smile on his face. "Sure."

"I talked to Megan again and she said yes. I also called Carrie. She wasn't sure, but when I told her Megan was going, she said yes. They both are happy we're not staying. They're glad to just do the Grand March, go home, and let us go to our party."

"Party?" Luke raised an eyebrow. "Oh, yeah! Never mind. Excellent." He chuckled, laying his head next to Jared's.

"Tomorrow we should order our tuxes." Jared ran to his desk and grabbed another paper. He pointed at the picture. "What do you think of these?"

"Nice." He smirked. "You'll look hotter in that tux than he does."

Jared giggled, punching him in the leg. "Be serious."

"I am being serious!"

"I know you're going to think this is cheesy, but if you wear this vest and bow-tie and I wear these, well... you know. They kind of match. They're just reversed." Feeling the blood rushing to his cheeks, Jared looked away. "You think it's stupid, don't you?"

Luke grabbed his hand, caressing it. "I think it's sweet."

"Really?"

"Really."

"I made reservations for all of us at Heidi's Place. Oh! And my dad's letting us take his Mustang. Isn't that cool?" He looked down. Luke's eyes were closed again. "Sweetheart? Are you all right!"

Luke jumped up, putting his hand on his shoulder. "Why? I'm fine."

"You seem really tired. We can do this later." Jared walked to his desk and put the papers down.

"No. I'm sorry. I just stayed up late. I had a stupid paper due this morning." Luke wiped his eyes and sat up. "I'm awake. I'm listening."

Jared pushed him back down and lay beside him. Grabbing Luke's arm, he wrapped it around himself. Luke pulled him close, snuggling his face into Jared's neck.

Jared didn't care that Luke was tired. He enjoyed having him near. *He's trying. We might just have a chance.* He felt Luke's breath on his nape then closed his eyes. *I'll make it worth it, Luke. I promise!*

AND THE BAND PLAYED ON

Jared winked at Luke on the other side of the car while he held the door for Carrie and Megan. The formalities were over. He was ready for the real night to begin.

"Where's your party, boys?"

Seeing Luke's blank expression to Megan's question, Jared came to the rescue. "It's out at Paul Jenkin's place."

"Sounds like fun." Megan elbowed Carrie. "Maybe you should go with them."

Jared stared at Megan's reflection in the rearview mirror. He glanced at Luke, unable to believe all their plans were going down the toilet.

"No, thank you!" Carrie pulled the clips from her hair. "That was quite enough revisiting high school for me."

Jared chuckled. "I don't blame you."

Luke smirked at him, turning to the girls. "Thank you both again for coming with us. I know it was painful."

Megan smiled. "It wasn't that bad. It could've been worse. You're not a bad date." She laughed, patting him on the arm.

Jared pulled into Carrie's driveway. He helped her out of the car then walked her to the front door. "Thanks, again. I had a really nice time."

"It was nothing. Don't tell anyone I said this, but it was actually kind of fun." She leaned in, kissing him on the cheek. "You guys have fun. And behave." She winked at him, disappearing into the house.

As Jared headed back to the car, he noticed Luke standing by the driver's side door. "What are you doing?"

"My turn!" Luke jumped into the driver's seat. "Come on. Get in."

Jared watched through his window, wondering what the night would bring. Luke had insisted that he would plan the after party, keeping everything a secret. His body tingled with excitement. When they arrived in the Montgomery's driveway, Luke got out, offering his hand to Megan. She got out and led him to the door.

"Wait!" Jared stopped them, running up to Megan. "Thanks, Meg. I owe you." He hugged her.

"You owe me big for this."

Jared went to the car and watched them say their goodnights. His heart raced seeing the huge smile on Luke's face as he walked to the car.

Behind the wheel again, Luke grabbed Jared's hand and kissed it. "Well, Sir? Are you ready for our date?"

"I can't wait."

As the car pulled out of the driveway, Jared tried to imagine every scenario that might be in store. He was shocked when the car turned off so near their houses.

Luke stared forward, a devilish grin on his face.

The car slowed as they neared the fort. As the car pulled off the road toward the trees, Jared braced himself, thinking something was wrong. "Luke? What are you doing? What's wrong?"

He was about to grab the wheel of the car when he saw a path had been made through the trees. It wouldn't have been noticeable to anyone else, just enough for the car to fit through.

Luke stopped, shut off the car, jumped out and disappeared.

THE VIEW FROM A RUSTY TRAIN CAR

Jared used the rear-view mirror to try to see what was happening. Luke was dragging branches toward the road. The branches were tied together and once affixed to the tree on either side of their tracks the car was completely concealed from the road.

Jared laughed. "I can't believe this! You've thought of everything!"

After finishing with the branches, Luke walked back to the car, smiling from ear to ear. "Would you grab the blanket from the trunk?"

Jared opened the trunk and took out a blanket that lay at the bottom.

Luke put the convertible top down then took the blanket from Jared and spread it over the back seat. "I have a surprise for you," he whispered. He reached into the backseat for a bag, opened it, then pulled out some wine and glasses. He poured, giving a glass to Jared then raising his own. "To us!" He lifted his glass.

Jared clinked his glass against Luke's and scooted close to him. "To us."

"I almost forgot." Luke reached into the front seat. Turning on the radio, he offered his hand. "May I have this dance, gorgeous?"

Jared stared into Luke's eye, holding his hand. "I'd love to." He was breathless at the sight of Luke's face in the moonlight. He wanted to remember that picture forever.

Luke placed their glasses on the trunk, jumped out, and put his hands on Jared's waist, lifting him to the ground. He pulled his date closer, caressing his cheek before kissing him.

Luke led. Jared, his head resting on Luke's shoulder, allowed himself to be swept away with the music, the scent of Luke's cologne, the strong hand on his waist moving him to the beat. When the music stopped, Luke pulled away "Is something wrong?"

"I'm fine. It's you I'm worried about. Are you all right? You're shaking."

Jared hadn't noticed. "I'm just a little cold. It's no big deal."

"Do you want to go home?"

"No, God!" Jared pulled him close. "I want to stay right here."

Luke kissed him before returning to the car. He grabbed the blanket and wrapped it around Jared. "There's no use catching a cold."

Jared rested his head on Luke's shoulder. Behind them, the edge of the train car reflected in the moonlight. "How about in there? We can take the blanket and wine and in there for the night."

"That's a great idea." Luke smiled as he grabbed the stuff from the car then put his arm around Jared to lead him to the train car.

Jared watched Luke climb inside. A light came on and Luke appeared at the bottom. He passed everything down before joining him.

Luke took his hand, leading him to the back room where the blanket was spread. He gave Jared a glass of wine then laid back.

Jared joined him, lying tucked against his chest. "Thank you so much. This has been an amazing night."

"No. Thank you." Luke brushed the hair on Jared's forehead. "Look at me. I ended up with the cutest boy at the Prom! I am awesome." He laughed, pulling Jared into a kiss.

#

The second bottle of wine was almost empty. They had said little, content with being close to each other. Jared felt hot and a bit light-headed. "I have to take this jacket off." He slipped it off, lay it in the corner.

"Good idea. I feel like I'm being strangled." Luke removed his jacket, bow-tie, and shirt then lay back down. "Phew! That's much better."

The sight of Luke lying close to him half-dressed made Jared's heart flutter. He hesitated a moment thinking the wine was affecting his decisions, followed Luke's lead and removed his shirt.

Luke smiled, motioning for him to lie down beside him. He ran his finger down Jared's chest, looking into his eyes. "What are you thinking about?"

Jared hesitated, taking a deep breath. He leaned on one arm, looking into Luke's eyes. "Make love to me."

Luke jumped, turning away from him. "Jed... I can't."

Jared grabbed his hand. "I'm sorry. Did I do something wrong?"

"No. It's not you. It's... I knew this would come. I knew you'd want this. I want it too. I do. But... I can't. I'm not ready. I'm sorry."

Jared moved to the other side of the room. "I don't know what I was saying."

Hands on Jared's shoulder, Luke turned him, face to face. "Jed, I'm honored that you want me to be with you like that. I just need time. I'm messed up. I'm just not ready for that yet. I'm sorry. I wish I could."

"You're absolutely right. I'm an idiot." Jared stared at the floor, unable to hide his disappointment.

Luke held his face, looking into his eyes. "Baby, it's not you. It has nothing to do with you."

Jared pulled Luke's hands away from his face. "I'm an idiot. I've ruined everything."

Luke shook his head, putting his arms around him. "No! Never! I love being with you." Taking Jared by the hand, he led him back to the blanket. "Will you just lie next to me?"

"Of course." Jared cuddled into Luke's side, placing his hand on his chest. "Thank you."

Luke rolled onto his side, looking into Jared's eyes, caressing his face.

Jared stared at Luke's face until he was sure he'd fallen asleep. He kissed him on the forehead. The evening had been so wonderful it didn't need anything else.

Luke reached out, pulling him close.

Jared closed his eyes, lying in his arms, wishing it wouldn't end.

A DESTINY OF SOULS

May 1994

Luke rushed around the train car, preparing for Jared's arrival. He looked at his watch. "Damn it, Mom! Why did you have to make me late? I want everything to be perfect." He slipped a tape from his backpack into an old player he found in the garage. "Come on. Please work." The music played. He took a much needed breath as he looked around at his work then listened to hear if Jared was approaching. Hearing nothing, he went back to his preparations.

The blanket was smoothed, pillows propped so they could relax while they ate. Satisfied with his work, he reached into a cooler, pulling out the food he'd made and plated it. To finish off the mood, candles were lit. All that was missing was Jared.

Luke lay down on the blankets. Another hour passed. The candles had been lit, extinguished, and relit three times. His mind wandered. *Has something happened? Maybe Jared changed his mind. What did I do wrong? Maybe I should go looking for him?*

Unable to wait any longer, he decided to take a look outside to see if there was any sign. As he neared the ladder, he heard the sound of someone climbing up the back of the train car. He smiled with anticipation, rushing to meet him.

He looked up toward the hatch then shielded his eyes as the sunlight poured in. "Jed?"

"Yeah, it's me."

Luke was surprised at the lack of excitement in his voice. Jared climbed down the ladder only using one hand; he reached up to help, but Jared pulled his hand away and kept his back to Luke.

Luke waited for him say something. His throat tightened seeing Jared put his hand to his head and moan. "Sweetheart? What's wrong?"

Jared took a deep breath. He turned to him, an ice pack held on his right eye.

"Oh, my God! What happened to you?" Luke lowered Jared's hand. His eye was swollen and dark purple. "What in the hell happened? Who did this to you?"

Jared walked past him, his face showing no emotion. "I got jumped in the hallway at school."

Luke wrapped his arms around him. "Come on. Come sit down." He led him to the back room and helped him onto the pillows.

Jared lay down, putting the ice pack back on his eye.

"Who was it? I swear to God I'll kill them!" Luke paced back and forth. "Jed, talk to me. What happened?"

"I was just standing at my locker. I opened it and found your wonderful note. I was so excited! I shut the locker and when I turned... there they were at the end of the hall. He had this horrible look on his face. I knew something was going to happen."

"Who was it?"

"Who do you think?" Jared gave a half-hearted chuckle, shaking his head. "Craig Johnson."

Luke's jaw tensed, pacing some more until he slammed his fist against the wall. "I'll kill that son-of-a-bitch!"

The sound filled the train car.

"Luke, please! My head hurts enough already." Jared reached out, smiling at him.

Luke knelt beside him. He held his hand and caressed his face. "He's not going to get away with this."

"I'll be fine. You'll just get in trouble. It's not worth it. I'll live."

Luke lay down beside him, stroking his arm. "How did you get away?"

"Well, he said, 'There's nowhere to run you little faggot', ran up to me and punched me in the stomach. I fell against the locker. It must've made a really loud noise because after he got on top of me and punched me a few times, I heard footsteps running up the stairwell. It was Mr. Miller. Thank God. He must've been there for the detention people." Jared sat up, staring forward. "He yelled at him to get off me and ran toward us. Craig jumped up, ran down the hall, and disappeared."

Luke swallowed hard. "Jared! He could've..."

"I know!" Jared took the ice pack off his eye and threw it across the room. "It got me thinking."

Luke moved close to him, putting his arm under Jared's head. "About what?"

"Us."

"What? I've been trying haven't I? Did I do something? I tried to make this a romantic night for you." Luke felt his heart pounding in his chest.

Jared's face filled with tears. "You've been amazing. This looks so wonderful. Thank you."

"Then what is it?"

"It's the whole thing. I was wrong. You were right to not want this. People... just don't understand. It's unfair to you. You're not even sure about it."

Luke put his hands on Jared's shoulders. "I'm not unsure about us! I love you. I go to bed every night thinking about you, about how much I love you, how much I miss you when I'm in bed alone."

"Luke, just stop! I'm not saying anything bad about you. I'm saying I don't know about it myself anymore – if it's even worth it." Jared wiped the tears from his eyes, putting his head on his knees.

"I know. I've been through all of this in my own head." Luke studied Jared's battered face. "I was afraid of this happening." He cradled him, rocking back and forth. "A lot of what I was afraid of is what would happen to us." He took a deep breath. "No one talks about what happens when you fall in love with the boy next door -- not when you're the boy living beside the boy next door. You just know that you can't even ask. You can't talk about it. Even though Mom says to forget about girls and focus on studying, you know she can't wait for you to bring a girl home. She wants to plan the proms and think about what the grandchildren will look like. Parents don't plan for their son to bring home the 'man' he loves. I don't understand why people get so angry about it. Why does it bother them? It has nothing to do with them." Luke caressed Jared's arm and took a deep breath. "I don't care what they think. I know what I want." He ran his fingers through Jared's hair. "It's just that simple. I love you!"

#

Luke stared at the ceiling, breathless, heart racing. He felt flushed and exhausted, but euphoric. It was his first time, and it was the right time with the man that he loved.

Jared reached over to wipe the sweat from Luke's forehead, and smiled.

Luke kissed his forehead. "You're an incredible guy. I do love you. I hope you know that."

"I do." Jared snuggled in, burying his face into Luke's side.

Luke pointed at the graffiti and initials of others who'd laid claim to the train car. "I think it's time we put ours up there, too."

Jared giggled, jumping on top of Luke, giving him a smirk. "Does this mean you're going to love me forever?"

Luke reached for his face, kissing him one more time before searching the heap of clothes for his backpack. He rummaged through it then pulled out a small jar of paint and a brush. He stepped over Jared, searching the wall for the perfect place. Sensing Jared staring at him, he raised an eyebrow. "Are you going to help me or not? I'm not the only one who should be walking around here naked. I wouldn't mind a look for myself."

Jared's face flushed. He seemed to hesitate, but eventually walked toward Luke.

Luke was breathless at the sight of the man he loved walking toward him. "God you're beautiful." He shook his head, turning to the wall.

Jared wrapped his arms around him and kissed the back of his neck.

"Don't look yet." Luke put his hands over Jared's eyes, moving him a few steps back. "Ready?" He removed his hands and held him.

Jared beamed, reading aloud what Luke had written. *"L Loves J – Forever"*

"We'll figure it out somehow. I promise!" Luke kissed Jared's shoulder, locking their hands together.

There was a loud bang above them. Luke pushed Jared against the wall, shielding him. He listened again. There was silence.

"What was that?" Jared held on to Luke.

"I don't know. Turn off the light!" Luke moved to the doorway, hesitated, his ears straining, heart pounding.

The hatch snapped shut. Something banged above, continuing down the back side. Then there was silence.

Luke ran to the pile of clothes. As he dressed, he listened for more signs of trouble. "Hand me the flashlight."

Jared fumbled around for it. He crawled over to Luke, handing it to him. "I'm scared."

Luke took the flashlight from Jared's shaking hand. He squeezed it, winking at him. Jared gave a weak smile then took a deep breath as Luke ran to the ladder. Looking back at Jared, he held his finger up, telling him to be quiet then gave another reassuring smile before he started up.

Climbing the ladder, he thought about who was on the outside waiting for him. *Craig? You come to finish what you started? That fucker's going to be sorry!*

He opened the hatch, scanned his surroundings. There was nothing. Wind blew the tree branches around. He climbed out, walking to the edge. A large branch hit against the top of the train car. He went back inside. "Jared. It's okay. Turn the light on."

Jared grabbed the lantern, switching it on.

"It was just the wind." Luke walked to the back. "There's nothing out there." He looked Jared up and down then started to laugh.

Jared frowned, hitting his arm. "What's so funny?"

"Nothing. You're just so cute with your hair all messed up and your shirt on backwards."

"Oh, really?" Jared smiled. "You look pretty cute yourself... in my jeans."

"Trade you your pants for my shirt."

Jared grinned, pulling the shirt over his head then offering it to Luke.

Luke spotted a mark on Jared's chest and touched it. "You may want to be careful who sees that hickey."

"Hey. That's not fair." Jared pulled Luke toward him. Giving him a devilish smile, he put his lips to Luke's neck.

"I think we're going to have to be more careful about where we spend our time together. That noise almost gave me a heart attack. I pictured about ten different people up there and I didn't want it to be any of them."

"I know. You're right."

Luke checked his watch. "Holy shit! It's late. We'd better get home." He unbuttoned his jeans so he could take them off.

"Wait." Jared looked embarrassed, turning away from him. "You're going to think this is really stupid."

"What is it?"

"Can I wear your shirt home tonight?"

"Why?"

"I don't want to be away from you. At least I'll have something of yours. I can smell your cologne on it." Jared couldn't look him in the eyes. "Is that too stupid?"

Luke walked to him. "It's not. Of course you can, but only if I get to wear your clothes. It's kind of cold, and it might be hard to explain why I'm coming home in just my boxers."

"Deal!" Jared kissed him. "Thank you... for everything." He held on to him, putting his head on Luke's shoulder. "I'm going to miss you."

"Me too." Luke remembered the time. "Come on. We'd better get things cleaned up and get home."

Jared picked up Luke's shirt, putting it back on. "Will I see you tomorrow?"

"Of course." Luke stopped, remembering what was planned the next day. "Wait. We're going to visit my grandma this weekend. We're leaving early tomorrow morning."

"Can't you just stay home?" Jared grabbed his hands. "Please?"

"I wish I could, but we're supposed to help her with some things around the farm. Mom's not going to let me get out of that."

"When will you be back?"

"Sunday afternoon. Just watch for our car. We'll meet here."

"Don't worry about this stuff. I'll clean it up this weekend. Let's just get out of here so we're not grounded."

Luke kissed Jared once more, staring for a moment into his eyes. "I love you, Baby."

"I love you, too."

Luke took one more look at him before heading up the ladder and out the hatch. He walked to the edge, looking up at the moon.

Following the well-known path, he felt the urge to yell. "It is worth it." He remembered the feelings of confusion, but tonight changed all of it. "There's no turning back now. That's just the way I want it."

The light was on in the living room. He thought it best to wait a moment, hoping his mother would go to bed. He didn't want her to ruin his happiness. He leaned against the house, trying to catch one more glimpse of Jared before he left for the weekend.

THE VIEW FROM A RUSTY TRAIN CAR

GOODBYE YELLOW BRICK ROAD

Sunday morning, Jared sat on his bed, awaiting Luke's return, ready to start the new course their lives were taking. He spent the weekend trying to imagine what might lie ahead, thinking about where they would go after graduation.

He walked down the hall, into the bathroom to shower. The steam rolled out the bathroom when he opened the door. He went to the kitchen for a bowl of cereal. From the corner of his eye he noticed a car pulling into Luke's driveway. He didn't think Luke would be home until much later in the day. A nervous excitement ran through his body. He dumped his cereal and ran to his bedroom to get ready.

Fussing with his damp hair, he bolted from his room and, in four giant steps, was at the door and out of the house. He knew he had rushed, but he was pretty sure he'd still look damn good to Luke.

Halfway down the driveway he noticed the back-up lights on Luke's mom's car come on, heading out of the driveway. He reached his hand up to his brow to block the sun, trying to see if Luke was in the car. The car turned onto the street, pulling parallel to Jared's driveway. Ellen stared at him, seeming to seethe with anger, before speeding off down the road.

Gravel flew from under his feet as he ran to find Luke. In moments he was through the garage, standing at the door. Shaking, he rang the bell twice. A strange feeling came over him when no one answered. He rang the bell again.

Susie appeared from around the corner, stopping when she saw him through the window. She stared for a moment before opening the door.

"Hey, Susie. Is Luke home?" He noticed her eyes were red and swollen. "Is something wrong?" He tried to read her face.

Susie sat in a chair at the table, struggling to hold back more tears. "Luke's not home."

"Do you know when he'll be back?"

More tears streamed down her face as she shook her head.

"Okay. Thanks, Susie." He turned to leave. Sensing she wanted to say more, he walked over to her, putting his hand on her shoulder. "What's the matter?"

Susie shifted in her chair, looking through the window and wiping her face. "Luke and Mom had a big fight. They fought in the car on the way to Grandma's. It was something about you."

Jared's heart sank. "Is he all right?"

Susie looked down at the table. "I don't know. He stayed in his room all night. Mom was so mad she couldn't stop yelling. She told Uncle Richard she had to do something about it. I know he could hear her." She reached out and held his hand. "I went to his room and knocked on his door, but he never answered. I heard him crying."

Jared wanted to hear more, but the look on Susie's face made him stop. "It will all be okay." He squeezed her hand then went to the door. "Will you tell Luke to let me know as soon as he gets home?"

"Wait!" Susie caught up to him in the garage. "Luke put something in my room during the night." The screen door slammed behind her as she disappeared into the house.

Susie came back seconds later, her hand in her book bag.

"He must've come in while I was sleeping. I found it this morning in my backpack." She handed him a small envelope addressed to him.

Jared stared at the envelope, wanting to open it. A shudder went through his body. Unsure if it was the fear in Susie's eyes or the look from Ellen, he knew something terrible had happened.

Turning to leave, he forced a smile at Susie. "Thank you. I'll see you later. Okay?"

"My mom was right, wasn't she? You did something to him. You did hurt him like she said you would." Susie shook as her face turned red, tears streaming down her face. "Why? I thought you were his friend. I thought you were my friend."

Jared reached for her. "Susie, no. I would never hurt..."

The sound of the garage door opening caused them both to jump.

A million thoughts ran through his head. Remembering the envelope, he tucked it into his back pocket, and looked for a way out.

Ellen flew out of the car, the door slamming closed, her eyes fixed on Jared. "What in the hell are you doing here?" She stared at him, teeth clenched.

Jared walked to her, knowing it was a long shot, but hoping there was a chance to explain. His hands shook, feeling for the wall behind him. "Ellen, I was just..."

Ellen cut him off, her voice quivering with anger. "Get the hell out of my yard, you sick little pervert."

"I was just looking for..."

"I know exactly what you were looking for, you little faggot." Ellen advanced toward him. "I know what you've been up to. You and Luke! You get away from my daughter. Just get the hell out of here!"

Jared's heart raced as panic set it. Knowing it was useless to talk to her, he tried to run. Ellen grabbed his arm, pulling him back into the garage. He lost his footing, landing hard against the wall.

Ellen stood in front of him, her finger in his face. "Now you listen to me. I don't ever... *ever* want to see you anywhere near me or my family again. If you step one foot onto my property, I'll call the cops." Tears welled in her eyes as her face tensed, turning a brilliant shade of red. "You make me sick. I hope you rot in hell for what you've done!" She looked down at the ground, holding him pinned against the wall. Without warning, she backhanded him. The force threw his head back; his face slammed against the wall. He could taste blood from where his teeth were forced into his cheek.

Ellen stopped. She appeared as though she was going to say more, but instead turned away, grabbing Susie and pushing her into the house. The door slammed and locked. Jared heard Ellen screaming inside the house. Paralyzed with fear, he knew he had to run before she changed her mind and came back for him.

Consciously pushing himself from the wall, he stumbled toward the door. His feet and hands were still numb, causing him to fall onto the cold cement floor. He picked himself up and ran for home.

Realizing his current state, he stopped in the driveway. *How am I going to explain myself? Or the blood coming out my mouth?*

He put his hands on his head. Pacing back and forth, he thought about what Ellen was plotting. *Oh, God! What if she calls my parents?* Everything was falling apart around him.

He ran through his backyard, into the tall grass. Stopping to catch his breath, he looked up and saw the train car. Tears ran down his cheeks. He ran to it, leaned against it as he thought of Luke. *Where is he? What the hell is going on?* Rubber legs sent him sliding to the ground, cradled in the tall damp grass that grew out from under the belly of his beloved hideaway. *This has to be a nightmare. What's happening to him? What's going to happen to me?*

Rolling onto his back, he tried to regain control. Gray clouds enveloped the sky. He reached into his back pocket to adjust his wallet that was digging into his back. Throwing it to the side, the envelope flew into the air, landing behind his head. In the rush to escape Ellen, he'd forgotten about it. He jumped up to see it blow around the back of the car. He crawled toward it, looked all around. Spotting it lying against the back wheel, he threw his body over it.

Jared's chin tensed as he picked it up, caressing it. "Luke. Where are you?" He feared the worst.

Large, cold drops of rain fell on him. He held the letter against his chest to protect it, climbed the ladder, and went into the train car. He closed the hatch, listening for a moment as the rain drops hit against the metal. In there, he felt safe again. The rain intensified. A noticeable chill was in the air. He looked toward the back room where he and Luke had been together two nights before. Everything looked just like it had when they'd left.

The closer he got to the back room, the more intense the smell of Luke's cologne became. It was irrational, but he hoped that somehow Luke had managed to get home and was waiting for him. He stopped at the entrance, praying for the impossible. He held the letter against his heart and closed his eyes.

Luke wasn't there. The smell wasn't coming from him.

Jared brought the letter up to his nose; the smell intensified. He found the lantern sitting by the door. The light was faint, in need of new batteries. With a deep breath, he put his finger in the corner and ripped the envelope. A piece of crudely folded paper lay stuffed inside. He sat on the blanket, unfolding the paper, hoping for answers.

My dearest Jed,

I don't have time to explain everything right now. I don't know when we'll see each other again. Just know that when it's at all possible, I'll make it happen. Until then, take care of yourself and be safe. I'll be thinking of you every moment.

Please know that I will always love you, no matter what happens. I'll be in touch as soon as I can.
   Yours forever, Luke

   Jared held the letter in his hand, his eyes fixated on the page. His hands dropped into his lap.
   There were no answers, just more questions. All he could do was hope Luke was all right and wait to hear from him.
   He put the letter back in the envelope and tucked it in his pocket. Curled into a ball, he lay on the floor with his face on the pillow. Luke's cologne still lingered there. His sobs echoed through the train car. He pulled the blanket over himself.

GODS & MONSTERS

Luke sat motionless in the front of his Uncle Richards's car watching the trees as they went by. The sky was a beautiful shade of blue. There wasn't a cloud.

The car slowed, turning down a small road. Luke glanced at his uncle, wishing he could say something to stop what was happening. He didn't know what to say. Up the road, he saw a sign pointing to the left.

His Way Camp – 3 Miles

Pulling his bag closer, he stared down at the floor. He wanted to cry, but he was determined not to let anyone see he was afraid. They didn't deserve the satisfaction.

Richard parked the car in front of a cabin with a sign over it that read *Registration Office*. An older man approached, followed by someone around Luke's age. Luke's uncle met them, engaging the older man in conversation. After a few minutes, they approached the car.

Luke clutched his bag. *Hold it together, Luke.* He tensed, trying to stop shaking.

Richard opened the door. "Luke. Come on. They're ready for you."

Taking a deep breath, Luke readied himself. He stood in front of them, staring at the ground.

The older man extended his hand. "God be with you, Luke. My name is Pastor Ron."

Luke stood expressionless, staring past him.

Richard took Luke by the shoulder. "Luke? Where are your manners?"

"That's all right. We'll be fast friends." Pastor Ron motioned for the younger man to take the luggage. "Mark will help you with your things and get you settled in. Once you get unpacked, we'll have a visit."

Mark walked to Luke, smiled, picking up the suitcase. He reached for the backpack Luke was holding. Luke pulled it back, putting it behind his back. "Don't touch it." He glared.

Mark turned toward a group of cabins. "Follow me."

Luke started to follow, stopping when Pastor Ron called to him.

"Luke, you must say good-bye to your uncle."

Luke walked to Richard. He looked him straight in the eye for the first time that day.

Richard gave a nervous smile. "Good-bye, Son. Take care of yourself." Luke stayed silent as Richard reached to embrace him. "How about a hug?" Luke put a hand up, blocking him. "Okay... well, we'll see you soon, all right?"

"Go to hell." Luke headed back up the path to Mark, his uncle calling after him.

"Luke, please! This is the only way. It's for the best."

Luke paused, fighting the urge to attack him. *He's not worth it*. Looking back, he shook his head before continuing down the path.

He studied Mark who walked ahead of him, wondering about his story. Somber faces of the other boys stared at him through the windows of their cabins. A chill went through his body. "What the hell is this place?"

THE VIEW FROM A RUSTY TRAIN CAR

Mark walked up to a cabin, opening the multiple locks on the door. Luke looked to the cabin next to them, noticing the sign above the door. *Pastor's Cabin.*

Mark opened the door, motioning for him to enter. "This is where you'll stay for the first few nights until you're ready to be assigned to your permanent cabin."

Luke looked around. He became queasy from the noxious odor of moth balls and the smell of damp, rotting cloth.

Mark stood at the door. "Your bed is the one on the left. Mine is the one by the window. I sleep there to make sure you don't try to escape. It's pointless to try. There are bars on the window." He piled Luke's things on the bed. "Pastor Ron and I have the only keys to get in or out. When you're alone, the door will be locked and someone will be posted outside."

Luke refused to acknowledge anything that was said. His jaw clenched. He kept his head down.

"I'll leave you alone so you can unpack and get settled in. If you need anything, I'll be right outside." Mark turned to leave. He stopped, looking at Luke one more time. "This is just a friendly word of advice. Do your best to get used to it. It'll be much easier on you. You won't be leaving here for a while."

The door closed, one lock clicked. The sound stole Luke's breath. Another click; his hands started to shake, struggling for breath. A third, final click; he was a prisoner.

The room had two beds, two desks with chairs, and a door leading to a small bathroom. There were no curtains on any of the windows and nothing on the walls except for a large picture of Jesus as the Shepherd. He started to unpack. *You just have to survive. Get this over with as fast as possible.*

A half an hour went by before Luke heard a knock at the door followed by the sound of keys in the lock. Luke stopped, stood at attention by the desk, his head down as the door opened.

"I see you're getting settled in." Pastor Ron smiled, closing the door behind him. "Please have a seat. We're going to go over the rules." He pulled out a chair, offering it to Luke.

Luke complied, sitting with his hands clasped together.

Pastor Ron took the chair from Mark's desk. He handed a booklet to Luke. "This is a list of the rules and what is expected of you. You will not be involved in any of the group activities tonight. After we go through the basics, I'll leave you alone and let you look through it on your own. Page Nine has your first bible study exercises. You will complete them tonight and have them ready for tomorrow morning's class. Did you bring your bible with you?"

Luke shook his head.

Crossing his arms, Pastor Ron leaned back in the chair. "I'm sorry. I couldn't hear you."

Luke looked at him, staring him in the eye. "No, Sir." He couldn't help the acidic quality of his voice.

"Fine. There's one in the top drawer of your desk." Grabbing the booklet away from him, Pastor Ron opened it to the first page. "These are the most important rules. They are to be committed to memory." He read them aloud. "Rule one: There is to be no physical contact with the other campers except for a hand shake when greeting each other. This includes high-fives, pats on the behind, and touching anywhere else on the body. Rule two: There will be no use of name brand clothes. These clothes are a tool of the devil used by mainstream society to feminize the men and to push forward the gay agenda."

Luke was stunned. He had to stifle a laugh. *Is this guy serious?*

"Rule three: Use of cologne, aftershave, lotions, or any products with a scent is prohibited. These products are designed to play on your sexual perversions. You will only be allowed to use unscented products for grooming. Rule four..."

"I'd rather read these on my own, if you don't mind." Luke couldn't take any more. The sound of Pastor Ron's voice was like nails on a chalkboard.

Pastor Ron stared at him. "I'll warn you that everyone is tested on these. You will be asked anytime and anywhere to recite a certain rule. I want to point out the end." He pointed to a paragraph in bold type and underlined. "Any infraction to these rules will be met with strict, swift, and severe punishment. The head counselor, which is me, will have final and absolute approval on what the punishment will entail." He grinned, sitting back in the chair. "Do you have any questions?"

Luke resisted voicing the plethora of rude comments that flooded his mind. "No, Sir."

"Good." Pastor Ron pushed his chair back to the other desk. "Mark will bring your dinner in a couple hours. I advise you to make good use of the rest of the evening. Oh!" He stood in front of Luke with his arms crossed. "I'm going to have to look through your things. I'll take what are the tools of the devil." Picking up Luke's bags, he dumped them on the bed. The items Luke had placed on the desk were thrown into the pile. Opening each bottle, he started a small pile on the desk. "I'll have Mark bring you acceptable replacements for these items."

Luke watched as his deodorant, aftershave, shampoo, and conditioner were put in the pile.

Pastor Ron glanced at him, a look of suspicion on his face. "Do you have any cologne with you? I find it hard to believe that you don't when you have all these other products."

Luke's heart sank, not wanting to give up the cologne that Jared had given him for his birthday. Surprised it hadn't been found yet, he remembered putting it in his suitcase instead of the toiletries bag. "No." His heart raced, hoping Pastor Ron would leave his suitcase alone.

Pastor Ron stared at him. Sighing, he pointed to the bed. "Open your suitcase."

Luke swallowed hard. Standing at his suitcase, he turned his back to him to open it, hoping he could find the bottle and hide it.

Pastor Ron pushed him aside, throwing the lid open. Checking the labels on each piece of clothing, he dropped the name brand ones to the floor. Luke watched him nervously. "What's this?" Pastor Ron's hand came to a stop in the back of the suitcase. He pulled out the bottle of cologne, holding it in front of Luke. "This sure looks like cologne."

Luke stared down at the floor.

Putting a couple articles of clothing back on the bed, Pastor Ron closed the suitcase. "That should do it." He looked Luke up and down. "Except I'll also need you to give me that shirt you're wearing."

Luke was mortified. "Right now?"

"Yes, now."

Luke stepped toward the bathroom, but Pastor Ron blocked the door. "No. You will take it off and give it to me right here. There's less chance of you hiding anything."

Luke stared at him. Turning away, he took off his shirt, his arms covering his bare chest. Pastor Ron stood with his hand out, a strange grin on his face. Luke handed him the shirt then ran to his suitcase, pulling out the only one that was left then putting it on. The look in the pastor's eyes made him feel violated. Pastor Ron gathered the confiscated items and headed for the door. Luke went to the desk, looked through what was left, standing them up-right, putting them in some kind of order.

"One last thing." Pastor Ron dropped Luke's things outside the door. "I'll need to see your wallet."

Luke reached into his back pocket, pulling out his wallet. He held it out.

Pastor Ron stood at the door, holding out his hand. "Bring it here."

Luke's hand shook, handing it to him.

THE VIEW FROM A RUSTY TRAIN CAR

Pastor Ron pulled out the contents and searched through them. "Looks good. Nothing too objectionable in here." He stopped. "Except... " Pulling out a picture, he held it in front of Luke. "Who's this in the picture with you?"

Luke could feel the tears forming in his eyes, seeing Jared's smiling face looking back at him in the picture. "Jared." His voice quivered knowing this would be taken from him too.

Pastor Ron looked at the photo, shaking his head. "So this is the one. You're mother told me all about him when she called. She said she'd warned you about him. It's really heartbreaking. He looks like a nice guy." He walked to Luke, putting his arm around him, holding the picture of Jared in front of them. "You see, it's not all your fault. The devil takes many forms. He uses these poor, pathetic people to do his bidding. He likes to use the ones who look sweet and innocent to lure others to his evil ways."

Luke chuckled, grabbing the photo from his hand. "You're insane! This whole damn place is a freaking joke!" He ran to the bed, throwing his things back in his bags. "I'm getting out of here. You can't keep me here!"

Pastor Ron pushed him, throwing Luke on the bed. "We can and we will. It's the will of God." He snatched the picture away from Luke. Holding it up, he ripped it into little pieces. "It's too late for him. We can't save him, but we will save you!"

Luke watched as the pieces piled onto the floor. He dropped to his knees, picking each of them up, holding them close as tears streamed down his face.

Pastor Ron walked past him. He pulled out a set of keys and looked through them. "Mark will be back here soon. I'll see you in the morning for prayers in the chapel."

Luke tried to ignore the sounds of the keys engaging the locks. Placing the pieces of the photo in his bag, he watched out the window as boys filed from their cabins and headed down the path to a larger cabin where a bell was ringing. He could hear bits of their muffled conversations, one of them mentioning dinner.

Luke sat at the edge of the bed. The feeling of numbness turned to fear as the realization of where he was started to sink in. "Jared... Oh, God. Why? Why is this happening to me?" He placed his hand over his mouth to muffle his cries.

#

A noise came from the other side of the door as Luke lay in bed watching the ceiling fan spin around. Mark entered, carrying two trays of food. He placed one on Luke's desk. "Dinner is served."

Luke continued to stare at the ceiling.

Mark sat down at his desk, taking the cover off the plate. "The food really isn't bad. It's much better hot though. You should eat it now. They won't heat it up for you."

Luke couldn't tell if he was hungry or not. His stomach felt like it was in knots. He sat at his desk, taking off the foil, examining the plate. The smell made him nauseous. Covering it, he pushed it away. He looked over at Mark who was reading the bible as he ate. "So this is your job? You babysit the newcomers?"

Mark turned, smiling at him. "There are a few of us chosen. We take turns. Each of us has the honor for a month."

"Take turns? How long have you been here?"

Mark thought a moment. "It's going on two years."

"What?" Luke could feel his heart race. Sweat formed on his palms. "There is no way I can make it here a year!" He jumped up from his desk, pacing.

"Don't worry. You'll get used to it. I love it here. I choose to stay."

Luke stopped, staring at him. *This guy's crazy!*

"I'm sure it sounds strange to you, but I'm classified as a 'terminal offender'. I'll never be able to live out in society. I tried, but..." Mark stopped. He looked down at the Bible in his hand. "It didn't work for me."

"If it doesn't work, why do you stay here? Why do you help them force it on other people?"

Mark smiled. "If we can save one person the fires of hell, it's worth it."

Luke sat on the corner of Mark's desk. "I have to get out of here. You can help me. I know you can. What do I do? Do you want money? I can send you money once I'm out..."

"You're not going anywhere." Mark put the Bible on his desk and leaned toward Luke. "The only way out is to let go and let God in. Let him take control. Only he can save you now. The devil has a strong hold on us, but God will win out in the end; that's if we give ourselves to him... fully to him." He picked up his fork and started eating again. "Besides, even if you got out, where would you go? Our parents put us here, remember?"

Luke stared at him, wondering how this guy could be taken in by it all. *He's brainwashed. That's it. That's what this place is for.* He went back to his desk, thinking about what Mark told him. *Okay Luke. You've got to figure this out. You just have to survive it.* His mind raced at the thought of what lay ahead of him. *Just play along. Make them think you've changed then you can get out of here and go home, back to Jared.* He took a deep breath, lay down on his bed, turned toward the wall. When he closed his eyes he could see Jared as if he was right there with him. He knew it was the only way he was going to stay sane. *You'll get me through this. I'll make it back to you. I promise.*

I TURN A PAGE

March 1995

"Luke was wrong. This year's not going fast." Jared stopped at the mailbox, just like he did every day on his way home from school. He kicked the post and slammed the box shut.

As he walked to his room, he thought about Luke. *We were supposed to get through this together.* The things he carried dropped to the floor as he sat on the bed, grabbing his head to silence the doubts that whispered constantly at him now. *He's staying away because he wants to. That's the only explanation. If he really loved me, he would've called, or at least written.*

Turning on to his side, he saw his reflection in the mirror over his desk. "It's time to move on. He's not coming back."

Jared went to his desk. He stared at a letter from the University of Washington that lay in front of him. He'd applied there a couple months ago, thinking it would be a good place for both of them. It was time to find out what it said. His hand shook as he ripped the envelope open. It dropped onto the desk.

Running up the stairs, paper in hand, he found his mom in the kitchen.

"Hey, you! How was school?" Candace put a pan in the oven.

"Fine." He walked to her, handing her the letter.

"What's this?" She leaned against the cupboard, read it, then beamed a huge smile at him. "Oh, Jared! Congratulations! I'm so proud of you." She threw her arms around him.

"Thanks! I'm pretty excited. It'll be good."

Her eyes filled with tears. "I'm sorry. I know. I shouldn't do this." She laughed, wiping them away. "You know I'm not thrilled that you're going so far away. We'll never see you!"

Jared put his arm around her. "We talked about this. I'll come back to visit any chance I get. I promise. It's just the best thing for me right now."

Candace went back to the food. "I know. I know. I'll be fine." She stopped to take another look at him. "Congratulations."

Jared smiled, turning back to his room.

"Oh, Jared?"

"Yeah?"

She walked to the stairs. "The strangest thing happened today. I saw Ellen in the store. I'd been trying to call her. I've gone over to the house but she never answers. I tried to ask her about Luke..."

Jared felt his pulse race. *This is it. Ellen told her everything.* He started plotting his rebuttal.

"... but she just looked at me and walked right past. I don't know what I did. She didn't say a word."

Jared grabbed her hand. "Mom, just leave it alone. I'm sure he's fine. They hadn't been getting along. Maybe he just chose to stay away."

Candace looked unsure. "Maybe. It still doesn't explain her acting so rudely."

"Mom, its fine. I'm sure we'll eventually find out what happened. I can't worry about it anymore. I've got too much to get ready for now." Jared studied her face, hoping he'd convinced her to leave it alone.

She smiled, squeezing his hand. "You're right. Dinner will be ready in about an hour. I'm sure your dad will be happy to hear the news."

Back at his desk, he thumbed through the information that came with the letter. *It does look amazing. You'll be fine.*

He stared at the letter, his fingers tapping, knocking over a picture. He reached for it; Luke and him in their tuxes at prom. A tear rolled down his cheek. He slammed the picture down, exhaling deeply. He stiffened. "No! It's time to move on." Running around the room, he grabbed everything Luke had given him or that reminded him of Luke. Opening the door to the closet, he threw them in, slammed the door then pressed his back against it. Tears rolled down his face. His knees gave out; he landed on the floor. "I'm sorry."

I WANT TO BREAK FREE

July 1995

"Damn!" Luke watched the clock turn to midnight, sitting at his desk working on the next day's assignment. He threw his pencil down and rubbed his face. "Come on, Luke! Only one week left in this wretched place."

Luke walked to the window, looking to the newcomer's cabin. The boy inside wasn't a newcomer though; he was a former student who'd returned to the camp. After catching him with another boy, his parents brought him back.

A tear came to his eye remembering the scene a couple days ago. He watched as the boy struggled, heard him scream and plead with his parents not to leave him. There was no emotion on their faces; they watched as he was locked inside.

In his cabin, Luke could hear the screaming and sobbing as if it were in the next room. Between those horrible sounds and the night terrors he'd started having since his own arrival, it was almost impossible to get any sleep the last couple of days. Finally, all was quiet. "God, I hope he's all right."

Luke stared at his homework. His attention kept going back to the window. Putting his pencil in the book, he closed it then pushed it away. He pulled the top drawer open, put his hand in, feeling around the underside of the desk. Carefully he removed the tape holding it from falling in the drawer. Luke pulled out a folded piece of paper, his fingers caressing it. "Hey, Jed." Holding his head in his hands, he stared down at the portrait he'd sketched. "Well, Baby. I'm getting out of here. Thanks to you, I've made it through this without going completely crazy. I'll be coming home soon." He chuckled as he traced the outline of Jared's face with his thumb. "But what am I going to do with you?" The smile disappeared when his stomach turned to butterflies. "I can't wait to see you! But... we have to talk. Okay, I'm not sure how to tell you this. I just don't know. I don't know anything. Shit! I don't even know who I am anymore. Or if I can be what you want... or need. I'm so confused. I hate to say it, but I think this fucking place has gotten to me. I tried my hardest not to let it, but I failed. I have so many doubts and fears. I don't think I can get over them. I don't know what's going to happen to me... to us." Wiping his tear-soaked face, he held the picture up, staring into Jared's eyes. "I don't ever want to hurt you, but maybe it's inevitable." The picture dropped back onto the desk. Luke paced around the room, trying to keep control. He took some deep breaths. Taking the portrait off the desk, he held it to his chest. "Hey. It'll be all right. We've been through shit before. You always know what to say to me. You'll help me, right? No matter what, I do love you." He walked back to the desk. "I'll see you soon, okay?" Putting the tape back on the corners, he stuck it in its hiding spot.

#

Hushed voices and a few loud thumps from outside roused Luke. The first light of the sun was bleeding into the room. He checked the clock. "5:32 a.m."

The voices sounded harried and panicked. Luke stood at the side of the window, being careful not to be noticed. Pastor Ron and a couple other staff members stood at the open door to the newcomer's cabin. One of the men held his hand to his head, staring inside. The other kept a nervous watch down the trail. He noticed Mark sitting around the corner. He stared blankly into the trees. His face looked white as a sheet.

Pastor Ron motioned. Two paramedics rolling a stretcher came running toward them.

Luke dressed and ran to the door. Cracking it open, he looked to see if he had a clear shot to get to Mark. About to dart out, he saw the door to the other cabin open. Pastor Ron and the counselors emerged, followed by the paramedics with someone on the stretcher. Mark didn't move.

Luke crept out, looking around the corner down the path. They had all disappeared. He ran to Mark, kneeling in front of him. "Mark? What happened? Are you okay?"

Mark looked up at him; the blank expression twisted into one of terror. He inhaled sharply reaching out to Luke.

"What happened?"

"Josh. He..." Mark's eyes searched Luke's face. He tried to speak, but choked on the words.

Luke put his hand on Mark's shoulder. "It's all right. You're fine."

"No! It's not all right!" Mark shook, tears flowing down his face. "I went in to check on Josh this morning. He screamed and yelled for two days, but then there was silence. I was so relieved. I hoped I'd find him sleeping finally. Poor guy." He pounded his fists on the ground. "When I checked on him, I found him in the bathroom. He was hanging from the light! I tried to help him, Luke. I did! I put my shoulders under him and tried to lift him up so he could breathe, but I couldn't; he was too heavy. I ran to get help!" He sobbed, continuing to pound the ground with his fists. "But it was too late. He's dead! I should've check on him earlier. I shouldn't have let him be alone for so long, but I couldn't take it! I couldn't stand the sound of him screaming and crying! I felt so bad for him."

Luke grabbed his hands and held them. "Mark, listen to me. This is not your fault."

"Yes, it is! Yes, it is! I locked him in there. I left him alone. He asked me to help him, but I couldn't. Oh, God, what did I do? I'm so sorry. I'm so sorry!" Mark put his head in his arms, resting them on his legs. "I just did what I was supposed to. I didn't want him to die!"

Luke could barely breathe. He put his hand on Mark's arm. "I know. I know you didn't. What can I do?"

Mark gasped, looking up at him, putting his hand to Luke's face. "Will you hold me? Please? I need someone to hold me."

Luke looked around making sure no one could see them. Taking Mark's hands, he led him to their cabin. He helped Mark lie down. Crawling in next to him, Luke placed his arm under Mark's head. "It's going to be okay. Shhh. Just close your eyes and rest. I'll be right here."

Mark grabbed onto Luke's shirt, pulling himself as close as he could.

Luke stroked the hair on Mark's forehead until he fell asleep. Hearing a noise outside, he jumped, his heart beat rapidly. *If someone catches us like this, I'll never get out of here.* He tried to get up so he could move to his own bed.

Mark stirred, his hands still wrapped into his shirt; he pulled Luke back down.

Luke looked at his face. The fear and terror were still there, even while he slept. He glanced at the window, taking a deep breath. *Screw 'em.* Pulling the blanket over Mark, he laid down, wrapping his arm over him.

HORIZONS WEST

August 1995

Jared looked around his half empty room. He caught a box as it was about to fall off one of the stacks. Opening his suitcase, he threw in one last pair of socks and zipped it shut.

Megan poked her head around the door. "Can I come in?"

"Of course."

She looked around the room and started to cry. "I can't believe it. You're leaving us."

Jared threw his arms around her. "Stop that. Don't make this harder than it already is."

"Sorry." She smiled at him, wiping away tears. "Have you been able to say good-bye to everyone?"

"Mostly. The family's been stopping by all day. I'm surprised I've been able to get this done. My friends threw a party a couple nights ago so I saw all of them there."

"What about Luke?"

He stared at her. "Luke?" It had been a long time since anyone had mentioned his name. "Meg, I haven't heard from him in a year. You know that."

Rubbing his arm, she rested her head on his shoulder. "I'm sorry."

Jared pulled away, chuckling. "What? It's no big deal. He was a friend and he moved away. It happens all the time. We were kids. Life goes on." He picked up a stack of papers from the desk.

"You don't lie very well. I know you. It's been bugging you." She put her hand on his arm. "Have you tried talking to Ellen and asking..."

Throwing the papers in a box, Jared turned away and started shuffling more in another pile, fighting the urge to cry. "It's no big deal! Can we just drop it? Yes, I was sad he was gone, but I'm over it. Now it's time for me to go. These things happen."

"Okay. Fine. Sorry." Megan studied his face. "Can I help with anything?"

"I was just going to take these out to the car. Can you grab a couple?" He picked up his luggage and headed toward the door.

"What are you going to do with the rest of this stuff?" Megan picked up his other bags, following him.

"Mom and Dad are shipping some of it to me. The rest will just have to stay here. It's sure not all going to fit in a dorm room." He stopped at the door, looking back into the closet. On the floor lay the presents Luke had given him. He pushed the closet shut before starting up the stairs.

Jared opened the trunk of the car and loaded his things inside.

Shaking, tears in her eyes, Megan stood behind him. "Well. I guess this is good-bye."

"I guess so. You'll call me, right?" Jared hugged her, holding her tight.

"Of course!" Megan walked down the driveway, drying her eyes. Looking back, she gave him a big smile. "I love you!" Her voice broke.

THE VIEW FROM A RUSTY TRAIN CAR

"I love you too." Jared wiped a tear away. He blew her a kiss, watching her drive away until the lights disappeared around the corner. Reaching down for his last bag, he caught a glimpse of the house next door. *God, I wish you were coming with me.* Closing the trunk, he took a long look across the street. *Good-bye.*

"Ready?" Mike stood at the door, waiting for Candace.

Jared snuck a final look, taking a deep breath before getting into the car. "As ready as I'll ever be!"

Sitting in the back seat, he took in as much as he could; trying to memorize everything. His heart raced when he saw the train car in the distance. "Dad, can you pull down the gravel road? I want one last look at the old fort. Who knows if it'll be there when I come back?"

"Sure, Son."

Jared's eyes welled up with tears as they got closer. Thoughts of Luke flooded his mind. *Don't do this to yourself!* He shook his head, looking away. "Thanks, Dad. That's all I needed."

WERE THE WORLD MINE

My hands shook. Writing the article about what Luke had gone through made me angry, but speaking it out loud made me furious. It was like hearing it for the first time and having that feeling of disbelief that morphs into a burning rage. I took a sip of water, wiping the perspiration forming at my brow.

"Most of you are probably shocked and appalled, not just about what Luke went through in that place, but that these places even exist at all. This isn't a fictional place I made up to add punch to my story. You can go on the internet right now and find them. They aren't a secret. In fact they are proud of what they're doing. I'm not going to mince words here... this is social engineering. In the good old U.S.A., gay young men and women are being tortured and brainwashed every day, yet no one does anything about it. Too many people don't realize these camps exist. That changes today. I may not have the power to shut them down, but I'll be damned if they continue and not answer for it! I have a great belief in the goodness of people and I know more will feel as furious as I am. Knowing first-hand what it does to people is part of the reason I am here today. I saw what it did to Luke. Writing that article gave me the excuse to talk to Mark to find out what really happened. He was there a lot longer than Luke. That poor guy never had a chance. I found out a couple weeks ago, when I was trying to check in on him, that he went back to the camp for his third stint. He finally escaped. Unfortunately, his escape cost him his life... just like Josh."

Shaking my head, I sat back in my chair. I needed just a moment to collect my thoughts and regain my composure.

"Mr. Montgomery, would you like to take a break?"

I looked into the eyes of the woman who'd been listening so intently. Her face was full of compassion.

I leaned forward against the desk. "No, thank you. I'm fine." I took a deep breath. "If we are going to have a discussion and debate about the rights of gay citizens in this country, people need to know the truth – all of it. So, no, the story doesn't end there. In fact, in some ways, this is where it begins."

TEARS OF LOVE'S RECALL

Luke shifted in the seat of his uncle's car, fingers tapping on his leg. His heart beat rapidly thinking about his reunion with Jared. They were only a few blocks away.

He jumped from the car before it had come to a complete stop in his driveway. "I'll be right back. I won't be long." He glanced over at Jared's house. "Hi, Jed. Long time no see." He shook his head. "That's not right." Walking to his room, he tried to find the right words. He stopped in the hallway, looking at a picture of his mother. His jaw tensed and he shook his head. "I hate you for what you've done to me."

He opened the door to his room. It looked as if no one had been in there since he left. There were still dirty clothes on the floor. Lying on top of the pile was Jared's shirt and pants. He picked them up, held them close, pressing his nose to the collar. "That's him." He tucked them into his backpack along with some other clothes and a few things from his night stand. Reaching behind his bed, he took out the pictures of Jared he'd hidden years ago. "It's so good to see your face!"

In the kitchen, he dug out a couple pots and pans from the cupboard. "I'm going to need these." He took a quick look around for anything he might have forgotten then glanced at the clock. "Time to get the hell out of here before that bitch gets home."

Opening the door of the car, Luke threw his bag along with the pots and pans into the back seat before getting in. "That's all I need from there."

Pulling the car out of the driveway, Richard glanced at him. "Luke, I know I've told you a hundred times now, but I'm sorry. If I could've known what that place was really like I wouldn't have..." He sighed, shaking his head. "I'll make it up to you."

Luke patted his shoulder. "I know. You already have. I mean, getting me that job at your friend's office... and I would never have been able to get my apartment if you hadn't co-signed. Thank you." He saw the apartment building come into view. "The best gift is that I don't have to live with her anymore. I don't blame you for what happened. I know who was responsible."

The car had barely come to a stop when Luke grabbed his things, exiting the car.

"Luke, wait!" Richard stood behind the door of the car. "Listen, I better get on the road. I'll come back in a couple days and help you get the rest set-up. You need some time to yourself."

Luke dropped his things then threw his arms around his uncle. "I can't thank you enough. I'm going to be okay." He picked everything up then opened the door to his new home. He turned, motioning to stop his uncle. Walking up to the window he leaned in. "Please tell Aunty Carol, thank you, too, and tell her thank you for the talk. It really helped me."

Richard nodded, smiling at Luke as he pulled away.

Looking up at the window to his new apartment, Luke took a deep breath. "Here we go!"

#

The next morning, Luke rode his bike down the familiar road toward his old neighborhood. As he approached the driveway to Jared's house he watched a vehicle arrive. "Hey, Montgomery family!"

"Oh my gosh! Luke!" Candace ran to him, throwing her arms around him. "It's so good to see you! How are you?"

"Fine! It's great to be back. I've missed everyone."

"You look great." Mike hit him on the arm, smiling.

"Thanks. You guys do too! So..."

"Jared's going to be sick that he missed you." Candace held on to his arm. "When did you get back?"

"Late last night. I've got an apartment over by the park. So when will Jared be back?"

Candace looked at Mike. "Well, we're not sure, Sweetie. We just put him on the plane to Seattle. He starts school in a few days."

Luke felt like someone had punched him in the gut. "I see." Not wanting them to see how upset he was, he picked up his bike. "When you talk to him, will you tell him I say hi? Maybe I can get his number from you sometime." He had to leave. "I'll see you around."

"Sure. Don't be a stranger. Come and visit. Anytime."

"Okay." He called to her, unable to look back.

At the baseball field, he jumped off the bike, letting it crash in front of him. He crawled up, sitting in the playground equipment on which he and Jared used to play 'spaceships'. Laying his head back, staring up at the sky, he shook. "You can't be gone!" He reached for his wallet, pulling out one of the pictures of Jared he'd rescued the night earlier. He stared at the face, caressed it with his thumbs. "Well. You made this easy on me. I had no idea how I was going to tell you that we would just be friends. I didn't know if I could even do it. Seeing you would've been really hard. At least now I don't have to hurt you again."

Luke pushed his bike down the road toward his apartment. "Luke, this is a sign. It's time to move on. You were making the right decision. This is for the best." He shook his head. "If that's true then why am I crying?"

TALES OF THE CITY

Jared unpacked some pictures, setting them up on the desk in his dorm room. He heaved the box out the window, watching it land in the dumpster below then made another note on his list of things he wanted from home.

Hearing a thump against the wall and what sounded like a curse, he ran to the door, opening it. "Sorry!" He grabbed one of the boxes his roommate, Chris, was trying to balance.

"This is finally the last of it." Chris dropped the boxes by his desk, collapsing onto his bed. "This is too much work for one day. I'm done with this moving shit."

"No kidding. I think I'm finally finished too." Jared fussed with the things on his desk.

Chris stood, raising an eyebrow. "You're one of those."

A wave of nausea flowed over Jared. His heart started to pound in his chest. He took a step backward. He examined the path to the door, looking for a clear shot out. *Run!* Swallowing the lump in his throat, he cringed at the smirk on his roommate's face. Not seeing a way past, he walked to the window, leaning out to take in some cool air. "I'm not sure what you mean." His voice quivered.

Chris laughed, kicking a mound of clothes on the floor under his bed. "Organized... everything all neat and tidy. I'm telling you now that I'm a slob, but I promise I'll keep it on my side of the room."

Jared laughed. "No worries. I don't care. It's just... habit, I guess."

Chris looked at the clock on his nightstand. "How did it get so late?" He jumped up, pulled off his clothes then grabbed some new ones from the pile, putting them on. "Some of my friends and I are running to get some food. Do you wanna come with us?"

Jared averted his eyes. "Sure. What the heck."

"Cool! Kelly wanted you to meet her friend Derek. She thought you'd have a lot in common. He's going into journalism too." Chris ran out the door, waving for Jared to follow.

"Great!"

Chris led Jared down the street a few blocks, meeting up with Kelly and Derek at a bus stop. Jared waved to Kelly as they approached. She smiled and waved back, whispering something to the guy next to her.

Chris put his arms around Kelly, kissing her. "Hello, beautiful!"

She smiled at Jared and gave him a hug. "Hey there, cutie! This is my friend Derek." She raised an eyebrow, smirking. "Derek, this is Jared. See what I mean?"

Jared watched their interaction. *What did she mean by that?*

Derek offered his hand. "Hi. It's nice to meet you."

"You too."

Derek stared him in the eye, smiling.

Jared pulled his hand away, hoping Derek hadn't noticed he was shaking from nerves. "Chris told me you're studying journalism."

"I am. Photo-journalism actually."

"Oh, cool. I'm going into plain old journalism... journalism." Jared turned away, beating himself up in his head. *Stupid. Stupid. Stupid.*

THE VIEW FROM A RUSTY TRAIN CAR

"You know, I heard they make us pair off for projects. We'd make quite a team. I need you and you need me. I might just get through this whole damn school thing." Derek put his arm around Kelly, chuckling.

"Sure. I mean... I guess." Jared caught Kelly winking at Derek. *See? They think you're an idiot.* Chris followed Jared. He took the seat next to him, Derek and Kelly the ones across the aisle. They whispered to each other, tossing glances in his direction. Jared stared out the window. *I wish this was over.*

Derek leaned over to Chris, whispering in his ear. Chris smiled as they exchanged seats. Jared inched closer to the window. Derek patted him on the leg. "I hope you don't mind. Kelly wanted to sit with Chris."

"No. Of course." Jared took a deep breath, staring back out the window.

The bus stopped. Derek stepped into the aisle, motioning for Jared to go ahead of him. "Thank you." Jared followed Chris and Kelly to the entrance of The Spaghetti House. Derek rushed ahead of them, holding the door.

"Kelly and I are going to play a game of air hockey. Will you guys hold our table?" Chris took Kelly by the hand, leading her to the back.

Jared took a seat on the opposite side of the table, pretending to look through the menu. There were a few awkward glances followed by equally awkward smiles. Realizing Chris and Kelly wouldn't be coming back as soon as he'd like, Jared put his menu on the table. "So, Derek, where are you from?"

"Maine. You?"

"A little town in North Dakota. Actually, every town in North Dakota is a little town. I'm not even sure why I said that. I'm sorry. I'm an idiot." He looked down at the table, feeling the blood rush to his face.

Derek laughed, touching Jared's arm. "You are just too damn cute."

Jared stared, finding it hard to breathe. "Excuse me?"

Derek pulled his hand away. Shifting uncomfortably in his chair, he looked down at the table. "I'm sorry. That was really forward of me."

"No. It's all right. I was just... shocked. That's all."

"No! It's not all right. We don't even know each other, or if you actually are... gay."

"If I'm..." Jared stopped, looking around to see if anyone was listening to them.

"It's just that Kelly thought you might be then I met you and you're really cute and sweet. I'm... I'm sorry. I made an assumption. I should've known it was too good to be true." Derek leaned forward, putting his head in his hands. "I hope I didn't offend you. If I did, I'm really sorry."

"No, no. You didn't offend me. It's just... well, am I that obvious? I thought I was hiding it so well." Jared touched his arm, laughing. "It's just that no one's ever told me that... that I was cute, I mean. Well, not in a long time anyway."

Derek winked. "I find that really hard to believe."

"Thank you. You just made my night. You're pretty damn handsome yourself."

"That's sweet, but what else were you supposed to say?" Derek sat back in his chair. "Listen, can I have a redo?"

"I guess."

Derek sat up, clearing his throat. "Jared? Would you ever go out with me? On a date? I mean... just the two of us?"

"I would love to."

"Really? Cool. How about tomorrow night? After class? I know this great little place by campus. Actually, Kelly showed it to me. Do you like Thai?" The words flew from his mouth. He was unable to contain his excitement.

Kelly popped her head around the corner. "Is it safe to come back?"

"It's safe." Derek offered his chair, taking the seat next to Jared.

Pulling Chris from behind the wall she took her seat. She looked back and forth between them. "Well?"

"If you must know we have a date tomorrow night." Derek placed his hand on Jared's.

Jared's heart raced, glancing around, wondering if anyone could see that their hands were touching. He fought the impulse to pull away.

"Sweet!" Chris punched Jared on the arm, smiling.

"Wait. You're okay with this?"

"Dude, this is Seattle! No one cares. Relax."

Jared's mind raced. *I can't believe this is happening. I have a date. And he's cute!* He jumped as Derek pulled his hand closer.

Chris leaned across the table, lowering his voice. "Kelly and I will be gone most of the night tomorrow. You have the place all to yourselves." Grinning, he put his arm around Kelly.

Kelly slapped Chris on the arm. "Stop it. Look at the poor guy. If he gets any redder his head will explode."

Derek winked, stroking Jared's face with his thumb.

Jared jumped up. "If you guys will excuse me, I've got to find the restroom." He followed the sign into the back, past the game room. Locking the door, he leaned against it and sighed. The cold water splashing against his face made him shiver. He stared at his reflection in the mirror. "What is wrong with you? This could be amazing. He's cute, sweet, and interested. You've dreamed of this. Why can't you just accept it?" He shook his head. "You know why: Luke. It feels like you're cheating on him." He dried his face. "No! He left you! You have to get over this. It's time to move on. You can do this!"

Jared threw the towel into the trash then joined Derek and the others at the table. "So? What did I miss?" He sat close to Derek, putting his arm around him. Derek smiled, snuggling into Jared's side.

I'VE NEVER BEEN TO ME

Luke walked into Heidi's Place, requesting a table with Megan as his waitress. Once seated, he noticed awkward gazes in his direction. *What is everyone's problem?* He forced a smile, looking around the room. *Go to hell.*

Megan placed a glass of water on his table. "What can I get you?"

Luke laughed, leaning back in his seat, arms crossed. "That's it? We haven't seen each other in over a year and all you can say is what can I get you? Kinda rude."

"What?" Frowning, Megan looked up from her order pad. "Luke? Oh, my God!" She threw her arms around him. "How are you? It's so good to see you!"

"You too! You look wonderful."

"Thanks for lying to me. It'll get you everywhere!" She sat across from him. "When did you get back to town?"

"A few days ago. I stopped in to see your mom and dad. They told me you worked here."

She put her hand to her mouth. "Oh, no! You missed Jared! He just left a few days ago. He's going to be so pissed."

"Yeah, I heard." Luke rolled a crumpled straw wrapper between his thumb and forefinger. "It's all right. I'll see him when he comes home."

Smiling, Megan put a hand on his. "I can't believe it's you! How long are you back in town?"

"For good. I moved back. I've got an apartment over by the park. A friend of my uncle's gave me a job working in his insurance office."

"That's great! I can't tell you how happy I am to see a friendly face in this town." She raised an eyebrow, looking around the room. "What can I get you?"

"How about a Coke?"

"Sure. I'll be right back."

Luke watched her walk away. *I finally feel like I'm home.*

Megan put the glass of Coke in front of him. "Here you go. The best Coke in town." She laughed, sitting back down.

"Well I suppose I should eat something since I took this table." He opened the menu.

Megan grabbed it away. "I'll get you the special. It's the only thing worth eating here today."

Luke grabbed her hand. "I actually did come here to see you." He sipped his Coke. His eyes stayed focused on the table. "I was kinda wondering... well, if you'd ever want to go out sometime."

"Are you asking me out on a date?"

"It doesn't have to be like that. I mean, you probably have a boyfriend. I was just wondering if we could hang out? You know, like the old days? It doesn't have to be a date, date." Luke looked away, feeling the blood rush to his cheeks.

"No. I'm not dating anyone." Megan thought for a moment then chuckled. "Wouldn't it be weird? I mean, I've always thought of you like a little brother."

Luke put his head in his hands, laughing. "Sorry. You're right. Bad idea. Forget it." He took another sip. "You know what? Maybe I should just go." He handed her some money.

Megan pushed his hand away. "Why not? I'd love to. You name the time and the place and I'll be there."

"Really?" Luke looked up at her smiling face. "Ummm... how about tomorrow night? Maybe we can catch the movie?"

Megan put her pad and a pen in front of him. "I'll call you."

Luke wrote his number and handed it back. "It'll be fun. We'll catch up."

"I can't wait." She smiled over her shoulder before going to check on another table.

What the hell am I doing? Megan's right. It's a bad idea. I know I've got to move on, but is asking Jared's sister on a date 'moving on'? He jumped when Megan touched his arm as she passed. He smiled.

#

Luke looked at Megan who was lost in the movie. Trying hard to be a good date, he took a deep breath and put his arm around her. *Why am I doing this? This is crazy.*

They went for a walk after the movie. Megan filled him in on everything he'd missed while he was gone. Whenever she mentioned Jared, his heart would start to race.

"Enough about me. What about you?"

"I told you, I have an apartment and a job. Not much else to tell." Luke gave her a smile, hoping the conversation would end there.

Megan wrapped her arm in his. "Luke. Come on. You know what I mean. What happened to you? Where were you all those months?"

He took a deep breath, trying to think of an explanation without telling what he'd really been through. "I went to school near my aunt and uncle. Mom and I hadn't been getting along and we thought it was best for me to be out of the house."

She stopped, turning to him. "Then why didn't you call to let us know? One day you were just gone. We talked about you all the time. We were so worried."

"I'm sorry. I tried, but... I just couldn't." Wiping a tear, he put his arm around her, continuing the walk. "Meg... how did Jared do while I was gone? Was he all right?"

"We were worried about him for a while. He didn't talk to anyone. I'd never seen him so depressed." She shook her head. "Then he was angry. He never talked about how he felt, but I knew. I could tell. I'd look in his room and catch him staring at the photo of the two of you from Prom. It took him a long time before he started acting more like himself."

Luke stared into the distance. Looking across the gravel road, he caught sight of the train car. "He's doing all right now though, right?"

"I think so. We don't hear from him much. He seems pretty busy with classes and projects. Sounds like he's made some friends. Seems like he's thriving out there so I guess he's doing all right."

Luke noticed her sober expression. "What? You don't look very happy about it."

"No. I am. I just... miss him. I didn't think I'd miss him this much. You know?" She wiped away a tear and chuckled.

Pulling her close, he kissed her on the forehead. "Yeah, I do know." He walked her to the door and kissed her cheek. "Thanks for coming out with me. It was great spending time with you. I've missed you all so much. You have no idea."

Megan took him into a hug. "It's good to have you home."

Candace opened the door, popping her head out. "Hey you guys. Did you have fun?"

"Yes, we did." Megan looked back at Luke, smiling. "I hope we can do it again."

"Anytime you want. It's getting old sitting in that apartment by myself."

"Luke, why don't you come over for supper tomorrow night? To celebrate your coming home. It's awfully quiet in the house now that Jared's gone and with Megan working all the time. It would be nice to have you around again. You're family." Candace reached out, taking his hand.

Luke gave her a smile. "I'd love to." His voice broke.

"Wonderful! See you tomorrow around six-ish." Candace disappeared into the house.

Luke wrapped his arms around Megan, holding her close. "Thank you so much for a great night. I'll see you tomorrow."

"Yeah, see you tomorrow. Thanks for everything." Megan went into the house and closed the door.

Luke walked down the driveway; a path he'd walked a hundred times before. Looking at his mother's house, he noticed the light on in the living room. He walked closer. Peeking through the window he saw his mom sitting on the couch. He stiffened, wiping the tears from his eyes. *How could you do that to me?*

Ellen screamed Susie's name, flying off the couch and disappearing into the hallway. "I'm sorry, Susie. I wish I could get you away from her." Staring up at the sky, he shook his head. "I've got so much to figure out."

ALWAYS ON MY MIND

May 1997

Derek and Jared sat on a blanket in their favorite spot in Seward Park. They'd taken the bus from campus in order to work on their final sophomore project.

Watching Derek reading, Jared kicked his foot. Derek glanced up, giving a knowing look before getting back to work.

Jared sat up, stealing the notebook away. "Derek, come on. Let's do something. We can work on this later."

"This is due next week. I just want to get it done, then we don't have to worry about it." He grabbed his notebook back.

Raising an eyebrow, Jared moved across the blanket and lay next to him. He blew in Derek's ear.

"Stop it."

Jared tickled him.

Derek closed the notebook with a sigh. "Why can't I ever say no to you?" He smiled, shaking his head. "Fine. What do you want to do?"

Jared jumped up, picking up their things, stopping when he heard someone call out.

"Jared Montgomery?"

Turning, he saw a familiar smiling face walking toward him. "Phillip? What on earth are you doing here?"

Phillip embraced him. "The same as you, I imagine. I heard you were here for school. How are you liking it?"

"I love it. Isn't it a great city? It's sure not like back home."

"No kidding." Phillip smiled, looking away. He rubbed his arm. "Speaking of back home, there's something I've wanted to ask you for years now." His face blushed.

Jared hesitated, looking back at Derek. "I know what you're going to ask. Yes. I'm gay." He stiffened, waiting for Phillip's response.

Phillip grinned. "I know. I was wondering if you'd ever go out with me sometime." He looked at the ground.

"Phillip? Wow. That's sweet, but..."

Phillip put his hand up. "Never mind. I didn't think so. You're still mad. He told you, didn't he?"

Jared stared at him. "Mad? Why would I be mad? I don't know what you're talking about."

Shaking his head, Phillip looked at him with a sneer. "You're still mad because I made-out with your boyfriend, Luke."

"What did you say?" Jared could feel his pulse race.

Phillip walked away from him. "I wasn't good enough for him. I don't know why I thought you'd be any different."

Jared lunged at him, grabbing his shoulders, turning him. "You did what with Luke?"

Phillip tried to pull away. "Oh, God. He didn't tell you."

Jared grabbed Phillip by the collar, pushing him against a tree. "When? When did it happen?"

Derek ran to them, putting his hands on Jared's shoulders. "Jared, stop! What's the matter with you?"

Jared pushed Phillip harder against the tree. "Tell me!" Hands tightening on Phillip's shirt, he shook him.

"It was before junior prom. I saw him walking and he looked upset so I asked him what was wrong. He said he had a fight with someone. I asked if it was with you. He was surprised that I knew. I told him I understood, then I asked him if he wanted to come to my place and..."

Jared threw him to the ground. "Enough! Shut up! Just shut the hell up! I don't want to hear it."

"I'm sorry!" Phillip got up and ran.

Jared watched for a moment, his body shaking with anger. People were staring. He turned to run the other direction.

Derek grabbed their things and ran after him. Finally catching up, he jumped in front of him. "Are you all right? What in the hell was that about?"

Jared pushed past him. "Nothing! I don't want to talk about it."

Derek dropped everything, grabbing his arm. "Who's Luke?"

"No one! Just leave it alone!"

Derek knelt down, gathering their stuff. "Jared? I think I deserve an explanation? Who was he talking about? Who's Luke?"

Jared turned. "The guy I'm in love with."

Derek's face dropped. "I see." Shoving everything in his backpack, he turned and walked away.

"Shit!" Jared smacked himself in the head. "That's not what I meant!" Derek disappeared into the crowd.

Jared ran, making it to the bus stop as it arrived. He stepped on, glancing behind him. There was so no sign of Derek. He found a seat in the back. Clasping a hand around his mouth to muffle his cries, he shook, tears streaming down his face. *What in the hell is wrong with you? You've just messed up the best thing that's happened to you.* He took a deep breath. *Derek, I am so sorry. You deserve better than this.*

TORCH SONG

Derek stared up at Jared's window. *Why the hell are you doing this? He doesn't want to talk to you.*

While he walked up the stairs to the third floor, he thought about what he was going to say. Knowing Jared, there would be a scene. *You just need answers. That's why you came.* He stared down the hallway. *I wish I could just let him go, but I can't.* He walked to the door, preparing himself for the worst. Jared wasn't answering his calls; he knew it wouldn't be the warmest reception.

Derek stared at the door, wondering if it was too late to walk away. *What do I have to lose?* He knocked then listened for a response. When none came, he knocked louder.

"I'm coming," Jared called from the other side. "Seriously, Chris?" The door opened.

"We need to talk." Derek pushed past Jared. Alcohol fumes made his eyes water. He took off his coat. "I was going to bring something to drink, thinking you might need it." He picked up an empty rum bottle. "Looks like you've done pretty well on your own."

Jared laughed, raising his glass. "I found that nothing seems to matter much after a couple of these." Shaking the ice in his empty glass, he smiled at Derek. "I have to say, I'm a little surprised to see you."

Derek crossed his arms. "Honestly, up until an hour ago I had no intention of seeing you again."

"I can't say I blame you." Jared sat on the bed, almost missing it.

Derek caught him by the arm. "You look like crap."

Chuckling, Jared collapsed onto the bed. "I bet I look better than I feel."

Derek sat next to him then struggled to find the right words. He leaned forward to take Jared's face in his hands. "I know you don't want to see me or talk to me. If you did, you would've answered your phone. I'm not going to take much of your time, but I need to know, for my sake." Pushing himself up, he moved to the other side of the room. "So... Luke? He's why you pushed me away. He's why you wouldn't commit."

Jared bit on his thumb nail, staring off.

"Listen, all you need to do is tell me you're in love with him, that it's over between us and I won't bother you anymore, but I need to hear it from you." Derek returned to his spot on the bed.

"I do love him. He was the one, you know? We knew each other since we were kids and... I fell in love with him. I thought he was in love with me. We had so many plans." Jared inhaled sharply, tears filled his eyes. "One minute we were in love, the next minute he was confused and needed to find a girlfriend, then we were in love... then he just left." He shrugged, shaking his head. "I never heard from him again."

Seeing the pain in his face, Derek, put an arm around him. "Oh, Sweetie. I'm so sorry."

Jared pushed him away. He went to the closet for another bottle that he cracked open. "I thought I was over it. I really did, but sometimes... I don't know."

"You don't just get over it. I understand that."

Jared shook his head. "You don't understand. Nobody does. *I* don't understand it. How the hell are you going to understand it? It's been confusing and difficult from the beginning. It still is."

"I do understand. He was your first love. I had one of those too." Derek sat on the desk.

Jared looked at him, surprise on his face. "What happened to him?"

"He was a year older than me. We spent all of our time together... until he graduated. He moved to college and I was supposed to follow after I graduated." Derek poured himself a drink. "I graduated and spent the summer getting ready to move. Then he showed up at my house to tell me he was moving to New York. He'd met someone on-line. That was that. All of my dreams and plans out the window."

"That must've been awful."

"It hurt, sure. I said good-bye, cried for a few weeks then knew I had to go on. There was someone else out there for me." He winked at Jared. "Or so I thought."

"That's just it. You said good-bye. I never got that. There was no ending, no closure; I just had to hope he was all right." Jared stared down at the floor, shaking his head.

"Maybe something did happen to him? Do you know where he is?"

"Yeah, I do. Mom told me he came back right after I left. Apparently he asked about me and she gave him my number. Still haven't heard from him." Jared reached for the bottle of rum. "He's had my number for two years."

Derek took the bottle away. He wrapped his arms around him, rocking him. "I'm sorry." *Luke is the biggest jerk alive and doesn't deserve you.* He stroked Jared's face. "Are you okay?"

"I will be. I think. I realized tonight, after glass number three of rum, that I got his answer. I got it a long time ago. It's just hard to move on, you know?" Jared patted Derek's leg. "I know how stupid I sound."

Derek kissed his cheek. "It's not stupid. It's exactly what I love about you."

"You know when you wanted to make love to me those times and I told you I couldn't? You know why?"

"Luke?"

"It felt like I'd be cheating on him." Jared laughed. "Boy, am I messed up."

"You'll be fine. Trust me. I've been through it." Derek kissed him again. "This may not be the right time, but I have to throw it out there."

"What?"

Derek stared into his eyes, holding his hand. "I've made no secret that I care about you... a lot. I don't expect you to answer this now, but... do you and I have a chance?"

Jared leaned against him. "I can't believe you even want to give me a chance."

"Unfortunately, I can't control my feelings for you anymore than you can for Luke." Derek caressed his hand. "Just think about it. I'm willing to wait for you to get things figured out."

"Why, Derek? What can you possibly like about me? I'm a jerk."

Pulling his face close, Derek looked him in the eyes. "Fine. At the risk of sounding like a love-drunk idiot, it's because when you smile, my heart races. When I make you laugh, it feels amazing. When you touch my hand and look at me with those beautiful eyes, I melt. For whatever reason, I want to make you happy. It's all I think about."

Jared pulled Derek's hands down, tears rolling down his face. "Then you're a glutton for punishment. I don't know what makes me happy. I've spent too much time worrying about all the bad shit in my life to figure that out. I may possibly be insane. You need to run fast and far, for your own good." He walked to the window. "I've been trying to tell you this for a few days. I'm going to be gone for a while. Mom and Dad are flying me home. I don't want to go, but I've run out of excuses. Actually, I do miss them. It's been a long time."

Derek cringed, knowing Jared would probably see Luke. "Maybe I should go with you. I'd love to meet them."

"Thank you, but no. I have to be honest. My parents don't know I'm gay. Besides, I don't know what's going to happen." Jared smiled. "I have to face him alone."

"I understand." Derek reached for him, but pulled back. "I'm going to leave you alone. You need to get some rest. Call me whenever you want, okay? I would like to know that you're doing okay." He leaned down, kissing Jared on the top of the head. He grabbed his coat then reached for the door.

"Derek?" Jared's voice broke. His face was soaked with tears.

"Yes?"

"For what it's worth, I do love you."

Derek forced a smile. "I love you too." Looking at Jared one last time, he closed the door behind him. "Goodbye, Jared." He got as far as the end of the hall before collapsing against the wall. "Luke, you son-of-a-bitch, you better take care of him." He collected himself and made it out to the street. He looked up at Jared's window. *Please come back to me.*

THE VIEW FROM A RUSTY TRAIN CAR

YOUR GAME

June, 1997

Jared was glad to be off the plane. The flight had been delayed twice, one of those times spent on the runway for two hours. He couldn't help thinking about the phone call from his mother the previous morning, telling him there was a surprise when he got home.

"Please, God, don't let it be a Welcome Home Party."

He picked up one of his suitcases then turned toward the door. It fell from his hand. Heart and mind racing, he stared at the man walking his way, smiling. *Luke!* His body started to shake and he felt light headed. "What...? What are you doing here?"

Luke smirked, standing in front of him. "That's it? 'What are you doing here?'" He held out his arms, taking Jared into a hug.

Being held by Luke for the first time in almost three years caused Jared to audibly inhale. He ran his fingers through Luke's hair. "What are you doing?" He pulled away to look at him, his arms still shaking.

"Your parents sent me to pick you up." Luke stared into Jared's eyes, caressing his face. "Damn, it's good to see you. You look wonderful. Come here." Luke pulled him back into his arms. "God, this feels amazing."

Jared laid his head on Luke's shoulder. "I've been dreaming of this for a long time."

"Come on. We should get your luggage and get out of here." Luke looked through the name tags attached to the luggage on the carousel. "How are you?"

"That one's mine." Jared pointed to a large dark green case. "Sick of traveling. I don't know how long I've been on planes today, but we were stuck on the runway in Denver for two hours because of some mechanical issues. I just need to sit and relax for a little bit."

"I thought you might say that. I took the liberty of getting us a hotel room." Luke smiled, raising an eyebrow. "It's late and I don't feel like driving another three hours. We'll leave early in the morning. I already called your parents to let them know."

"That sounds wonderful. As long as there's running water and a bathroom bigger than a shoe closet I'll be happy. A bar wouldn't hurt either." Jared chuckled, touching Luke's arm.

"I'm sure we'll be able to find something."

"I could really use a good night's sleep before Dad starts in on me." Jared grabbed for his cases, but Luke had already picked them up.

Leaning into his ear, Luke whispered. "Sleep? Really? We see each other for the first time in three years and you want to sleep?"

"Well, maybe just a quick nap." Jared laughed. "Eventually."

"I'll get the car and meet you at the door." Grabbing the rest of the luggage from Jared, Luke kissed him on the cheek. "See you in a minute."

Jared watched him disappear through the doors. "I sure wasn't ready for this." He stood outside, looking at the familiar landscape. It was home.

A car pulled up, stopping in front of him. Luke jumped out and walked around to the passenger side to open the door. He reached for Jared's arm.

The skyline of Gaylesburg came into view. Jared saw the lights of The Fort Kingston. The building had been converted from an old fort, turned into a hotel. "I love that building. It's gorgeous."

"It is beautiful, isn't it?" Luke reached over, grabbing Jared's hand. "See that dimly lit window up there on the right."

"Yeah. Have you ever been in there?" Jared strained to look as they pulled near the hotel.

"Just once... when I checked us in." Luke turned into the parking garage. "I remembered you talking about it. I thought now was the time. I took the liberty of ordering us a late supper."

"God, how I've missed you." Jared picked up Luke's hand, kissing it.

Luke leaned into Jared, giving him a long, passionate kiss. "Welcome home, Sweetheart." He got out of the car and took the luggage from the trunk.

"We have so much to talk about. I don't even know where to start? How's your family?" Jared rushed to hold the door for him. "How's your mom?"

"I'm sure she's fine." He pressed the button for their floor; Luke turned serious. "I don't really know. We haven't talked for quite a while."

"I'm sorry to hear that." Jared studied his face. "Was it because of us?"

Luke took a deep breath. "Jed, that was part of it, but don't worry about it. It doesn't matter." He smiled again. "I just want to enjoy the fact that you're finally home!"

"For a little while anyway. I still have to finish school. But seeing you again... it's going to make it pretty hard to get back on that plane." Jared bumped up against him.

"Then what?"

"Well, that all depends." Jared winked. Luke closed his eyes, drew a deep breath. "Luke? What's wrong?"

"There's something I really need to tell you..." The elevator doors opened.

Jared looked into the hall. "Oh, my God. Look at this place! This is incredible!" He grabbed Luke's arm to pull him out of the elevator. "Come on! Which room is it?"

"624." Luke motioned to the left, putting one of the bags down to dig the key out of his pocket. He threw it to Jared. "Can you get the door?"

"Of, course!" Jared fumbled with the key, his hands shaking. "I can't believe this. Look at this food. It smells incredible." Jared walked to the table in the middle of the room. There was champagne chilling in a bucket. The scene was very romantic.

Luke put the bags down, grabbed a lighter and lit the candles. "You approve?"

"I don't know what to say." Jared walked behind Luke, wrapping his arms around him. When he opened his eyes he saw the bed was covered with red rose petals and a dozen red roses sat on the night stand with a note attached. He opened the card.

'Welcome home, Sweetheart. Love always, Luke.'

"Thank you. It's really good to be home."

Luke pulled out a chair. "Hungry?"

"I wasn't, but how could I pass up all this great food? First, I need to get into some fresh clothes. I can't imagine what I look like, or what I smell like." Grabbing his suitcase, Jared ran into the bathroom. "It feels like I've been in these for a week."

Luke sat on the edge of the bed. "How are you? I mean, how do you like Seattle?"

Jared turned the water on, splashing it over his face. "I'm fine. It's a lot different than I thought it would be, some good, some not so good. It took more time to adjust than I imagined; I missed everyone terribly." He walked out of the bathroom and grabbed his carry-on.

"Well, it must agree with you because you look amazing." There was a silly grin on Luke's face as he looked him up and down.

Jared blushed, realizing he'd left the bathroom stark naked. "Are you flirting with me, Sir?"

"Yes. Is it working?"

"Absolutely." Jared winked, fastening the buttons of his shirt. He motioned to the table. "Shall we?"

Luke seated him. "Champagne?"

"Please."

He poured, handed one glass to Jared then raised his. "To seeing each other again after all these years."

"And to you being as gorgeous as ever." Jared clicked his glass against Luke's.

"Why thank you." Luke removed the cover from the serving tray.

Jared burst into laughter. Nearly spitting champagne across the table, he held the napkin to his mouth. "Cornish game hens?"

"Don't worry. I didn't cook them. They should be edible." Luke laughed, placing one on Jared's plate.

"Thank God. So, you mean, they won't be raw this time?"

"I should hope not." Luke smiled. "So you do remember that night?"

"Remember? I got so sick I thought I was going to die." Jared held his stomach, laughing.

"Your mom accused us of drinking because we were throwing up so much."

"Oh, she was mad. Then again, she thought it was odd enough that you tried cooking for us." Jared sat back in his chair. "That was a tough one to explain. I should've just said we were drunk. It would've been much easier."

The smile melted from Luke's face. "I know what you mean."

Jared stared into his eyes. "Okay, I need to know. What happened between you and your mom?" He reached for Luke's hand.

Luke pulled away, reaching for his plate instead. "It's nothing. I don't want to talk about it."

"Luke, it's me. I know you. It's not 'nothing'. Every time she's mentioned, your whole demeanor changes. You look like someone punched you in the gut."

"Jed, please don't do this. Don't spoil it." Luke pushed away from the table. He walked to the window, staring out at the night skyline.

Jared put down his napkin and went to him, wrapping his arms around him. "She must have really hurt you. I'm sorry if I had anything to do with it."

Shaking his head, Luke reached up, holding his hands. "It's not you."

"Then what is it? What happened?" Jared turned him. Luke said nothing, staring past him. "I deserve some explanation. Why did you just disappear? Susie told me about the fight."

Luke sat on the bed, holding his head in his hands.

Pulling a chair near the bed, Jared sat facing him. "I really need to know why you left. Why you never called me or wrote me. I waited for months, hoping you were all right. When nothing came, all I could do was assume you wanted nothing to do with me. It hurt so much." He bowed his head, looking down at the floor.

Luke looked up at him, his face and eyes red. "I had no choice." He wiped away tears. "You're right. You do deserve the truth." Taking a deep breath, his fists grabbed onto the bed linens and twisted. "That weekend I left to go to Grandma's, Mom and I fought all the way there. She said she'd had enough and told me I was going to live with my aunt and uncle. She'd come out looking for me that night. She suspected that I'd been hanging out with you so she'd been watching me. After an hour of looking for us, she was about to head home when she heard noises coming from the train car. She climbed up and listened through the hatch."

"Oh, my God. She... heard us?" Jared's heart raced and his throat tightened.

"My uncle Richard didn't know what to do with me. Mom found a place that would take me so she sent me there. It was a camp for boys who were gay... to make them straight." Luke shook. "I didn't see anyone for months. I tried to write. I did try to write you, but they found out and they..." He swallowed hard. "I just did what I could to get out of there."

Jared moved closer to him. "I had no idea."

"You think my mom was going to talk about it? Tell people she sent her gay son away to a place like that?"

Jared paced then threw his hands up. "I'm sorry. I don't know what to say. I can't wrap my head around it. It's too crazy! A camp for...? What happens? What did they do to you?" He sat next to Luke, holding his hand.

"Mostly, they told me how evil I was. Bible verses were always used to prove it. It doesn't sound like a big deal, but it was all day, every day... constantly. There were rules, most of them completely stupid, just to make sure you didn't act inappropriately with the other boys." Luke stared into the room. "The counselors didn't have rules. They did whatever they wanted. Fucking hypocrites. We were bad for being gay, but they could..." He looked at Jared, squeezing his hand. "They didn't touch me, Jed! I swear! I wouldn't let them. They knew. They could tell they wouldn't get away with it."

"Luke!" Jared sobbed, putting his arms around Luke. "I'm so sorry! How can they...? How is this being allowed to happen?"

Luke didn't react. He kept staring at the wall, shaking his head. "That wasn't even the worst part. The worst was the 'therapy sessions'. They seemed pretty harmless at first; just the same, constant berating. Then they decide you need more help. It doesn't matter what you do or what you say. Everyone needs more help. They sit you in a room with a screen, your arms and legs tied down. Pictures start showing on the screen. First they show you nice pictures, like of mountains and streams and things like that. Then they show you pictures of women. Not just every day photos, but pictures of them in sort of sexy poses, you know? They tell you how 'natural' it is to feel attracted to them. They encourage it. Then..." His jaw tensed. "Then come the pictures of guys. You know, nice looking, well-built guys in sexy poses. Suddenly, zap! They push something against your neck and a shock runs through you. It's like a tazer or something. It doesn't matter what you say or how you react. Whenever a picture of a guy comes up, you get shocked."

Jared's stomach churned. His hand shook as he held Luke's face. "Luke, I..."

"It works. It really does. You find yourself hating the guy in every photo and praying for a woman's picture, just to stop the pain. It burns your skin and they don't give you anything to put on it." Luke sobbed.

Jared led Luke to the bed, helped him to settle then ran to the bar to pour him a drink. He set it on the nightstand, crawled into bed and rocked him in his arms.

"You know what's really messed up?" Luke rolled over, looking into Jared's face. "The whole time I was going through it, all I could think about was you. I wanted you just like this, just to hold me. You made it all okay."

"It's okay. I'm here now." Jared pulled him close, stroking his hair as Luke wept.

Luke pulled away from him, got off the bed. "Then I'd feel guilty about being with you all those times. I was sick. The people at camp were right. I never blamed you, though. I blamed myself, that somehow I'd made you gay. I molested you. It was all my fault. I'm so sorry!"

"No, no, no. Don't think like that. I was with you because I love you. You didn't do anything wrong. Neither of us did. It's just who we are."

Luke touched Jared's face, his eyes searching. "I've missed you so much. I thought I was going to die if I didn't see you again. I love you so much... but it feels so wrong now. I don't know how to explain it." He turned away. "Why does it have to be like this?"

"It's not wrong, Luke! I've thought about you every single minute of every day since the last time I saw you." Jared turned Luke's head toward him and kissed him. "I'm here now. We're together again. Everything's going to be all right. I promise. I won't leave you. We'll get through it."

Luke lay back on the bed, wiping his eyes. He reached up, touching Jared's lips. Sitting up, he grabbed Jared by the shoulders, throwing him down beside him. He kissed him hard, touching every part of his body.

Jared unbuttoned Luke's shirt. Luke pulled it off the rest of the way then slid his hands down to Jared's waist, pulling their bodies together. He yanked the collar away from Jared's neck and kissed it.

"Make love to me." Jared unbuttoned Luke's pants, slipping his hands down his hips.

"No!" Luke jumped from the bed then moved to the other side of the room. "What am I doing? We can't do this!" He grabbed his shirt off the floor and put it on.

Jared followed him out of the bed. "What's the matter? Did I do something wrong?"

"No. God! It's not you." Luke paced back and forth. He sat down at the table, putting his head in his hands. "Jared. I'm so sorry. I shouldn't have done any of this. Oh, God, I'm so sorry. I didn't mean to."

"Luke? What's the matter? I want this. I really do." Jared put his hands on his shoulders, but Luke jumped. He took a step back.

"We can't do this. You don't get it! I'm not that guy anymore."

Jared put his hands up. "I'm sorry. I shouldn't have pushed you, especially after a story like that. I'm awful."

"Oh, God, Jed. You have to forgive me. I'm sorry. Please. You have to forgive me." Luke beat his fist against his chest.

"Luke. Stop it. What's the matter?" He grabbed Luke's hands. "You did nothing wrong! Everything's all right."

"No! It's the surprise... the surprise that your parents flew you home for."

"What about it?"

Luke crossed his arms, his hands clenching into fists. "You're here... God!" Looking at Jared, he spoke with no emotion. "I'm getting married tomorrow afternoon."

Struggling to breathe, Jared blinked, putting his hand to his head. "Excuse me?"

"You heard me." Luke's voice was low, speaking through clenched teeth.

Jared chuckled. "You're kidding me, right?" Luke shook his head. "I don't know what to say. This sure wasn't the reunion I'd imagined." He poured himself another drink. "I guess congratulations are in order, huh?" He sat on the bed, staring at the floor. "At least it can't get any worse, right?"

"I'm sorry. It does." Luke looked away, swallowing hard. "I'm marrying Megan."

"Megan who?" Jared slowly raised his head to look at him as realization set in.

Luke shot him an apologetic glance then buried his face in his hands.

"Luke? Please tell me this is a joke. Please!" Jared slammed his drink down on the table. "Meg? You and Meg? Tell me you're not seriously going to do this."

"Jed, please?"

Jared marched up to him, shoving his finger into Luke's face. "Do you have any idea how fucked up this sounds? This is crazy! You're standing here, telling the man you love...

wait... the man you were about to sleep with, that you're marrying his sister in the morning? You're insane!" Grabbing his drink from the table, he emptied it, and poured another. "Look, I'm sorry about what you went through. It was beyond awful. This isn't going to fix it! You can't just pretend it all away... everything we've been through. For God's sake, admit it, Luke! Admit it. Admit it to yourself. You're gay!"

Luke grabbed him by the collar, throwing him against the wall. "Shut up! Just shut up! It's not true! " His fist hit the wall by Jared's head. Closing his eyes, he slammed the wall again. "You don't understand. Meg and I hung out a lot after I came back. She's good to me. She was there when I needed someone. Megan loves me."

Jared shoved him away. "Oh, really? What about you? Are you in love with her?"

"Yes, I love her."

Jared grabbed his arm. "That's not what I asked. I asked if you were in love with her."

Luke looked away. "I think so. Yes."

Grabbing him by the shoulder, Jared shook him. "Then what in the hell was all this about, huh? This room? The food? The rose petals on the bed? What? You were trying to get me to sleep with you!" He took Luke's face in his hands. "It was that camp. Those bastards played with your mind. They confused you. You're in love with me and you know it!"

Luke ran from him, downed his drink then slammed it back on the table. "The camp showed me that I was right! The whole thing between us was impossible... and wrong. It was never going to work!" He looked to Jared. "This is the way it has to be. It's best for everyone."

Jared stared at him, unable to help the sneer he felt forming on his face. "Don't you dare. No! You mean it's easier for you. That's what it's always been about. You don't give a damn about anyone else!"

"That's not true." Luke turned to him. "I love you."

Jared's body tensed, his body shaking "Fuck you!"

"Jed, please. You have to understand." Luke took Jared into an embrace.

Collapsing into his arms, Jared sobbed. He pushed Luke, throwing him against the table. "Don't you touch me! Don't ever touch me again." He ran to the bathroom, slammed then locked the door. "You son-of-a bitch. How can you do this to me?" He fell against the door, sliding to the floor, sobbing. He put his arm against his mouth, muffling his screams. His other hand in a fist, he slammed it against the floor.

THE VIEW FROM A RUSTY TRAIN CAR

SHELTER

Jared noticed sunlight coming in from under the bathroom door. All was quiet in the other room. Cracking it, he saw Luke lying in the bed, his back to the door.

He gathered his things, threw them into a bag then tiptoed out, grabbing his luggage. He took one last look at Luke. "I loved you, you bastard." Fighting back tears, he quietly closed the door and ran to the elevator. He kept watch over his shoulder in case Luke had heard him leave.

There was no one at the front desk. He rang the bell, hitting more aggressively than he had intended. The desk attendant arrived, pulling the bell away from him. "Can I help you, Sir?"

"Yes. I'm checking out of room 624." Jared reached for his wallet.

"The total comes to two hundred forty six dollars and thirty cents."

Jared's head whipped up. "What the hell? Do you charge by the hour?"

"No, Sir, we don't." The desk clerk looked over Jared's shoulder. "Do you?"

The elevator doors opened. Luke appeared.

"He'll take care of it." Jared gathered his things then bolted for the door.

"Jared. Wait!" Luke ran into the lobby.

"Sir! What about the bill?" The attendant stepped in front of Luke, stopping him.

"Shit! How do I get out of here?" Jared spotted a taxi waiting across the street. He ran to it and jumped in. "Please, just start going."

As the cab pulled away, Jared looked back. Luke came running out, waving his arms. He took a deep breath, relaxing into the seat.

"Are you in some kind of trouble?" The cab driver stared at him in the rear-view mirror.

"No. Avoiding it."

The driver smiled. "So, where are we headed?"

Jared looked at himself in the mirror. "Where am I going?"

"Sir? I need to know where to go?"

"You wouldn't by any chance go as far as Sheldon, would you?"

"If you've got the dime, I've got the time."

Jared grimaced at the cliché. "I've got it." He watched through the window, trying to decide how he was going to handle everyone back home. *What in the hell am I going to say to Meg? Why didn't anyone tell me anything?* He thought back to the previous night. *This is crazy. I almost slept with him.* Derek's face flashed through his mind. *What am I going to say to him?*

Jared's stomach churned when he saw the first houses leading into his hometown. It was hot and humid; a strange haze hung in the air. Seeing the train car again after all these years was too much for him. He looked away, his eyes filling with tears.

Approaching his parent's house, he saw cars parked up and down both sides of the street. There wasn't a single place left for anyone to park.

THE VIEW FROM A RUSTY TRAIN CAR

The cabbie pointed toward a large group of people gathered in the driveway. "Is this it?"

"That's it. Just pull up to the driveway and I'll jump out." Jared got out of the cab, grabbed his luggage, and paid the driver. The door of the house slammed behind him.

"Jared? Is that my little Jared?"

Taking a deep breath, he forced a smile as he turned to her. "Hi, Aunt Grace."

She threw her arms around him, lifting him off the ground. "You look great. It's so good to see you. How's Seattle? Have you seen the Space Needle?"

Jared tried to respond, but Aunt Grace was notorious for never allowing anyone to answer her questions. The barrage continued as she pulled him to the house.

Candace appeared at the door. She held out her arms, a tear in her eye. "Welcome home, Sweetie!" She took him in her arms. "Where's Luke? We sent him to pick you up."

Here we go. Jared kissed his mother on the cheek. "It's all right. I've seen him. I took a cab thinking he had things to do before the wedding."

"Well, does he know you're here?"

"Yes. He knows I took a cab. Where's Megan?" The noise from all the people was driving him crazy. He could barely think.

"She's downstairs in her room getting ready. She wanted to see you as soon as you got here, so go! You might as well take your bags down. You'll be staying in your old room."

Picking up his bags, he ran down the stairs. He looked down the hall at Megan's room, trying to build up his courage. *You can do this. You have to!* Throwing his luggage into his bedroom, he took a deep breath and knocked on Megan's door. "Meg? Are you in there?" His knees shook.

"Who is it?"

"It's me, Meg. Can I come in?"

The door flew open and Megan took him in her arms. "Jared. Oh God! I've missed you so much." She rocked him back and forth. "Come in. Come in." Taking him by the arm, she rushed him into the room, closing the door behind them.

Looking around the room, Jared felt queasy. One side looked like a small salon had been moved in. The other had decorations and stacks of wedding magazines. A dress was laid out on the bed.

Megan walked up behind him, putting her arms around him. "I know what you're going to say. Yes, it's Mom's dress. She talked me into it."

"You're going to be beautiful." Jared held her hands.

Megan sat on the edge of the bed, pulling him down beside her.

Feeling her shake, Jared forced a smile, brushing her hair away from her forehead. "So, you and Luke, huh?"

"I'm sure you were pretty surprised. It surprised me."

Clearing his throat, Jared tried to relax. His jaw ached from clenching his teeth. "You have no idea."

"I didn't want anyone to tell you we were even seeing each other. It felt so strange. I don't know how to explain it." She went into the small bathroom then reappeared with a veil. She held it close to her, picking at the lace. "Jared? I'm sure it's just cold feet, but I'm still not so sure I should be doing this. Something doesn't feel right. Maybe it's just nerves?"

"I'm sure. It's a big decision. I'd be freaking out!" Jared laughed. *Come on. Tell her.*

Megan's face turned solemn, putting the veil back on the counter. "You know him better than anyone. Am I doing the right thing?"

Heart beating rapidly, Jared stared at her.

Megan paced back and forth. "I know he's a great guy, and I do love him, but our relationship has been so up and down. One day he was so sure we should get married. The next day he'd tell me that he was no good and had really screwed up and wasn't worthy of me." She wandered to the bathroom for a tissue.

Jared followed, standing in the doorway. He could feel his heart pound in his throat, took several deep breaths, trying to calm himself.

"I know you don't want to hear about this, but it's just that... well... we've never even... you know. I tried, but every time we'd get close he'd have to leave or it wasn't the right time. I don't know."

Jared closed his eyes, cringed thinking about it.

"It took me the longest time to not feel creepy about holding his hand. He was like a little brother for so long. Maybe he can't get past that. Maybe he thinks of me like a sister and he's only marrying me because there's no one else left!" Megan looked at Jared's reflection in the mirror. "Jared. Help me! What do you think? Should I marry him?"

Jared looked down, thought a moment then looked back at his sister. "No, I don't think you should."

Megan's face turned pale. "What?"

"I know you think it's just nerves." He took her by the hand. "But you're right; you shouldn't marry him. He's not right for you."

Megan sat on the bed. "Why? What do you mean?"

Jared knelt beside her, taking her hands in his. "Meg, he's..."

"What in the hell do you think you're doing?" Mike's angry voice yelled from the doorway. Candace and Mike stared at him. His father looked angry, his mother mortified.

Candace darted in, pulling Jared to his feet. "Why are you doing this to your sister?" She pushed him into the hall toward his father.

Megan followed, reaching for him. "Jared. Why? Why shouldn't I?" Her voice sounded desperate.

"Don't listen to him, Megan. You just get ready. There's a lot to do. I'll be right back to help you." Candace pushed her back in the room and closed the door.

Looking at his parents, Jared took a deep breath. He ran to her door and pounded "Don't do it, Meg. Just trust me. Please!"

Mike grabbed him by the back of the shirt and dragged him down the hall. He threw him into his room. Jared fell over his luggage, landing on the floor.

Candace ran into the room, her face red and twisted. "What in the hell is wrong with you?"

Jared ran to her, holding her by the shoulders. "You don't understand! I can't let this happen!"

Mike shook his head. "I know exactly what you're trying to do. You're jealous. I know all about what you really think of Luke."

"What are you talking about?" Candace looked at him, a puzzled expression on her face.

Mike opened the top drawer of the desk and took out a notebook. "I found this when I was cleaning out his room. I didn't want you to see it." He tossed it to Candace.

Jared tried to grab it from her. "No! Give me that. That's private." Mike restrained him.

Candace paged through it. "Michael? What is it?"

"Go ahead. Tell her, Jared. Tell her about how you dreamed of you and Luke... all the sick, perverted shit you have written in there."

"You had no right to read that!" Jared pulled away from him.

"It's a bunch of filth. It made me sick. I didn't want your mother to know about it. I thought you getting away from here would help, that you would outgrow it. Obviously I was wrong." Michael stormed off leaving Candace staring at Jared.

He buried his head in his arms and slid down the wall.

Candace put the journal on the desk. "What does all this mean?"

"Come on, Mom. Do I have to spell it out? I'm gay." Seeing the shock on her face, Jared sobbed.

Candace reached for the wall to steady herself. "No, God. Jared, it's not true." Covering her mouth, she muffled her cries. She closed her eyes and took a deep breath. "I'm very sorry. Your sister is getting married in two hours. Your tux is in the closet. We'll talk about this later." Her face was devoid of emotion.

Jared wiped his eyes. "What tux?"

"This one." Candace opened the closet door, took out a garment bag, and laid it on the bed. "You're the Best Man." She left the room.

"Over my dead body! There's no way I'm going to that wedding!" Jared caught her on the stairs.

Candace put her hand up. "Jared, please. I'm begging you. Don't ruin this day any more than you already have."

Jared was about to follow, but stopped in his tracks. His parents were arguing on the landing. He heard a car pull up outside. Holding his breath, he went to the window. Luke parked the car in the middle of the street, leaving the door wide open. Jared could hear Luke ask about him then Candace say he was there and getting ready. Footsteps came down the stairs; Jared grabbed his luggage and burst into the hallway.

Seeing Megan standing in her doorway, Jared looked at her then up the stairs at Luke.

Luke reached out to him. "Jared, I really need to talk to you."

"I have nothing left to say to you." Holding his luggage in front of him, Jared pushed him to the side and made it to the front door. He took one last look at his sister. "I love you, Meg."

Megan ran up the stairs. "Someone, stop him!"

Already down the driveway, Jared looked over his shoulder and saw his father pushing her back into the house. He blocked the door.

"Let him go. He's not wanted here." Mike was now restraining both Megan and Luke.

Jared jumped into Luke's car that was still running.

Luke struggled to get free from Mike. "Jed! Stop! Please!"

Shaking his head, Jared put the car in gear and sped-off. His eyes burned, sore from the tears. He watched in the rearview mirror for anyone who might try to follow him. "God, why? Why is this happening?" He slammed his hands against the steering wheel.

THE VIEW FROM A RUSTY TRAIN CAR

TRUE COLORS

Luke lifted his hand to knock on Megan's door. Hearing her crying on the other side, he stepped back and sat down on the stairs. *What did you say, Jared? Why is everyone so upset?* A thousand scenarios ran through his head. *Please, God! Don't let it be that he told them about last night. It was just a moment of weakness. I was just confused!* He shook his head, placing it into his hands. *What was I thinking? I thought I was past this with him.*

Megan's bedroom door opened. She jumped seeing Luke on the stairs. "Luke! You scared me. What are you doing out here?"

Luke studied her face. "We need to talk."

"Yes, I know." Megan opened the door, motioning him inside.

He thought about where to start as he walked into the room.

Megan sat on the bed, looking up at him. "So you must've heard."

"No, actually, I haven't. What happened?" Luke swallowed hard.

"Jared's gay." She stared out the window. "It was strange to hear it, but I already knew. My dad's furious. Mom hasn't said much of anything. She's just been crying." Turning to him, she raised an eyebrow. "Did you know?"

"Yeah, I did."

"So you knew he was in love with you?" Megan paced around the room. "Oh, my God. Is that why you left? He told you, didn't he? That's why you left... why you never called or wrote him."

Taking her arm, Luke led her to the bed. "Leaving wasn't my choice. Yes, I knew he was gay, but I didn't care. He was my best friend. I love him." He caressed her face. "What about you? Are you okay with it?"

Megan thought a moment. "Yeah, I'm fine. I don't care. As long as he's happy I don't care." She smiled at him.

"You still want to marry me?"

"Of course I do... if you still want to marry me." Megan looked in his eyes.

Luke kissed her hand. "I better let you finish getting ready. I'm going to see if I can find Jared."

Megan looked at the clock. "No! You can't go. We've got to be at the church in twenty minutes." She shook her head. "This is not the way I wanted my wedding day to be. I wanted Jared there."

"I know. I did too." Luke kissed her cheek.

"I hope there's no truth about it being bad luck to see the bride before the wedding." She winked at him. "Now go. You've got to get ready."

"Okay. See you in a few. My tux is at the church. I'll see you there." Luke closed the door and went up the stairs.

Candace caught him at the door. "Luke! Are you two all right?"

"We're fine. I'm just heading to the church to get ready." Stepping out the door, he stopped, turning back to her. "Any chance I can borrow a car? My car seems to have disappeared."

"Of course." Candace ran to her purse, pulled out some keys then threw them to him. "Take mine."

"Thanks. See you later." Luke looked around as he pulled away, hoping to see Jared. "Where did you go?" Approaching the gravel road, he stopped. "The train car. That's where he always goes when he's upset." Looking at the clock, he shook his head. "I have to check." He pulled the car over and ran to the train car. "Jared? Jared, are you in there?" There was no response. He turned to head back to the car, but stopped, looking at the train car again. "I have to make sure." He climbed to the top, opened the hatch and dropped inside. Jared wasn't there.

Alone in the train car, Luke's thoughts turned to what was happening. "What am I doing? I'm supposed to be getting married and I'm chasing after Jed?" He shook his head, leaning against a beam. His gaze fixed on their initials on the wall. Walking over to it, he traced them with his finger; thoughts of that night swirled in his head. "I do love you. I wish I could be who you want me to be. I just can't." Tears rolled down his cheeks. He looked at his watch, realizing everyone was probably gathering at the church and he was nowhere to be seen. "It's too late. I can't do that to her, Jed. I've made my decision... now I have to live with it." He took one last look at the wall.

"L Loves J – Forever"

Wiping tears away, he climbed the ladder to the top. "You must hate me so much right now, Jed. I'm so sorry. I never wanted to hurt you." He stared into the distance. One question plagued him: *Why didn't he tell anyone about what happened between us?* Walking through the tall grass, heading for the car, he looked back at the train car. *He didn't tell because he loves you... and this is how you repay him? He's better off without you.*

LEAVE YOUR DREAMS BEHIND

"What do I do? Where do I go?" Jared saw the bar, cranked the steering wheel to turn into the parking lot. He pulled around back where he wouldn't be seen. With a quick glance, he checked to make sure he had a clear shot for the door. Before he could start across the pavement, someone yelled. He jumped then realized it wasn't at him.

He looked through the dim light inside. Years of smoke had stained the walls a sickening shade of yellow. The smell of stale beer and musty curtains overwhelmed him. Avoiding eye contact with anyone, he found a booth that was tucked away in a corner on the empty side of the bar. It was out of view from the front windows.

"What can I get you?"

The waitress looked like she just walked out of a movie. Her hair was blonde, permed to within an inch of its life. The lines in her face revealed too many long nights of boring stories and attempts at 'brown bottle' psychology for the drunks crying into their whiskey.

Knowing his options would be limited, he thought of the simplest drink he could. "Whiskey/Coke?"

"Sure."

Nothing changes. I knew they wouldn't ask for any ID. Jared glanced up when he heard whispers at the bar. People were staring at him.

After a few moments, one of them got off his stool and approached him. "Aren't you Mike and Candy's boy?"

"Yeah. Jared." He offered his hand.

The old guy shook it. "I told them you were the Montgomery boy, but they kept arguing with me." He gave his friends at the bar a thumbs-up. "Ain't your sister getting married this afternoon? You having a little pre-celebration celebration?"

Jared chuckled. "Something like that."

"Tell everyone congrats from Ernie." Smiling, he went back to his seat.

The waitress placed the whiskey/Coke in front of Jared. "You want to start a tab?"

Jared took a sip while he considered the suggestion. "Yes. Thank you."

An hour and four drinks later, Jared looked at his watch. The wedding would have started. "I better go give my best to the newlyweds."

He stumbled over his own feet, fell back into the booth then laughed; everything seemed funny. His entire body felt numb. With the help of the table, he pushed himself up. He swayed while groping for his wallet, catching himself before toppling over. Unable to count the money, he handed over the wad of cash to pay his tab. "Thanks." The door jamb jumped up in front of him. His foot caught it, throwing him to the ground.

The waitress rushed to him. "Sir? Are you all right?"

"I'm fine. I gotta get to my sister's wedding." Jared tried to sound as sober as possible.

"I think I should call someone for you." She grabbed the phone then started dialing.

"No, no, no. I'm all right. The church is just down the block." Back on his feet, Jared waved at everyone. "Thanks for everything. Nice to see you guys. Take care of yourselves." They laughed, waving back.

Convinced he was doing a great job passing as stone-cold sober, Jared chuckled as he climbed into the car. As he grabbed the steering wheel, everything outside appeared out of focus, swirling. "She was right. I shouldn't be driving." He looked down the alley, he could see the church. "It's not that far." Jared drove to the church where he found a spot that required little effort to park. He could hear music as he walked up to the front doors. With one last deep breath he steadied himself. There was no one in the entryway, so he slipped in, hiding behind the door.

The priest instructed Luke and Megan to turn to the congregation. When they did, the smiles melted from their faces at the sight of Jared standing in the back. The entire congregation followed their gaze, watching as he teetered back and forth.

"It's my pleasure to present to you, Mr. and Mrs. Lucas and Megan Morrison." Father George started the applause. The congregation joined in as the recessional music started.

Luke and Megan strolled down the aisle, smiling to the people as they passed. The ushers opened the doors, pushing Jared to the side. He reached out to Megan.

"Thanks for being here." Megan tried to take his hand, but Jared was swallowed by the surging crowd that was trying to get to the newly married couple.

Fighting his way through, a firm hand on his shoulder stopped him.

"My God, Jared! You reek of booze! Get out of here." Mike shook him.

Pulling away from his father, he turned to face him. "Not until I say congratulations to my sister." Before Mike could grab him again, he disappeared into the crowd.

Megan and Luke stood in the receiving line, hugging people and engaging in small talk as they made their way to the church basement for the reception.

Luke looked at Jared, leaned in and whispered to Megan. Smiling, he approached Jared, placing a hand on his arm. "Jared, it means a lot that you came."

Jared grabbed his hand, threw it off. "Don't touch me." He stared into Luke's eyes as he walked past. He reached out once more for Megan. "Congratulations, Sis. I'm sorry. I didn't mean to ruin everything."

Megan cried, pulling him into an embrace. "I'm just so glad you decided to come."

"We both are." Luke placed his hand on Jared's shoulder.

Jared pulled away from Megan. "I said 'don't touch me'." He swung, planted a fist on Luke's jaw, throwing him backward.

The church erupted into chaos. Megan pushed Jared aside, running to Luke. She helped him up, glaring at Jared, a tear in her eye. "Why are you doing this?"

The ushers dragged Jared from the church, throwing him onto the sidewalk.

"Get the hell out of here! You're not welcome." Mike held Candace in the doorway, her face buried in his arm.

Jared rolled onto his side, looking at his parents as he tried to get up. "I..." There was nothing he wanted to say. He scrambled to stand then ran for the car.

"Jared." Candace ran toward him. "Where are you going?"

Mike grabbed her arm, ushering her back to the church. "Who cares? I don't care if I ever see him again."

Pushing away from him, Candace ran toward Jared, stopping at the top of the stairs that led to the street. "Why, Jared?"

Jared looked at his mother. "It's too late. It doesn't matter." He got into the car then pulled away.

An hour later Jared passed the sign telling him he was halfway to Gaylesburg. "Don't fall asleep." He turned up the radio and rolled down the window for fresh air. "I need to get the hell away from here."

Feeling drowsy, he stopped at a liquor store, across the street from a little motel. He purchased a large bottle of whiskey and a pack of cigarettes. The parking lot of the motel was nearly empty. Jared pulled up to the door leading to the front desk. "Do you have any rooms available?"

The old woman behind the desk was watching TV. She seemed annoyed to be interrupted. "Yeah."

"I'd like a room away from people. I need some peace and quiet." Jared stared at her.

She threw some keys, pointed at the end of the building, saying nothing then went back to her chair.

Jared jumped in his car, pulling it in front of the door to his room. The screen door was missing and the door was frayed at the bottom, looking as if someone had tried to kick it down. "Charming."

With the whiskey, cigarettes and his overnight bag, he dug the key from his pocket and fought to open the door. He despaired when it was just as difficult to get it closed again.

The room was small and dark, decorated with 60's décor. The walls were covered with dark paneling on the top half and orange carpet on the bottom. Jared choked. The smell of dirt mixed with years of cigarette smoke overwhelmed him.

He grabbed a glass from the counter then poured a drink. It burned going down. In the bathroom, he turned on the tap at the sink. The faucet spurted and sputtered, until amber colored water ran out, smelling of sulfur.

As he wiped his face, the reflection in the mirror stared back. His eyes were red and swollen with dark circles underneath.

The water cleared. Jared put the glass of whiskey under it, topping it off. Forcing down a large gulp, his body shook and his stomach turned. The sulfur didn't help the taste. He rushed to the cigarettes, hoping that would cover the horrible aftertaste in his mouth; he took a long drag. Sitting on the edge of the bed, Jared stripped down to his boxers and t-shirt, throwing his clothes at the wall. The TV buzzed when he turned it on. A fuzzy picture came on the screen. He flipped through the channels, but the reception seemed to worsen. One channel had come through clear enough to make out what was on. It was the local Public Television station broadcasting *Madame Butterfly*. Cigarette and ash tray in hand, he lay down, staring at the ceiling.

'I don't care if I ever see him again!' His father's words echoed in his mind, mixing with the ethereal sounds of the aria coming from the diva on the television.

The scene from the previous night and Luke's words also flooded his memory. "Well... I got my closure, Derek. Be careful what you wish for." He shook his head. "Derek, I've made a mess of everything. I would've slept with him if he hadn't stopped it. I didn't care what that would do to you. I'm no better than Luke."

Jared swallowed his drink then poured another. The bottle was soon half empty. "Nobody wants you around, Jared. Why would they? You're an asshole." He reached for his cigarette and took one last long drag on it. Smoke stubbed out, glass drained, he went to the bathroom. Every inch of his body trembled under the assault of voices of the past few days. Their rejections echoed.

The lights above the sink flickered. He glared at them, daring them to go out. Jared knelt down and turned on the rust colored tap in the bathtub. Once the water was heated as much as possible, he plugged the drain. With one hand against the mirror, his chest heaved with sobs, locked in a hate-filled stare at his reflection.

The steam rolled out of the bathroom, filling the entire room. Jared grabbed his overnight bag and dumped it on the counter. He placed the razor on the edge of the tub, locked the door then walked to the bathtub to test the water. His foot turned bright red. "That should do." After removing his clothes, he lay down in the tub. "I'm sorry. I'm so sorry." He picked up the razor, looked down at his wrist; his body tensed, knowing the pain to come. As the blade sliced into his skin he screamed. "God forgive me!"

I DON'T WANT TO FALL

The wedding dance was in full swing. Luke sat in a corner watching the festivities. He wiped his brow with his sleeve and tried to catch his breath. The room was sweltering and he hadn't stopped dancing since the music started. It kept him distracted from thoughts of Jared.

"Hey, Handsome." Megan sat on his lap. "Anything wrong?"

"No, just tired." Luke put a hand to his chest.

"Me too. It's been quite a day." She threw her arms around him, leaned in and whispered. "Maybe we should get out of here and go to the hotel?"

"I think that's a great idea."

Megan grabbed him by the hand. "Let's find Mom and Dad to let them know we're making a break for it."

Luke followed Megan, who said goodbye to people on their way through. He was still unable to catch his breath; his chest felt tight. *Come one, Luke. Calm down. You've been through a lot the last few weeks.*

Megan found her parents then embraced them. "We're going to get out of here. We're exhausted." The loud music made it difficult to be heard.

"All right, Sweetheart. We'll take care of things here." Candace smiled at Luke. "You take care of her."

"I'll do my best." Luke kissed Candace on the cheek.

Michael took Luke by the arm, leading him outside. "Don't worry about the car. I'm taking care of it."

"What do you mean?"

"I have a friend on the police force. They're looking for Jared. He won't get far. I may need you to come with me to the jail tomorrow to get this all straightened out."

"Jail? What?" Luke's pulse raced causing his chest to tighten more. "Jared will be all right, won't he? I'm not going to press charges or anything."

"We'll see." Michael patted his shoulder. "Don't worry about it. You two go and have a good night."

"I'm ready." Megan took Luke by the arm, smiling up at him.

Halfway down the sidewalk, Luke stopped. "What do we drive? I gave your mom her keys back?"

"Wait!" Michael came running toward them. "Here's the key to the Mustang. Be careful with her." He threw them to Luke.

Catching them, Luke waved. "Thank you." They found the Mustang parked at the end of the parking lot. It was decorated with streamers and had 'Just Married' written on the windows. He helped Megan into the car then jumped behind the wheel.

Megan grabbed his hand. "I haven't been in this car since you took me to your prom." She chuckled. "Hey, that was our first date."

Luke forced a smile at her, remembering the look on Jared's face as they lay next to each other. "That was quite a night."

Luke rushed ahead to hold the hotel door for Megan. The lady behind the counter smiled, nodding to their attire. "You must be Mr. and Mrs. Morrison."

Megan gave a broad smile, looking into Luke's eyes. "That's us."

Luke forced a smile back at her, scolding himself. *For Christ's sake, stop thinking about Jared! It's your wedding night.*

Luke unlocked the door then stopped Megan from passing through. "Wait! Isn't the groom supposed to carry his bride across the threshold?"

Megan laughed. "Seriously? All right, but I gotta warn you, this dress is heavy."

Pushing the door open, he scooped her into his arms. A spasm in his chest, followed by a sharp pain, caused him to hesitate. He bit his lip, hoping Megan was oblivious as he set her back down. "Here we are." He sat on the edge of the bed, leaned forward, massaging his chest as he slipped off his shoes.

Megan turned her back to him while she took off her earrings. "Can you help me out of this?"

Luke pushed himself up and started to undo the buttons on the back of her gown. Megan watched their reflections in the mirror, biting her lip. "Luke. I hate to bring this up, especially tonight... I'm worried about Jared."

Luke closed his eyes, steadied himself by putting his hands on her shoulders. He took a deep breath and wiped the sweat from his forehead. "I know. I am too. I shouldn't have let him leave."

Megan slipped out of her dress. "It's not your fault. I don't think there was anything we could've done. It was just so strange. It's not like him." She walked into the bathroom, leaving the door cracked open enough to still talk.

Luke sat at the edge of the bed, straining to concentrate on what Megan was saying. Another sharp pain shot through his chest. He clutched his hands to his heart, leaning forward, hoping to relieve some of the pressure. Unable to speak, he reached out to her. Another sharp pain sent him to the floor.

"I was a little surprised to hear that he was in love with you, but I guess it makes sense. You guys spent all of your time together. Of course he fell in love with you. I did." Megan returned to the room. "Luke? Oh, my God! What's wrong?" She knelt beside him, holding his head.

Everything was a jumble. Luke tried to speak, but the words wouldn't come out. The room was spinning; his focus went in and out.

Megan laid a pillow under his head then rushed to phone 9-1-1. "I need an ambulance! Hurry!"

Luke winced as a severe pain shot through his chest. His body started to go numb.

Megan ran to him and rubbed his arm. "Hold on, Sweetie! They're coming. Just hold on!"

It was becoming increasingly hard to breathe. Another pain shot through his chest. The sound of Megan's voice was growing distant. Gasping for air, he pulled at his shirt. He fought to stay awake, but there was another sharp pain. Everything went black. All was silent.

DeeJay Arens

SONG FOR THE LONELY

Jared slowly opened his eyes. The bright lights caused him to flinch. He could make out a woman leaning over him.

"Mr. Montgomery? I'm Doctor Evans." She spoke slowly, deliberately. "Do you know where you are?"

Jared looked around the room then nodded.

"Where are you?" Pulling his eyelid wider, she shined a light into his pupil.

The light gave Jared an instant headache. He tried to pull his head away, but had no strength. His throat was sore and the inside of his mouth felt like leather. He cleared his throat. "The hospital." The voice didn't sound like his.

"That's right." The doctor patted his arm. "Do you know why you're here?"

Tears welled up in his eyes. He looked at the bandages on his arms. "Yes."

The doctor wrote on the chart. "You're in the emergency room. You're in critical condition. We thought we lost you." She hooked the call button onto his gown. "If you need anything, just press this button and a nurse will be here. We'll be moving you to the ICU in a few minutes. Anything I can get you?" Jared shook his head. He looked into her face at a

THE VIEW FROM A RUSTY TRAIN CAR

mixture of sympathy and sadness. "I'll check on you in a little bit. We have a few things to talk about, but I'll let you rest. Okay?" She gave him a smile before leaving the room.

EMT's passed his room, pushing someone on a gurney. Their voices carried down the hallway. "We're losing him!"

Jared struggled to get the glass of ice water to his lips. Weak from the loss of blood, his hand shook, spilling the water all over himself.

Candace stepped into his room, wiping tears from her eyes. Michael stood, looking over her shoulder.

Jared leaned forward to put the glass back on the table. Missing it, the cup fell to the floor. "Fuck!" He lay back, breathing heavily. His arm dropped and hung off the side of the bed. Startled by a sound at the door, he turned to see his mother. Tears streamed down his face. "Mom, I'm so sorry!" He reached out to her, but the IV caught on the blanket. He screamed in pain, carefully putting his arm down

Candace ran to him, sat on the bed, touched his face and kissed his forehead. Michael leaned against the wall, his face expressionless.

"I'm so sorry! I don't know why I did it." Jared grasped her hand.

"Shh." Candace stroked his hair. "You're all right now. Everything's going to be fine." She looked to Michael.

Michael moved closer to the bed, stopping a few feet away. His jaw clenched. "The doctor said she found a place for you at a treatment center once you're well enough to leave the hospital. We've already signed the papers."

Jared struggled to sit up. He grabbed Candace's arm. "No! You can't! I don't need treatment. Mom, please?"

"Jared! Just stop!" Candace squeezed his hand. "My God! Look at yourself!"

Jared lay back, shaking his head. "I know. It was stupid!"

"You cut your wrists, Jared! If that wouldn't have killed you, the amount of alcohol in your blood would have!" Candace looked down at the bandages. "They said you died twice in the ambulance." She jumped up, staring him in the eyes. "You need help. If the cops hadn't found the car and found you, you would've..."

Jared looked back and forth between his parents. "Wait. How did the cops find me? How did they...? The car." He put his hands to his face. "Oh, my God. Luke called them, didn't he? That son-of-a-bitch called the police."

"Luke didn't call the police." Mike finally looked at his son. "I did."

Jared chuckled. "Too bad you didn't know about the razor. You got them there too early."

"Don't you dare..." Mike shook with anger, glaring at him "You stole a car and you were drunk off your ass. What were we supposed to do, huh? Let you drive off and kill someone?"

"Sweetheart?" Candace took a step toward him, touching his arm. "We're going to check in with Megan. We'll see you a little later."

Jared's heart raced. "No! God! Don't tell them I'm in here. Don't tell them anything."

Candace walked towards the bed again. "But, Jared..."

"Please? I'll do anything you want, just promise you won't tell them anything! Don't ever say another word about me to them again." Jared lay back then turned his face toward the window.

"All right, if that's what you want, we won't tell them. We'll see you a little later. We love you." Candace turned to give a half-hearted smile as they left the room.

The blinking lights of the monitors caught Jared's gaze. The rhythm was hypnotic. It made him feel drowsy, even with so much to think about. "I know one thing. I'm not going to some stupid treatment center. I've got to get back to Seattle. I'll figure things out."

THE VIEW FROM A RUSTY TRAIN CAR

AN IDEAL HUSBAND

Luke stared off into the distance, glad to be conscious again. He'd thought it was all over. There was still a slight nagging pain and he felt weak, but it was nothing like what he'd experienced earlier in the evening.

After a knock at the door, the doctor entered. "It's good to see you awake. How are you feeling?" He pulled a chair to the bed.

"Tired, but other than that, not too bad." Luke struggled to sit up.

"No. You just stay there. You need to rest." The doctor pushed him back down. He looked at his chart. "Well, we've run all the tests I could think of. There are a few abnormalities on your cardiac tests, but nothing that could cause this episode."

"So, what's wrong with me?"

"Right now, I have no idea." The doctor recorded the readings from the machines onto his chart. "I'm consulting with some specialists. You're going to need to see one of them. Something is obviously wrong. We just have to figure out what."

Luke stared at him, his heart rate starting to increase. "It's got to be just stress, right? I mean, I've had a couple stressful days. I got married this afternoon. I probably just need to get some rest."

"Mr. Morrison, you had no heartbeat when you got here. It was touch and go for a while. Stress can do some horrible things, but it's not going to cause your heart to stop... at least, not by itself." The doctor checked the IV's. "I'm afraid it's quite a bit more serious than that."

"Excuse me." Megan peeked around the door. She offered her hand to the doctor. "Hi. I'm Luke's wife, Megan." Taking the chair next to the bed, she leaned forward, kissing Luke on the forehead. "It's good to see you."

Luke squeezed her hand. "You too."

Megan looked up at the doctor. "I was listening at the door. So what do we do? What happens now?"

"We make sure he's stabilized and that he's going to stay that way. Then we decide which specialist is the one for him. That's about all I can tell you." The doctor put his hand on Megan's shoulder. "We'll do everything we can for him. I promise." Looking at Luke, he raised an eyebrow. "For now he needs rest. No extraneous movement, definitely no running or lifting. You have to be very careful until we know what's going on."

"Don't worry. I won't let him move unless it's absolutely necessary." Megan looked at Luke.

"Until I know more, I want him to stay here for observation, at least until one of the specialists gets back to me and we figure out a course of action." He patted Luke on the arm. "I'll be back to check in with you in a couple hours. We gave you something to put you out for the night. By the look of your eyes, I think it might be taking effect. You need rest. We'll re-run the tests in the morning just to see if we missed something. Okay?"

Fighting against the medication, Luke shook his head. *How do I know I'll wake up?*

"You should go get some rest as well. He'll be out soon. There's no use in sticking around here. We'll take care of him." The doctor smiled at Megan. As he opened the door to leave, he ran into Candace and Mike.

"They let us come in to say goodnight. Is he asleep?" Candace put her arms around Megan.

Luke took a deep breath and forced a smile. "No. Come in." Trying to sit up, he reached for her arm. "Did you find Jared? Is he all right?"

Mike stood over him. "Everything's being taken care of. Nothing you need to worry about. You just worry about getting better."

"Where is he? Is he coming back? I need to talk to him." Luke kicked off the bedding, stood on wobbly legs then fell backwards into the nightstand.

Mike grabbed him. "You're in no shape to do anything." He helped him back into the bed. "Jared's fine. He needs to take care of some things. He headed out of town."

"Does he know I'm here?"

Mike shook his head. "No. We didn't think we should tell him yet. He's still pretty upset with me about calling the cops on him, but he'll be fine. We thought it best to let him deal with his things first. We didn't know what to tell him, anyway."

With Mike's support, Luke laid back. "Thank you. I don't want you to tell him. Okay? He needs to do his thing. He'll just get upset and worry. I'll be fine." He turned his head away, closing his eyes. A tear rolled down his cheek. *I wish he was here with me.*

Mike reached for Candace and Megan. "Now, we all need to get some sleep."

"No!" Megan pushed him away, grabbing on to Luke's hand. "I'm staying right here. I'm not leaving him."

"He's right. You go with them. It's been a long day." Luke squeezed her hand. "I'll be fine. I'll be asleep any minute. You need to get some rest. I'll see you in the morning."

"But..."

"Go!" Luke looked to Candace. "Can she stay with you tonight?"

"Of course." Candace took Megan's hand. "You can just take a nap. We'll be back in a few hours once he has a chance to rest."

Megan kissed Luke then looked in his eyes as she caressed his face. "Good night, Mr. Morrison!"

"Good night, Mrs. Morrison." Luke chuckled, forcing a smile. It was getting harder to keep his eyes open.

She gave him one last kiss on the forehead then led her parents out of the room.

Luke lay in the dark room, listening to the muted sounds coming from the hall. "What the hell is wrong with me?" He sighed. *Jared, I think I made the wrong choice. Now I'm paying for it, aren't I? I wish I could do it all over again, but it's too late. You'll never speak to me again. I don't blame you.* He tried chasing away thoughts of Jared. "I have to accept it. I promised Megan." As he imagined the life ahead of him, the tightness in his chest worsened. Rubbing it to relieve some of the pressure, he glanced down at his wedding ring. He turned onto his side, tears in his eyes. "What in the hell have I done?"

THE VIEW FROM A RUSTY TRAIN CAR

THE PLACE THAT CRADLED ME IS BURNING

July 1997

The days went by slowly for Jared. It had taken him longer to stabilize and recover than had been expected. It was also a lonely time: he refused any visitors including his parents. Looking at the same four walls was taking a toll.

The nurses had packed his luggage. He went through it, making sure nothing was missing. Another bag lay at the door. One of the hospital staff had delivered it, telling him his mother had dropped it off. It was a small comfort knowing he had more of his belongings; he didn't feel as much like a hobo. The feeling of real clothes would be a luxury after all those days of wearing hospital gowns.

As the minutes ticked by, Jared got more uncomfortable, more nervous about going to treatment. "I don't need to go! I'm fine. I had every reason to be upset." He looked up at the clock. Only three minutes had passed since he last checked.

There was a knock at his door. A man entered, wearing a green shirt with 'DeBain Recovery Center' printed on it and the name 'Brian' embroidered underneath. "Jared?" Brian held a file in his hand, smiling as he walked into the room.

Feeling a sneer form on his face, Jared rubbed his mouth. "Yeah. That's me."

"I'll help you with these." Counting the luggage, Brian wrote in the file. He picked one up.

Jared lunged at the bag, pulling it out of his hand. "Listen. I don't need this.... treatment, I mean. I'm only going for a little while. I don't want to go at all, but I don't have anywhere else to go right now." He gathered his luggage. "I'm not quite ready to go back to school and face the music there, and I'm certainly not going to my parent's house, so I don't know if I tell you or what, but I'm staying a week then I'll be on my way. I just need to clear my head and get everything together before I head back to Seattle."

Fumbling through the file, Brian pulled out a form. "Actually, Sir, your papers say that you're registered for the 28 day program."

Jared chuckled. "Yeah, I'm sure my dad would love that. No, thank you."

Brian handed him the papers. "You don't have a choice in the matter."

Jared threw his luggage down. "What in the hell do you mean I 'don't have a choice'? I'm over eighteen. I can do whatever I want. No one can make me stay there!"

Brian put the file down on the bed, sliding it toward him. "Your father went to court and had it ordered."

Jared picked up the papers, read through them, his heart pounding. "How in the...?" Shuffling through the file, he looked for answers. "He can't do this!"

Taking the file back, Brian pulled out one of the papers and handed it to him. "He asked for temporary power of attorney over you since you had attempted... you know... to take your own life. The judge granted him sixty days or until completion of a full stay in a treatment facility."

THE VIEW FROM A RUSTY TRAIN CAR

"That son-of-a-bitch!" Jared threw the papers on the bed, then grabbed his things. "I'm not going! I'm not. This is a bunch of shit. I'm going home." He rushed for the door.

"Jared, don't do this. Don't make this harder on yourself."

Jared opened the door then stopped. A policeman was standing outside it. He turned back to Brian. "Are you kidding me?"

"This way, Mr. Montgomery." Giving Brian a knowing look, the officer took Jared by the arm.

Jared jerked his arm away. "You don't have to do that. I'll go."

"Either you let me take your arm or I put you in these." A pair of handcuffs swung from the officer's finger.

The thought of something wrapped around his wrists after all those weeks wearing bandages wasn't appealing. He offered his arm. "Let's just go."

Brian gathered Jared's things and walked into the hall to lead them.

Turning to follow, Jared saw his mother standing at the end of the hall. "What is she doing here? Get her out of here!" He turned away.

"No, Jared, please! I had to see you." Candace's voice broke, reaching out to him.

Jared stepped back into his room. "I'm not going any farther until she's out of here. You'll have to drag me out."

The officer motioned to a woman standing with Candace. She grabbed her arm, pushing her down the hallway. "Come on, Ma'am. It's best to leave. He's got to go. Come on."

Candace fought back, keeping her eyes on Jared. "No. I have to see him. Please?" Her face was streaked with tears. The woman motioned and another police officer took Candace's other arm. They pulled her toward a room behind them.

Hearing the commotion at the other end of the hall, Jared peeked around the corner.

"No. Stop. Please!" Candace struggled to pull away from them, her fingers wrapped around the frame of the door. Before she disappeared into the room, she looked back to Jared. "I love you." The door slammed shut.

The officer took Jared's arm again. "Let's go."

As they walked past the door where his mother had disappeared, Jared could hear her sobbing and moaning. He closed his eyes, fighting the urge to go to her. He was led to a van. Brian was loading his luggage in the back.

The officer took the passenger seat and made a call. "This is Tanden. Mr. Montgomery is in the van. We're getting ready to leave." He looked over his shoulder at Jared. "Are you all right? Do you need anything?"

"No. I just want this over."

He watched out the window as the van pulled away from the hospital and toward Sheldon. It seemed like only days ago he'd taken the taxi from Sheldon to home. The once familiar things somehow seemed different. He no longer felt at home when he looked at the buildings he'd seen a thousand times before. *This isn't home anymore.* He longed to get on an airplane and return to Derek and Seattle. *I swear to God, I will never come back here again. There's nothing left.* Remembering the happier memories wouldn't erase the hurt of the past month. Looking at his reflection in the rearview mirror, Jared thought about what he was leaving behind. *I'm done. You won, bastards. But guess what? The guy who came here isn't the same guy who's leaving. I don't need any of you. I'm going to be fine.* There was no sadness at the realization.

#

Jared filled out the paperwork. Passing over the last of the forms, he put his hand to his head. He had a horrible headache. "Can I go to my room now?"

The guy at the desk nodded, giving him his room assignment.

The rooms were dormitory style, but he'd lucked out, ending up in a room by himself.

Luggage unpacked, he set about organizing his things. If he had to be there for four weeks he was going to make it feel as comfortable as possible.

Once everything was in place, he sat on the bed, looking around the room. He picked up a folder laying on the night stand with his name on it. *The Path to Sobriety*. He laughed out loud. "Sounds exciting." Tossing it aside, he laid down, imagining what was ahead for him.

DESPERATE LIVING

August 1997

As Luke walked into their apartment building, he took a deep breath as he stared up the flight of stairs ahead of him. He was returning from his fifth emergency trip to the hospital in four weeks. He was growing weary of being sick and not getting answers. The call came the day before, telling him the second specialist was sending him on to another. The only bright side was that he was given a medication to try. *Please, God, let it work.*

Watching Megan pull the car into their parking space, he waited in the entryway; he'd become so weak that Megan had to help him up the stairs.

She walked in and took his arm. "Ready?"

"I'm sorry you have to do this."

"Don't be silly."

Unsettled by the absence of emotion in her voice, he stopped then sat on the stair. "Meg, wait..." He reached up, pulling her down to join him. "You shouldn't have to keep doing this. This is beyond what you signed on for."

Megan stood, trying to get him to stand. "Whatever. Don't be an idiot."

Luke looked into her eyes. "Listen to me. I think you need a break. You need to go somewhere, get away from this... take some time for yourself."

"Are you kidding me? I can't leave you alone. Knock it off. I'm fine." Megan leaned against the banister, staring out into the parking lot.

"Meg, I'm sick, not dead. I can see what this is doing to you. You're exhausted. You need a break." He reached up, touching her arm.

Megan took his hand, smiling at him. "That's sweet, but even if I wanted to, I don't know where I'd go... or what I'd do."

Luke pulled himself up with the banister; he wanted her to see he could still manage to do something. "I happen to know that Shannon is in town. All the girls are heading out for a girl's weekend."

Megan's headed whipped around. "How did you know about that?"

"I overheard you on the phone the other night."

Staring off, she seemed to consider it then shook her head. "No, I'm not leaving you alone. Come on. Let's get upstairs. I have to start supper."

Luke wrapped his arms around her. "I won't be alone. I called Susie yesterday. She was excited about coming to stay with me. She's wanted to do something to help out for a while. Plus we haven't had hangout time in ages. It'll be good for her... for all of us." He raised an eyebrow.

A smile stretched across Megan's face. "Are you sure? I would like to see the girls again."

"I'm positive. In fact, I'm not suggesting it; I am telling you that you have to. You don't have a choice. I already told Susie."

Megan held him, whispering into his ear. "Thank you, Sweetie." She pulled away, taking his arm again. "Let's go upstairs. I have to call Shannon and let her know."

Luke kissed her then walked to the door. "Go on ahead. I'm going to sit out in the sun for a while. It's a beautiful day." He turned back. Megan was staring at him. Her face was filled with questions and doubts. "Go. If I need help I'll yell up to you. I'll be fine. Go!"

Megan smiled at him before running up the stairs.

Sitting on the grass in the sun, Luke sighed, relieved his plan to get Megan out of the house worked. *Now... to finish the surprise!* His health issues had forced him to come to terms with his own mortality. If it happened that they couldn't find out what was wrong with him, he wanted to know Megan would be okay.

He thought back to his conversation with Mike, he'd told him they had been turned down for a mortgage. Mike called the bank and told Luke he would co-sign on it. "She deserves it."

A horn honked as a car drove by. The driver waved at him as the car came to a stop in the parking lot. Waving back, Luke got to his feet.

"Hey, big bro!" Susie ran to him, her arms stretched out. "God, it's good to see you."

"I am so happy to see you! I've missed you."

Susie watched as he sat back on the grass. Sitting next to him, she laid her head on his shoulder. "How are you? Really? ...And don't lie to me. I know you."

Luke forced a smile. She was right; few people knew him like Susie. "I'm scared, frankly. I'm tired of hearing that no one knows what's wrong and I'm tired of feeling like shit."

Squeezing his hand, Susie's lip quivered.

"But... I started a medication that should help a lot. They feel pretty optimistic about it."

Susie looked at the ground. "You've got to get better. You've got a wife to take care of."

"I know."

"Speaking of that, I hope you know that I wouldn't have missed your wedding if I could've helped it." Susie shook her head. "I had a screaming match with Mom. She refused to let me out of the house. She said if she wasn't invited, I wasn't invited."

"She hasn't changed at all."

"You have no idea. She's gotten worse! She's a complete bitch! I don't know how I'm going to take one more year in that house."

Luke put his arm around her. "You'll make it because you always have a place to come when things get too rough."

She smiled and held him. "I could always deal with it when you were in the house. Of course, that was because most of it was directed at you... or Jared."

Luke took a deep breath. "It was a rough time."

Susie jabbed him with her elbow, grinning. "I heard he made quite an entrance at the wedding. Grace's mom was there and told us about it."

"That he did. It was pretty... shocking."

Susie looked him in the eye. "Seriously? You were shocked? The man you love crashed your wedding in a drunken stupor. What exactly did you expect him to do?"

Luke gave a quick look up at the window to the apartment. "Could you keep your voice down?"

Susie followed his gaze, looking up at the open window. "Sorry. It was supposed to be a joke."

"You're awful, you know that?"

Grabbing on to his arm, Susie laughed. "I know. I've learned from the best." She looked into his eyes. "How's he doing? I mean, about all of this? It can't be easy for him."

Luke stared off into the distance. "I don't know. I haven't seen him since. I'm really scared for him. He must feel like he has no one."

"What? You mean to tell me you haven't checked on him? What's wrong with you?" She pushed him away. "What am I saying? This from a guy who expected him to be the best man at his wedding? I have to tell you, that was pretty damned low."

Staring at his sister, he shook his head. "When did you grow up on me?"

"Next, I suppose, you're going to try to tell me you were never in love with him."

"I just don't think he wants to hear from me. He was pretty upset. I don't want to bother him." Luke walked down the sidewalk.

Susie caught him and linked arms. "Don't even try to tell me you haven't thought about him."

Luke put his head down, closing his eyes. "Of course I've thought about him." Looking back at her, he sighed. "I think about him every day. He must absolutely hate me. He should." He leaned against the fence that went around the parking lot.

"You'll never know unless you talk to him. You're not going to be satisfied until you do." Susie winked at him.

"I tried calling his Seattle number. Some guy named Chris said he hadn't seen him since he'd left for home. I don't know what to do. I don't even know where he is. He could have this guy lying for him for all I know. Who the hell is this Chris, anyway?"

Giggling, Susie hit his arm. "Someone sounds jealous."

"What? I'm not jealous. I just don't know who this guy is."

"Stop worrying. It's his roommate."

"How do you know?"

"Don't be mad because I didn't tell you, but... I wrote him. I was worried about him and wanted to know how he was. I was surprised to actually get a letter back. He told me all about Seattle and he mentioned Chris."

"Wait. When did you do that? What did he say?" Luke's pulse raced.

"Don't get excited. It was months ago. We exchanged a couple letters then I stopped hearing from him. He never said much." Susie laughed. "The last time I heard from him, he emailed me a photo after I asked him to my prom."

"You did what?"

"Well, you took his sister. I just thought that's how things were done around here." Susie smiled at him. "Luke, it was a joke. He thought it was funny. He emailed me the photo from his prom with my face put on his date's body." The smile disappeared from her face. "That was the last I heard from him. I emailed a couple times and heard nothing back. I tried again a month or so later and my email bounced back, saying his email address no longer existed." Looking up at him, she dug in her coat pocket. "So, knowing you and knowing what a loser you can be, I took the liberty of looking up his mailing address on-line." She handed Luke a slip of paper.

Luke looked at the paper in Susie's hand, contemplating what taking it would mean. *If I do get a hold of him, I'll know what he really thinks.* He bit his lip. *I have to know.* Taking the paper, he unfolded it and stared at the information.

Susie smiled, pulling him away from the fence. "I know what we're doing this weekend." Raising an eyebrow, she smiled. "Face it; you need my help with this."

"You're probably right." Luke tucked it in his pocket, walking Susie to her car. "See you tomorrow."

"I can't wait." Susie leaned out the window and kissed him. "I love you!"

"I love you too." Watching her drive away, he laughed. He'd thought that any memory of his relationship with Jared had disappeared when he left. Not only did Susie know their history, she seemed to understand it. *It feels good being able to talk about him... for real.*

He walked up the stairs to the apartment, struggling for breath. He stopped on the second floor to rest. Luke took the paper out of his pocket, stared at the information, his thumb caressed Jared's name. *I miss you so much.* Taking a deep breath, he put the slip back into his pocket, grabbed the banister and pulled himself up the stairs.

WOULD IT MAKE YOU MORE COMFORTABLE

Two weeks into his stay at DeBain, Jared made the decision to get back to his writing. This time it wasn't for homework or school projects. It would be for him. His mind was clearer when he wrote, allowing him to think things through. After all, it was his chosen profession, not to mention he had quite a bit of time on his hands in the evenings to think and work.

After attempting a few stories to get back into the rhythm, it occurred to him to write about his experience in a treatment facility. He was getting firsthand knowledge of what it felt like and of the process. Writing about these things was part of the program, so he was able to kill two birds with one stone. It made the time go quickly. His nights were spent working into the wee hours of the morning.

#

Jared shut off the alarm. Attempting to summon the energy to get up, he lay in bed, staring at the ceiling. It was another restless night. He was so focused on his story that he spent most of the night tossing and turning, writing and editing in his sleep. For a brief moment his head was clear as he enjoyed the peace that came before the others were up.

Jared's eyes shot open. He checked the clock. "Late again! Why today?" He ran to the bathroom. Brushing his teeth, he looked into the mirror. "Time to get the hell out of here!"

There was a knock on the door. A small and sturdy man entered. "Today's the big day! How are you feeling?"

Jared appreciated Jerry's calm and gentle attitude. He was the kind of person he needed around when dealing with all the thoughts and questions swirling in his head.

"I am definitely ready to go." Jared rushed to his desk, grabbing his books.

Leaning against the door frame, Jerry watched as he hurried around the room. "Good. You have one more thing to do before we can let you go."

"Can you give me a couple minutes? I woke up late. I'll hurry and get dressed."

"Sure. I'll wait for you in the hall."

Pulling out clothes from the dresser, Jared thought about what Jerry had said. *What's left to do?* He'd known others who'd left there and didn't hear about anything. A sinking feeling hit him. *Please don't let it be one more group therapy session.*

Finally ready, he met Jerry in the hall.

"Follow me." Jerry led him down the hallway.

It had become a routine walk every day for the last month. Remembering how helpless and scared he felt for the first couple of weeks, Jared was relieved it was one of the last times down that corridor. They passed the group therapy room. *Thank, God! We're going to his office.* One last therapy session with Jerry wasn't a bad thing. He enjoyed talking to him.

Turning the corner, Jared saw his parents sitting at the desk. He stopped. "No! I told you. I don't want to see them."

Jerry grabbed his shoulders. "We talked about this, Jared. You have to let go of the anger. You have to forgive."

"I know! I've forgiven them, but I'm not through being angry! That takes time and work. You should know that. It's what you've been preaching for the last few weeks."

"If you want any chance at staying sober and getting through life, you need people with you. You need people to support you."

"That's fine. I get that. But it's not going to be them." Jared turned away from him.

Jerry pointed to the door of his office. "Your mother has called every single day to see how you were doing. They love you, Jared. They just want to see you and talk to you. Often times the people on the outside do just as much thinking and making changes as the person in here. I think you should give them a chance. That's all I'm asking."

Jared looked toward the room and saw his mother's face smiling at him. "Fine. Let's just get this over with." Taking a deep breath, he walked into the room.

Candace ran to him, taking him in her arms.

"Hi, Mom."

Mike rose from his chair. Walking to him, he offered his hand. "You look good, Son."

"Please sit down." Jerry took his seat at the desk and looked at Jared. "Part of what I do while you're here is talk to your loved ones. It's routine that we offer support and guidance to the patient's family. I've explained all that you went through and told them how well you've done here." He looked at Candace and Mike. "You should be very proud of him."

Candace grabbed Jared's hand. "We are."

Leaning back in his chair, Jerry turned to Jared. "I also shared with them what they can do to be supportive of you through your recovery and that it's a life long journey." He looked to Candace and Mike. "Do you have any questions about that?"

Candace grabbed her purse, pulling out some books and pamphlets, laying them on the desk. "I don't think so. I've read everything I could to find about what to do. We're ready for him to come home." Smiling, she patted Jared's hand.

Jared pulled away. "Wait. Is that why you're here? To get me to come home? I'm not going home with you."

"What do you mean? Where do you think you're going?" Mike's tone betrayed his anger.

Jared closed his eyes, trying to control his reaction. He wanted to scream. "I'm going back to Seattle. I've got school to finish. I need to move on. I can't do that at home."

Mike stood, throwing a pamphlet on the desk. "You're coming home with us and we're going to help you through this. The alcohol, those feelings you have toward... other..."

Jared felt the blood rush to his face as his fists clenched. He stared Mike in the eyes. "Now I get it – the real reason you sent me here. You thought they would change that part of me? Well, I hate to be the one to tell you... they didn't. If you want to support me and love me then you'll have to accept that I'm gay. I make no apologies for that. It's part of who I am."

Mike slammed his hands on the desk. "So, you're not even going to try to fix this?"

Jared stood in front of his father. "Dad, there's nothing to fix!"

Jerry moved between them. He pointed a finger in Mike's face. "Mr. Montgomery, that's not why he came here. He needs your support and love without strings attached. He doesn't need you trying to fix him."

Mike sneered, snatched up his jacket then went to the door. "That's it. I'm going home. I've had enough. Candace?" He left the room.

Candace went to Jared, taking his hands. "He tried, Jared. He just can't understand."

"He's never tried to understand me. That's not what he does. He wants me to be what he thinks I should be. He always has." He pulled his hand away. "It doesn't matter. He has a new son now. He doesn't need me. Luke's more the son he always wanted anyway."

"Jared, stop! That's not true!" Candace held his arm.

"I'm sorry. That was unfair. I'm still working on things. It's my natural reaction." Chuckling, Jared went to the door. Taking another deep breath, he turned back to Candace. "I'm done, Mom. I'm not doing this anymore. I do love you, but I'm not going to change for you or Dad or anyone else. If this is the way it's going to be, don't expect me to be a part of it." Slamming his hand against the door, he ran to her, embracing her. "Take care of yourself." He kissed her cheek then ran from the office. Ignoring Candace's pleas and sobbing, he walked back to his room to pack, angry at his father and saddened that he was right. "That answers that. This isn't where you belong anymore."

THE VIEW FROM A RUSTY TRAIN CAR

A MARRIAGE MINUS HEART

Megan wrote the information on a notepad then turned off the answering machine. Sitting at the kitchen table, she admired their new home as she rubbed her tired feet. Picking up extra hours because Luke was unable to work full-time was taking its toll.

The clock chimed six o'clock. "I know, I know... Supper." Megan thought about getting up, but she didn't have the energy. "There has to be something in the freezer to warm up."

On her way to the fridge, she heard the garage door slam. Luke was on his way to the mailbox. She watched as he made sure no one was looking and placed a letter inside, timing it so that the postman would pick it up within a few minutes.

When Megan had asked about it, Luke would tell her it was business stuff or sweepstakes, but she could tell there was more to it. "Just one more thing he won't talk to me about."

He looked down the street. Megan thought about what had been happening recently. Luke had become more withdrawn from her than usual. Leaning, hands against the counter, she shook her head. "He's not a husband. He's a roommate."

The door slammed. Megan jumped as Luke came in the side door. "Oh! Hey." She walked to the fridge and dug through the freezer.

"Hi. I didn't see you come home." Luke kissed her on the cheek. "How was your day?"

"Same as always. Run, run, run." Forcing a chuckle, Megan took out some containers and put them on the counter. She examined each one trying to figure out what the contents were. "How was your day?"

Luke sat at the table, going through the mail that had just been delivered. "Oh, fine. I took your advice and started on some projects. You were right. It does help to have something to take my mind off things."

Facing away from him, Megan wiped the sneer she felt forming. She picked up a container, the only container that was marked, and put it in the microwave. "That's great. What kind of project?"

"Just a wood project."

There was a noticeable change in his demeanor. He stared at a letter, his back turned as if trying to hide it. "Anything good in the mail today?" She walked to the table.

Luke jumped. "The usual." Sliding the letter into his shirt, he added the rest of the mail to the already tall stack on the table.

Sitting next to him, Megan touched his arm. She studied his face; words escaped her.

Looking away, his eyes shifting nervously, Luke jumped up. "I'm going back out to the garage to work a little more. Call me for supper?" He ran to the door.

"Wait!" Megan grabbed the note from beside the phone. "Doctor San's receptionist called. You must've been in the garage. She wants you to call and schedule an appointment. They want to do a Transesophageal echocardiogram. At least I think that's what she said." She passed him the paper. "Here's the number."

Luke stared at it. "Oh, goodie... more poking and prodding. I can't wait." Putting it in his pocket, he disappeared out the side door.

THE VIEW FROM A RUSTY TRAIN CAR

Megan walked to the door, watching him disappear into the garage. She felt horrible for him going through all the testing and never getting answers. It had to be wearing him down. Taking the bowl from the microwave, she stirred the chili, thinking about the letter Luke slipped into his pocket. "Wait! He knows something. The doctors have told him what's wrong. He just doesn't want to tell me."

Throwing the bowl back into the microwave, Megan leaned against the counter, taking measured breaths. "What is he not telling me? It has to be something horrible!" She ran down the hall and into Luke's office. "I'm sorry. I hate myself for this, but I have to know." Glancing out the window, she saw Luke working in the garage. Before she could consider what she was doing, she dug through the stack of letters sitting on the desk. There were bills and work related information. Dropping into his chair, her hands grasped the arms as she scanned the office. The piles were neatly stacked, everything was organized. "If Luke was keeping something from me he wouldn't just leave it on the desk." She sat back in the chair, a finger tapping on her chin, hoping something would come to her. A noise came from the kitchen and Megan jumped. Looking at the garage again, she saw Luke still engrossed in whatever it was he was doing.

She pulled open each drawer, scanned the contents, keeping an eye out for anything from one of the doctor's offices or the hospital. "Nothing."

With a silent prayer, she pulled open the last drawer. There was a stack of envelopes, laying face down toward the back. She picked one up and turned it over.

Megan inhaled sharply, reading the name of the recipient: Jared Montgomery. *Return to Sender* was scrawled across the envelope. All the others were the same.

Now it makes sense. Luke's demeanor, his being withdrawn... he's worried about Jared. No one had heard from him in a long time.

Standing at the window, Megan watched as Luke smiled as he worked. "You are so sweet. I'm sorry I didn't trust you."

She returned to the desk, gathering the stack of envelopes. Ready to shut the drawer, she noticed there was a letter lying on the bottom. There was no envelope with this one. At first glance she could tell it was one Luke hadn't finished yet. Holding it close, she thought of Jared. "We'd both feel better if you would just answer one. Just let us know how you're doing."

The microwave signaled that the food was ready. Megan opened the drawer, ready to put the letter way. A couple words caught her attention. "No." She shook her head, reaching for the drawer. Holding the letter in front of her, she sat down and started to read. Her pulse raced.

My dearest Jed,
This seems ridiculous to say, but I am so sorry for everything. I know now I've made the wrong decision. If I could take it all back I would, but I can't. It's too late. I hope it gives you some comfort to know I love you and I always will. I hope you are well and life is giving you everything you deserve. Please write me or call. I really need to hear from you.
All my love,
Luke

Megan placed the letter and envelopes back in the drawer. Closing it, she put her head in her hands then leaned against the desk, crying. "It can't be..."

The door closed in the kitchen; Megan jumped. She wiped her tears, trying to collect herself.

"Meg? I'm going to eat in the garage." Luke disappeared out the door with a plate.

She wandered into the kitchen, her eyes taking in their home – the furniture, the pictures on the walls. "Everything's a lie."

She ripped the wedding photo from its nail, stared at is as she dropped onto the couch. "How could you do this to me?

THE VIEW FROM A RUSTY TRAIN CAR

You bastard! The hours of work to pay for this lie, the hours of sitting beside you in the hospital, the cost..." From the kitchen door she could see him. She wanted to run out, scream, pummel him with her fists. "I've got to get out of here." She grabbed the keys, dashed to the car. As she pulled out of the driveway, Luke popped his head out of the garage, smiled, waving at her. She sneered, her foot hitting the gas pedal.

Megan saw a light on in the living room; her parents were home. She started to pull into their driveway. "No, I can't. I can't dump this on them. I don't know for sure. I have to talk to him first."

As the car crept through quiet downtown streets, her fist slammed against the steering wheel. "I gave you so many chances to tell me! You son-of-a-bitch!"

The parking lot of Heidi's Place was full of cars. Megan parked and went inside. She'd never seen so many people in the restaurant. It took some time to push through to the bar.

She tugged on the sleeve of the bartender. "Greg?"

"I thought you got out of here hours ago."

"I did." It was so loud, she had to yell. "I just need a drink. A gin and tonic."

"Coming right up." Greg made the drink and set it in front of her. "Four fifty."

"I'll take care of that." Reaching over her shoulder, someone put money on the bar.

Megan turned, looking up at her benefactor. "Matt?"

"Long time no see." Winking, he gave her a big smile.

She scooped the money off the bar then tried to give it back to him. "You don't need to do that."

Matt dropped it back on the bar. "I insist. Can't your old boyfriend buy you a drink?" He motioned for her to follow him.

Hesitating a moment, she followed him to a small table near the back. It was far less noisy.

"When did you get back to town?"

"A couple weeks ago. My dad talked me into coming back to help him on the farm. My career was going nowhere so I thought what the hell. It was better than nothing." He looked her up and down. "God, you look good."

Megan put her arms in front of her, trying to feel less exposed. "Thanks."

He reached across the table for Megan's hand. "I've missed you."

"I'm married, Matt!" She showed him the ring on her finger then pulled her hand away.

Matt chuckled, sitting back in the chair. "I know. I heard. You can't be happily married. You're sitting in a bar alone. Where's your husband?"

Megan didn't appreciate the Cheshire cat like smile on his face. "He's at home working. I just wanted to get out of the house for a while." She looked away from him.

"So all's well with you two, huh?"

The sarcastic tone of his voice made her cringe. "Listen, Matt. If you've got something to say to me then say it. I'm not going to sit here and..."

"I know your husband. I know a lot about him. My cousin, Phillip, told me some interesting things." Matt leaned across the table, raising an eyebrow.

Megan jumped off her chair. "I don't care what you've heard. I wouldn't trust anything you hear in this town. It's all a bunch of rumors. Luke is a good man. I'm sure you don't know this, but he's also very sick, so I will thank you not to be such an ass."

Matt smirked, looking up from his drink. "Sick, huh? Did he catch something from your brother?"

Jaw clenched, Megan picked up her glass then threw its contents at him, before slamming it back on the table. "Go to hell!" She stormed to her car. Her body shaking, she leaned over the steering wheel, sobbing. "What in the hell? Does everyone know? How was I so blind? Why didn't anyone tell me?" A tap on her window caused her to startle. "Matt, just leave me alone!" Fumbling for her keys, she wiped the tears from her face.

"Megs, I'm sorry! I'm a jerk. Come back inside. Please?"

Cracking the window, Megan stared straight ahead though the windshield. "What? You're not done yet? Haven't you had enough fun at my expense?"

"I've had too much to drink. I didn't mean anything. I was upset to hear that you're married and when I saw you... I don't know. I'm an idiot." Leaning against the car, Matt held his head in his hands. "Will you just come back in? I won't be stupid any more, I promise. I just want to talk."

Megan took a deep breath, got out of the car and leaned against it. "I don't want to go back in there. I shouldn't have had a drink anyway. I was just upset."

"And I didn't help anything. I know. I'm sorry." Matt moved closer to her. "I'm just jealous. Someone else got you and I'm pissed."

Megan put her head against his shoulder. "You're such a jerk."

"I'm happy for you. I really am. I'm sorry to hear that he's sick. Is everything going to be okay?" Matt put his arm around her shoulder.

She took him into an embrace, softly crying. "I don't know."

"Well, isn't this a cozy scene?" A chill ran down Megan's body, recognizing the voice. "Does your husband know where you are?" Ellen walked up to them.

Megan pulled away from Matt. "I don't have to explain myself! Certainly not to you." She got back into her car and started it.

"Ellen, it's not what it looks like." Matt put himself between Ellen and Megan. "We're just friends."

"My son's sick at home and she's here making out with you. I think it's exactly what it looks like." Ellen pushed Matt aside, leaning into the window of Megan's car. "You're a slut, just like I told him you were. You and your brother are a lot alike."

"You need to get the hell out of here, Ellen. You have no idea what you're talking about. Go!" Matt pulled Ellen away from the car.

Pushing Matt aside, she smirked at Megan as she went into the restaurant.

Matt reached into the car, put his hand on Megan's shoulder. "I'm sorry. I shouldn't have followed you. I caused a lot of trouble tonight."

"It's fine. It doesn't matter anyway."

"Are you going to be okay? Should I come and explain it to Luke before she calls him?"

"No, It'll be okay. Don't worry about it." She shifted the car into gear. "Thanks for the drink."

"If you need anything, just let me know. Call me. I'm here for you. I'm at Mom and Dad's until I find a place so it's the same number as before." Matt smiled waving to her.

"Thank you. I will." Megan waved as she pulled away. "Stop thinking about Matt!" She slammed her palm into the steering wheel. "You can't do that to Luke. It's not right!"

#

The light was still on in the garage when Megan pulled into their driveway. "You can do this, Meg. You deserve an explanation. He owes you that much." Trying to build the courage, she walked up to the garage door. "Luke? Can we talk?" There was silence. Out of the corner of her eye, she could see Luke's arm.

"Luke!" He was lying on the floor, unconscious. She shook him, but there was no response. "Hold on, Luke. Please don't do this. Not now." Running into the house, she picked up the phone. She hesitated. *What if I don't call for help? What if I just let him go? Life would be a lot less complicated. He has to be tired of fighting.* She shook her head. "What am I thinking? What is wrong with you? Oh, God!"

"9-1-1. What's your emergency?"

She dwelled as she said the words; calling for the paramedics had become routine. Her voice was measured and calm. "I need an ambulance. My husband is unconscious. The address is 236 Valley View Drive."

She answered the usual questions, went back to the garage and sat beside Luke. She stared at his face as she waited for the ambulance to arrive. The day replayed in her head. The letters... what Matt had said... how she allowed herself to find comfort in Matt's arms, and how she considered, for a brief moment, letting Luke lay on the floor and die.

A shiver ran down her spine. She picked up Luke's arm, feeling for a pulse. She couldn't find one. "You can't die, Luke. We've got too much to sort out. Everything's going to be okay. I promise." She stroked his face. "I love you. I know you love me, too. We'll get you better and figure everything out. We'll beat this, do you hear me?" She leaned down and kissed his forehead, hearing the ambulance pull into the driveway. "Please, God. Don't let it be too late."

She went to the door, waved her arms. "He's in here! Hurry!"

#

Doctor Carter came into the waiting room.

"How is he? Did he make it?"

Taking a seat next to Megan, he nodded his head. "Yes, just barely." He held her hand as he looked her in the eyes. "It's getting very serious. The medication is obviously not working anymore. These episodes... having to defibrillate so often... he can't take much more. It's not good for his already weak heart. It's going to make things worse in the long run."

"What do we do?"

"I spoke to the specialist. She's on her way. She wants to examine him and if she feels he's up for it, she wants to do the transesophageal echocardiogram. Remember us talking about that? It can't wait any longer. We need answers and we need them now."

"Absolutely." Megan stared off, trying to collect her thoughts. "Can I see him? Before all this happens?"

Doctor Carter stood up. "If you want, you can go in, but just for a few moments. I have to warn you that he looks pretty rough, and he's not fully conscious. He doesn't make much sense."

"I understand." Megan followed him down the hall. The look on the doctor's face told her the desperation of the situation. At the door to his room, a tear formed in her eye seeing Luke hooked up to so many machines. Their sounds made her anxious. Luke lay motionless, his mouth wide open under a mask, gasping for air. His skin was a pale purple and his eyes were dark.

Putting her hand on his arm, Luke twitched. His whole body shook as if each part of him was desperately working to keep him alive. Struggling, his eyes opened.

"It's okay, Sweetie. Just relax. It's going to be all right."

Luke stared at the ceiling, his hand grasped onto Megan's arm. "Jared? Where's Jared?" His voice was weak and desperate.

Megan's lip trembled. "We'll find him. He's all right. I'm sure of it." Her words seemed to calm him. Luke nodded his head, closing his eyes again. His breathing was less frantic and his body relaxed.

A new anger consumed her. *Jared, where the hell are you? If you loved him, you'd be here. Maybe he'd fight harder.*

Doctor Carter entered, motioning for Megan to come into the hallway.

Giving Luke a kiss on the forehead, she followed him to a conference room. She recognized the specialist sitting at the table. "Thank you so much for coming." Shaking her hand, Megan sat across the table.

"Mrs. Morrison, I just wanted to run you through what's going to happen." Opening a folder, she slid a diagram to Megan. "The transesophageal echocardiogram is like a normal echocardiogram except that, in theory, we get a much better picture of what's going on in his heart. We'll be able to see how each part is working, or in his case, not working. We should get a pretty good idea of what's going on."

"That's wonderful! So this should give us answers?"

"I sure hope so. I'm sure you're aware that we're running out of options... and time." Doctor Sans stood. "I'm going to examine him before we do the test, but I also want to examine him to make sure he can withstand any sort of surgery. If we find something and we have the ability to do something about it, I would like to do it immediately."

"Of course. Do anything you can. I'll sign whatever you need." Megan swallowed hard, looking up at both of them. "Thank you for everything you're doing."

"If you don't have any questions, I'm going to get started."

Megan reached for Dr. Sans' hand, squeezing it. "No, please. Go ahead."

Doctor Sans left the room. Sitting Megan in the chair, Doctor Carter put his hands on her shoulders. "Megan, you can wait here if you'd like. Is there someone you can call to be with you?"

"Yeah, I'll call someone. Thank you." Megan watched as he left, dazed at how quickly everything was happening. She went to the couch, picked up the phone and dialed. "Susie? It's Megan. Can you come to the hospital? I'll explain everything when you get here. I need your help. Yes. Just hurry. I'm in the ER. Ask for me at the desk. Thank you... See you soon... I love you too."

DeeJay Arens

THE RIVER OF NO RETURN

The room was silent when I finally looked up from the desk. *Did I lose my audience?* I had to make sure they were aware of the reasons surrounding everything that had happened so far in the story. Happy to see my pitcher of ice water being refilled, I smiled my thanks to the young man. His smile back and the seemingly proud expression on his face and the touch on my shoulder as he passed gave me the courage to continue.

"I take full responsibility for my actions during that time... the drunkenness, the scene at the wedding, the suicide attempt... but you have absolutely no idea the immense stress I felt. Keeping everything about me a secret, living a lie, watching others live their lives, knowing the consequences if I was found out... I loved a man deeply; that was my crime... loving someone. I point out again, had there not been the societal pressures and the abuse that is still tolerated against the gay and lesbian community, a lot of this would not have happened. If we were allowed, without fear of physical harm or rejection, to love and to care for those we fall in love with, there wouldn't be this need to conform to what society expects. There would be no need to deny who we are. I was, of course, affected by it, as was Luke, but in making the decisions that Luke did, so were Megan, our parents, Susie, Derek, the people we work for, our friends, the hospital staff... the list goes on and on... which is my point. If you think for one second that decisions about freedoms and rights, or hate-filled statements about our minority population affect only us, you can see that is not the case. So many people, most of whom have no say in the matter, are affected and hurt. Think about the pain and confusion I was feeling to make me believe my only option was to end my life. It was real. I'd been rejected by everyone I loved, in one twenty-four hour period." Feeling the touch of a hand on my shoulder, I turned my head, and gave a smile. "Or at least, that's what I felt at the time. Luckily, not everyone had abandoned me."

SCARS THAT WON'T HEAL

Every time Derek heard a noise from the front door of the coffee shop, his heart would pound. Jared had requested they meet here. He sipped a mocha, then looked at his watch. *I knew it. He changed his mind.* He'd heard from Chris that Jared had been back for a couple weeks but up until yesterday, there had been no word from him. Now he wondered what it was that Jared had to say. *Calm down, Derek. You have no idea where this is going. You don't even know where you want it to go.*

He checked the time again. *Twenty minutes late. How long do I wait for him?* He looked at his phone, checking to see if he had somehow shut off the ringer and missed a call or a text message. There was nothing. *He's not coming.*

Taking one last sip from his cup, he got up, grabbed his napkin then turned to throw them in the garbage. He almost dropped them when he saw Jared standing near him. The hours of thinking about what he was going to say proved useless. Words escaped him.

"Hey, you!" Jared smiled, taking off his sunglasses. "Sorry I'm late. I had to drop off some papers at school and I got a little lost. It's amazing what you forget when you've been gone for a while."

"No. It's okay. It's fine." Derek looked him over trying to figure out what was different. *He looks tired. Is he sick?* He forced a smile. "Can I get you something?"

"A mocha would be great." Jared sat down at the table, taking off his jacket.

Derek dumped his garbage in the trash then went to the counter to order. He looked back at Jared while he waited in line, staring at the back of his head. *God, I've missed you.* He wished he could throw his arms around him, but he didn't dare.

He set Jared's coffee down then took the seat across the booth. Jared took a sip. "Oh, God! Thank you. I haven't had a real coffee in weeks. Back home they think mocha comes out of a dispenser at a gas station." He chuckled, met Derek's gaze then looked away. His face reddened.

Derek laughed, happy the ice was broken. He noticed the dark circles under his eyes. "How are you? Are you okay? You look tired."

Leaning back, Jared raised an eyebrow. "Wow. I must look like shit."

"No! You look great. You're just as beautiful as always." Derek grabbed his hand. "That's not what I meant. I'm just worried. Something's different about you. You just don't look well."

Jared squeezed his hand. "Don't worry. I'm fine. I'm just having some trouble sleeping. I'm getting readjusted to being back here." He looked in Derek's eyes. "How are you? You look amazing."

"I'm fine. Great, now that I've seen you and know you're still alive and not laying in a corn field somewhere in the middle of the prairie or whatever the hell it is out there in North Dakota."

"Ah. Touché." Leaning forward, Jared wrapped his hands around his mug, staring into it. "I don't know how to say this.

There are no right words to apologize for not letting you know what was going on. I'm sorry. You must be furious."

"Furious? No. I was desperately worried about you." Derek looked at him. "Although now that I do know you're okay, I am feeling more upset with you."

"I know. Like I said on the phone, I owe you an explanation. I'm just not sure where to start." Jared rubbed his face. Leaning back, he stared at the table. "Once I got home I had a few... things to take care of."

Derek studied his face. Jared seemed to be guarding his words.

Pushing his coffee away, Jared took a deep breath and shook his head. "Look, I had it all planned out what I was going to say to you, but I just don't feel like going through it all. It's a very long, tedious, ridiculous story. I'm just going to give you the short recap of, how I like to refer to it, 'Gays of our Lives'. Ready?"

Derek could tell Jared was uneasy. He felt guilty at his earlier comment. "You don't have to tell me now. If you'd rather wait, I understand. I'm fine just sitting here with you." He smiled at him.

"Thank you, but I'd rather get this over with." Jared crossed his arms and sat back. "So, I was met at the airport by none other than Luke. It started out well... he explained what had happened to him... why he was gone. Then it turned into a rather huge blow-up once he told me that the big surprise I was coming home for was that he was getting married... to my sister... that weekend."

"Wait, wait, wait! He what?"

"Oh, no. You heard right." Jared patted his hand, a strange smile on his face. "I made it to my parent's house and my dad 'outed' me to anyone who was within earshot of him, screaming and yelling while everyone was getting ready for the wedding. Next I had a melt-down, got drunk, and crashed the wedding... where I was told no one wanted me around. I headed out of town, got drunk again, did something completely idiotic, ended up in the hospital, was whisked off to court-ordered treatment... courtesy of my father, and, voila, I'm back here where, in hindsight, I should have stayed." He thought for a moment. "Yeah, that pretty much sums it up."

Derek stared at him. His mind raced trying to take it all in. The short version was confusing enough.

"Okay, your turn." Jared laughed. "What happened with you while I was gone?"

"Oh, right! How the hell am I supposed to compete with a story like that? The most exciting thing I did was buy myself some new underwear." Derek laughed. The smile was gone from Jared's face. He took Jared's hand. "I, um... Wow. I... I just don't know what to say to you." The images of the story bombarded his mind. "For starters, are you okay? That seems like a really stupid question, but how are you? I can't believe you can laugh about it? I mean, holy shit! Treatment? The wedding? I'm just... stunned. I'm sorry. That's all I can say. I'm stunned."

"You know me. If I do something, I do it with all the drama I can throw at it." Jared pulled his hand away. "Well, at least I got what I wanted. I wanted closure and I got closure. You know, I now understand why they say 'be careful what you wish for'." He chuckled looking down at the table.

Caressing Jared's hand, Derek tried to make eye contact with him. "I know there are a lot of things you haven't told me... and that's okay. It must've been hell." Jared nodded, a tear running down his face. Unable to hold back, Derek moved next to him, put an arm around him, pulling him closer. "I wish I could have been there for you. I can't stand thinking about what you went through. I missed you so much."

Jared's body shook. "I missed you, too." He pulled Derek's other arm around him, leaning against him. "If it's any consolation at all, I wanted to call you... I did, but when I wanted to, I couldn't... literally. I couldn't make long distance calls from treatment, not without a calling card and there wasn't anywhere I could get one. When I could finally call you... I wasn't sure what to say." More tears filled his eyes. "Then when I got back here, I wasn't sure what to expect. Part of me hoped you moved on, knowing you deserved better. Another part of me just wanted to see you. I didn't want your sympathy... well, I don't know what I wanted."

"Stop. Don't say that. I'm just glad you called. I wanted more than anything to see you." Derek kissed the top of his head.

"You may or may not believe this, but I thought about you often. I had a lot of time to think." Jared laid his head on Derek's shoulder. "You got me through some really tough times."

Derek felt a smile form on his face hearing those words. Picking up Jared's hand to kiss it, his heart stopped when he saw the mark on Jared's wrist. He pulled away and grabbed Jared's arm, pushing up his sleeve. A lump formed in his throat as he stared at the scar. "Jared. My God! What the hell...?"

Jared pulled his arm away, rolled down his sleeve, then moved as far away from Derek as possible. "I'm not saying I dealt with it well." He chuckled. "Just for future reference; Jared, horrible situations, and whiskey do not mix."

"This isn't funny!" Pulse racing, Derek grabbed his shoulders, turning Jared to him. "Listen to me. That bastard isn't worth it. Do you hear me?"

"I know. I know." Wiping his eyes, Jared looked past him. "It wasn't just him, you know? It was... my parents, what they said to me, how I was hurting you... everything."

"None of it would've happened without him in the equation." Derek jumped out of the booth. He kept looking at Jared then down at his wrists as he paced. He wanted to scream; his body shook with rage. He dropped back into his seat, put his arms on the table to hold his head. "I'm so angry, I want to get on a plane, find Luke, and beat the shit out of him!"

"Derek, no. Come on." Jared reached for Derek's hands. "You're absolutely right. He's not worth it. None of them are."

Bringing a clenched fist to his mouth, Derek cleared his throat. He touched Jared's face. "I know you love him, but to think about what he did to you for you to consider... I hate him! I don't know what it's worth right now and I really don't care, but I love you... more than anything. If you ever start to feel like that's your only option, I need you to remember that. No matter where you are or who you choose to be with." His eyes filled with tears. Picking up Jared's hand, he kissed it.

"You have no idea..." Jared's voice broke. He tried to clear his throat. "You have no idea how much I wanted to hear you say that." He sobbed, holding his head in his hands. "I love you too."

Wiping his face with his arm, Derek moved to the other side of the booth. He put his arms around him, holding him close. Lifting Jared's head, he stroked his cheek, staring into his eyes then pulled him into a gentle kiss. Jared clutched his shirt as he leaned his head against Derek's.

Kissing him on the forehead, Derek stroked Jared's face. "How about we get out of here?"

Jared looked around. "You've noticed people staring at us, too?"

Derek took Jared's hand, pulled him up. "I don't care about that. I just want some alone time with you."

"How about walking me home?"

"Sure, but isn't that a bit far? I could just drive you? You didn't walk all this way, did you?"

"I knew there was something I meant to tell you." They were on the sidewalk. Jared put his arm around Derek's waist. "When I got back here, I decided I needed something more. I couldn't live in the dorms. It wasn't because of Chris. He's moving too. So I took a job at that gift store around the corner and found an apartment. It's just up the street."

"That's wonderful! Even more alone; you know... without interruptions." Derek followed Jared up the stairs of the apartment building to a door at the end of the hall on the top floor.

Jared opened the door then switched on the lights. "Well? What do you think?"

The apartment was small, but quaint. Derek looked through the window at the view of Puget Sound and Mount Rainier. "It's just gorgeous."

Jared walked behind Derek, wrapped his arms around his waist, resting his chin on Derek's shoulder. "I was hoping you'd like it, because I have a question for you. I hope I'm not rushing you and I don't know where you're at with everything right now, but I was hoping you'd move in with me. If you need to think about it, I understand. I threw a lot at you tonight."

Derek stared at him. "Jared, this is a really big step."

Jared put his finger to Derek's mouth. "I've given this a lot of thought. Frankly, it's another reason it took me so long to call you when I got back. I had to be sure that if you, by some miracle, wanted anything to do with me again, I knew what I wanted. Every time I'd think it through, I came to the same conclusion. I want to be with you."

Taking Jared's hands, Derek pulled him onto the couch. "This is a lot to think about."

"If we're going to try to make a relationship work I think we have to start by being open and honest, so before you say yes to this, I want to tell you that I'm still working through things. It sounds a little crazy after everything that's happened, but, every once in a while, I have a moment of weakness and I think about Luke."

Derek dropped his gaze to the floor.

"I know it's in the past. It's over. He made his choices. I still... I don't know... mourn for it, I guess, but it gets easier as time goes on. That's because of you. I realized that when I get depressed and think about not having him in my life like I'd planned, I start to think of you – the one guy who's loved me with no strings attached, and did so knowing what a train wreck I could be, how selfish I could be, and how much of a pain in the ass I am."

Derek laughed.

"That should've been enough for me. Hell, that's more than I could've expected from anyone and it was right there in front of me. How self-destructive can I get?" Jared got up to look out the window. "When I came back, I hoped more than ever that you still felt about me the way I was feeling about you. I was scared to find out. That's why it took me so long to call you. I didn't want to face the possibility that I'd screwed up my only real chance at a relationship."

"Sounds like you've really tried to work through things. You don't sound like the same guy I was in love with a few months ago."

"A lot's happened. I hope I'm not fooling myself into believing it, but I think I've changed. I hope it's for the better."

"Since you're being honest, I'm going to be honest. My first thought was 'no'. With all you've been through, it's not a good idea. I want to protect myself. I got nervous about what you went through and how you were handling it." He noticed the look of panic on Jared's face. "Don't get me wrong; I meant everything I said before. I do love you... more than I can tell you. I want more than anything for us to be together and to make it work like I know it can. But..."

Jared shook his head. "I understand. It was a lot to expect of you since you had no idea where we stood until a couple hours ago."

"I'm so proud of you. You amaze me. You're much stronger than I ever gave you credit for. I believe you do want us to work."

A smile formed on Jared's face as he sat back down. "So you're saying 'yes'?"

Derek pulled him into a hug. "I'm saying 'thank you'. I'm thrilled you want me to live with you."

"Yes! You won't regret it! I promise!"

"But I think we need to talk more. A lot's happened. Out of respect for each other, we owe it to ourselves to make sure this is what we both really want." Derek pulled away, sat back on the couch. "I know you don't want to hear this and you're going to try to argue with me, but a part of you is still in love with Luke."

"No! Derek, I..."

"That's not a bad thing. I'm not saying you don't love me. I'm saying all the stuff that happened to you... that was only a couple months ago. You need some time. You said it yourself; you're still mourning it... as you should. My being here is not going to make it go away. All those feelings will still be there."

Jared's voice broke. "Derek, please..."

"I need time, too. I've got to process everything. I want to make sure that I can be what you need. I thought I lost you once to Luke. It was unbearable. I can't do that to myself again." Derek kissed him. "Jared, I'm not saying 'no'. I'm saying 'not yet'. Let's both think about it, okay? We'll take it slow. It will be better in the long run."

Jared wiped his eyes and nodded, looking away.

"I know this isn't the answer you had in mind, but I really think it's the best, for both of us. I do love you. That hasn't changed." Derek kissed him before going to the door.

"I love you, too."

"Call me tomorrow, okay? We can get together and talk some more."

"I'd like that."

Halfway down the hall, Derek questioned if he'd done the right thing. Walking away from Jared was one of the hardest things he'd ever done.

MAYBE THIS TIME

May 1999

Megan poured a bowl of soup, placed it on the tray while watching out the window for the mailman. Weeks had gone by since she'd sent a letter to Jared and still hadn't heard anything. She wanted to tell Luke that she'd heard from him and that he was all right. Luke needed some good news after all he'd been through. He seemed to be losing his will to keep going after the third surgery in eight months.

Sneaking into the office, Megan looked at Luke, who was asleep on a hospital bed that had been moved in for him. The last surgery had been hard. He wasn't bouncing back as quickly as before. When she set the tray on the desk, the spoon clanged against the bowl.

Luke stirred, opening his eyes. "What time is it?"

"It's twelve-thirty. I'm sorry I woke you." Megan sat at the edge of his bed, caressing his arm. "Feeling any better?"

Luke struggled to push himself up. His arms shook. He grasped the rail for support. "Thanks to you, I am feeling a bit better."

Megan chuckled, putting pillows behind him. "All I do is bring you soup. You do all the rest."

Caressing her face, Luke stared into her eyes. "I couldn't do this alone. Thank you."

Megan stood, offering her hand. "Well, why don't you try walking? Are you up to it?" She pulled on his arm.

"No, not right now. I don't think I'm ready for that quite yet." Luke stared out the window.

"Okay. I'll let you rest. Let me know if you need anything." As she closed the door, a reflection roamed through the house. Megan ran into the living room to see the postman at the mailbox. As the truck pulled away, she ran out. "Come on, Jared!" Her heart pounded as she rummaged through the stack. She stopped, staring at a manila envelope addressed to her in Jared's handwriting.

She ran back to the house, threw the rest of the mail on the table then ripped open the envelope. As the contents landed on the counter, her heart dropped at the sight of three letters she'd sent him. Each one was unopened. Her body shook, anger welling up inside. "I didn't do a thing to you, Jared. Yes, shit happened, but it's time to get over it. Stop being so damned selfish!"

Her mind raced as she approached the office; she was trying to think of what to tell Luke. She had to say something. Luke stared out the window, his face void of any emotion.

"Am I bugging you? Can I come in?"

Luke reached out to her. "Of course you can come in."

Realizing she was still holding the envelope, Megan looked at it then back to Luke. "I need to tell you something." She sat on the side of his bed, holding his hand. "I wrote Jared. I've been trying to get hold of him to let him know what you were going through and to make sure he was okay."

Luke sat up again, the smile spreading across his face. "Did you hear from him? Is that what you're holding?"

"Not really. He sent back my letters." She handed them to Luke then looked down at the floor.

"He's all right." Luke chuckled, staring at the writing. He threw the letter to the side then pulled his blankets off. "Does that offer still stand to help me walk?"

She got him sitting on the edge of the bed then reached around his waist. "Ready?" Luke nodded. He put one arm around her and the other on the railing. Legs wobbling, he rose to his feet.

Looking into his eyes, Megan noticed a determined look as he took his first steps. There was an instant sweat on his brow, but the smile never disappeared. He had a reason to keep going.

DeeJay Arens

LOSING MY MIND

August, 1999

Jared pulled the car into his parking spot next to Derek's. He walked to the mail box then shuffled through the stack of bills and letters as he walked up the stairs. He stopped when he saw one addressed to both of them. It was from *Time Magazine*. He ripped it open and read it. "Oh, my God!" He ran up the stairs, threw the door to the apartment open. "Derek?"

The paper Derek was reading dropped onto the kitchen table as he ran to the living room. "What? What is it? What's the matter?"

Jared threw his arms around him. "We did it! We're going to be published!" Grabbing Derek's arm, he pulled him into the living room and down onto the couch. "Read it! It's from Time freaking Magazine! They've accepted our piece!"

Letter in hand, Derek's eyes widened as he read it out loud. *"Your submission will be published in next month's issue. We look forward to a long and productive working relationship."* He stared at Jared. "I can't believe it! I can't... believe it! We did it." He grabbed Jared's hands, pulling him into a kiss. They both screamed with excitement.

Jared picked up the letter and read it again. "It's hard to believe... but it's real, isn't it?" He grabbed the phone. "We have to celebrate! What should we do? Order Thai or Chinese?"

"I know what we have to do." Taking Jared's hands, Derek stared into his eyes. The smile and excitement had disappeared. "Now listen to me. Don't say 'no' until you've heard me through. I've been thinking about this for a while now; about what we would do if this ever happened."

"Derek? What? What's the matter?" Jared swallowed the lump that formed in his throat, as he studied the face before him.

"Nothing. It's just that..." Derek picked up the letter and held it before him. "...We have credibility now. People will take us seriously. This is the ticket to jumping in head first!"

"Yes, and...?"

"Okay, I'm just going to throw it out there." Derek took a deep breath. "This might sound crazy at first, but we need to go to the Middle East. With all the shit happening over there... we have to be there to cover it. I say we pack up and go!" He touched Jared's shoulder. "Well? What do you think?"

Jared stood shaking his head. "Wait. Are you serious? I mean, how do we... how? It's not just that easy. You don't just jump on a plane. There's a lot to consider and plan, not to mention the costs involved. You're right. It does sound crazy!"

Derek gave him a sheepish smile. "I know I should have told you, but I've been saving money. Actually, it's the savings account I started when I was ten. My mom and dad and I have been adding money to it for years. We have more than enough to get started. This is what it's for! Let's do it! We'll figure it out." He put his arms around Jared. "We can do it! I know we can. What do we have to lose?"

Jared chewed on the corner of his lip then stared into his eyes. "Let's do it! What the hell?"

Derek kissed his face, shaking him by the shoulders as he did so. "Thank you. Thank you. Thank you. I promise I'll get everything organized and taken care of. You won't have to worry about anything!" He gave him one more kiss. "What do you say? Should I order that Chinese so we can celebrate?"

"No! I'm taking my boyfriend on a date. We're going out!" Laughing, Jared walked down the hall. "Let's get dressed up!" Glancing over his shoulder, he saw Derek still in the living room, a worried expression on his face. "Derek? What's wrong? You don't want to go out? That's fine."

"We have to talk." Taking Jared's hand, Derek led him to the couch, sitting him down. He sat on the coffee table in front of him. "Before we get too involved in this plan, I have to tell you something." He looked down at his hands, attempting several times to speak. Derek was unable to find the words.

Jared leaned forward, caressing his face, used his thumb to dry a tear that slipped down Derek's cheek. "Talk to me. What is it?"

"It's just hard. I'm worried you're going to hate me." Derek's face contorted as he fought back more tears. He tried to turn away.

"I doubt very much that there's anything you could do to make me hate you." Jared held Derek's face. "...Unless you're going to tell me you're leaving me for someone else. That can't be it because you wouldn't be planning a trip overseas with me." He wiped Derek's tears. "Now come on. What is it?"

Derek moved to the window and looked out. "I need to be honest with you before you actually decide to do this with me." He took a deep breath. "The truth is, I go check the mail before you every day before you get home. I never bring all of it in because I didn't want you to know that I was going through it." He sat at the kitchen table, holding his head. "There were things in there I didn't want you to see."

Jared sat next to him, holding his hand. "Derek? Are you in some kind of trouble? If you are, I'll help you figure it out. It can't be that bad."

"No. It's not that." Derek shook his head, pulling his hand away. "They were letters to you. I told myself I was helping you by keeping them from you, because you'd just get upset. The truth is I did it for me, not you."

"What are you talking about? What letters?"

Derek disappeared into the bedroom. Jared heard the closet door open and papers shuffling. Derek reappeared with a letter in hand. "This one came today. The others I marked 'Return to Sender' and put them back in the mail." Tears streamed down his face. He put the letter on the table. "Please forgive me."

Jared inhaled sharply as he read the return address. *Luke Morrison.*

"I never opened any of them. I swear to God."

Jared picked up the letter then stared at Derek. "Why would you do that?"

"I was scared. I didn't know what he said in them. I was worried he was asking you to come back to him. I couldn't live with that."

Jared slammed the letter down on the coffee table.

"Jared, I'm..."

"Stop! I can't talk to you right now. I need to think. Just leave me alone." Jared could feel the blood rushing to his face as his body tensed.

Derek backed away from him. "I'm sorry." He disappeared into the hall.

What do I do now? Do I open it? Jared reached for the letter. Looking down the hall, he shook his head. *Why did you do this to me?* Ready to have it out with Derek, he headed for the bedroom, but stopped in the hall. *Don't do this. Not yet. You need to think through this.*

#

The clock in the kitchen read 7:05. Jared realized he'd been trying to decide about the letter for an hour. There'd been no word from Derek.

As he opened the door, Jared saw Derek lying on the bed. He stood in the doorway, arms crossed, leaning against the wall.

Derek jumped hearing the door open. His eyes were red and swollen. "I've been laying here trying to figure out a way to tell you how sorry I am for what I did. It's unforgiveable, I know. I wish I could take it all back, but I can't. You must hate me."

"Up until a few moments ago I would have agreed with you." Jared stared at him. "But I don't hate you. I'm furious with you, yes, but I don't hate you. I've had a hard time figuring out why I was so upset. You don't know this, but you did exactly what I've done to the letters I've gotten from Megan and my mom. I probably would've done it to Luke's. I'd like to think so anyway. It should've been my choice."

"I know. I'm sorry..."

"Just wait. It's my turn to talk." Sitting next to him, Jared stared at the wall. "I'm furious with you because it shows that you don't trust me. I thought we had a better relationship than that. I've always been so proud that we talk about things and don't keep secrets. It's what I never had with Luke." He looked at Derek. "However, the more I thought about it the less angry I was. I mean, with my history with him, you had a right to be concerned. Every time Luke's name used to be brought up or I had some sort of interaction with him, I was sent into a tailspin. I'd want to avoid that too, but it doesn't excuse you for not trusting me. We have to trust each other, if we have any chance to make our relationship last."

"It was wrong and I know that." Wiping away more tears, Derek looked down at the floor. "Can you forgive me?"

Jared put his hand on Derek's leg, moving closer to him. "I do. I'm just going to need a little time to get over it."

"Thank you! I'm sorry. I love you so much! I don't know what I'd do if you left me. I'll be better. I promise." Derek threw his arms around him.

"I love you, too." Pulling Derek off the bed, Jared caressed his face. "Now get ready! We're going out on the town!"

"You still want to go out?"

"Now more than ever. We need to get out for a while." He pulled off his shirt and winked.

"I may be pushing my luck here, but now that we're talking and we're supposed to be open and honest, I have to tell you that I'm dying to know what was in that letter."

Pulling on a new shirt, Jared stared into his eyes. "I'd tell you, but I don't know. I didn't open it. It's going to join the rest of his letters. This time, though, I'll take care of it."

DeeJay Arens

REBEL WITHOUT A CAUSE

Luke laid his tools out on the workbench to organize them. He still tired easily. His strength was coming back, but he was unable to go back to work. It left him with free time to do projects and a lot of time to think.

The new shelves in front of him would be perfect to showcase his finished projects. Putting down his power drill, he admired his work. He began to line up each piece. As he reached up to place another one, he looked out the window. Just down the hill he could see the top of the train car, Mike and Candace's house, and his mom's house. He looked at the small carved train car in his hand, tracing the letters painted on it with his finger: *J & L Railroad*.

Luke moved a step stool to reach the special place he'd saved for his creation. Reaching up, he felt a sudden pain in his chest and slumped over against the bench. He measured his breathing and relaxed his body, trying to work through the pain. It was one of the tricks he'd learned over the months.

God damn it! The episodes were becoming an issue again. The latest surgery had made them subside for quite a while, but they'd come with increased severity and frequency now. *They've never been this bad.*

THE VIEW FROM A RUSTY TRAIN CAR

Once the pain subsided, Luke stood, shaking his head. He wiped the sweat from his brow. A flash of light drew his attention to the window, then outside. He looked around, but didn't see anything. Turning to go back to the garage there was another flash. This time he could see some activity down by the train car. A large truck pulled into the driveway. Two men guided the truck up behind the train car. The tow cable was lowered and they attached it to some chains.

"No!" Luke ran to his car. Heart pounding, he drove down the hill then pulled into the junkyard. Luke jumped out of the car, yelled, waving his arms to get the men's attention. They didn't notice him over the sound of the truck.

The driver of the truck saw Luke and shut off the motor. He motioned through his back window and the other two men came around to the front.

"What's going on here? Who's in charge?" Luke looked to each for answers.

"I am," a voice called from behind him.

Luke turned. "Mr. Hanson."

"What can I do for you, Luke?"

"I saw the truck pulling up. What's going on?"

"Finally getting rid of this thing. I found a guy who's going to cut it down and sell it for scrap metal."

"No! You can't!" Luke's body shook as he looked at the chains enveloping the train car.

"I have to. It's time to downsize. I'm ready to sell the place." Mr. Hanson raised an eyebrow. "I don't mean to sound rude, but why do you care?"

Luke tried to explain, but he couldn't seem to come up with the right words.

Mr. Hanson smiled. "Let me guess. You were one of the kids who fooled around in here." He hit Luke's arm, winking at him. "You fool around with your first girl in here?"

Luke blushed, looking down at the ground. "Something like that."

A hand on Luke's shoulder, Mr. Hanson laughed. "It's time for it to go, and I need the money." He motioned to the men to continue.

"Wait." Luke pulled his check book from his back pocket. "How much are they giving you for it?"

"What?"

"The train car. How much did you sell it for?" Luke's hand shook, searching his pockets for a pen.

Mr. Hanson looked at Luke's check book. He gave him a smile, putting an arm around his shoulder. "Luke, I understand. It's tough, but be serious. You have to let go."

The lump in Luke's throat grew bigger. He looked at the train car, the remains of the old fort behind it then back at Mr. Hanson. "I can't. How much?"

"I'm getting eight hundred bucks for it. Don't waste your money." He patted Luke's arm then turned away. "Go home. You'll always remember it, I'm sure."

Luke held out the check. "Here! Eight hundred bucks, and you don't have to pay to get it moved."

Mr. Hanson stared at him, shaking his head. "Where are you going to put it?"

Luke thought for a moment. He made out another check and offered it to him. "A thousand bucks and it stays right where it is... until you sell the place; then I'll figure out what to do with it."

Mr. Hanson pushed his hand away. "This is crazy. Put your money away. I..."

"Please!" Luke fought back tears. "I can't explain it, but this is important to me. Please do this for me."

"It means that much?"

He couldn't say anything for fear of crying. He nodded. Mr. Hanson took the check. Luke felt a smile forming as he watched the chains being removed. The men jumped into the truck and pulled away. Mr. Hanson waved to Luke then climbed into his pick-up. He followed the truck down the road.

THE VIEW FROM A RUSTY TRAIN CAR

Memories flooded back as Luke leaned against the side of the train car. He stared at the sunset over the hill. "Best view in the world." The scene hadn't changed in all those years. There was some rustling in the tall grass. His heart beat rapidly. "Jared?" A bird flew from the grass, landing in the tree that held their fort. There was very little left of it now. A piece of the flooring hung on by a couple nails. The rest of the structure had disappeared. Things had changed. Jared wouldn't be meeting him there.

A sob rose up from within. Luke slammed his fists against the train car. "Damn you, Jared. I need you." His fingers scratched down the side of the train car as he collapsed to the ground, tears streaming down his face.

A FOREIGN AFFAIR

Jared watched through the window as their jet taxied down the runway. The Kuwaiti desert wasn't like the pictures he'd seen. It looked endless and barren.

Derek grabbed his hand. "I can't believe we're doing this. We're crazy!"

Jared's stomach turned. "We are freakin' crazy!" His mind ran a hundred miles a minute. *Come on, Jared. You wanted to be a journalist.* He couldn't help the rush of second thoughts.

"Next thing we do is look for a ride; find a taxi or shuttle or something." Derek reached into the overhead compartment and handed down their bags.

"What? You mean you didn't check to see if our hotel had a shuttle?" Jared grabbed his arm, pulling Derek down beside him. "What the hell are we going to do? What if they don't have taxis? How far is it?"

Derek put his chin on Jared's shoulder, whispering in his ear. "Honey, it's all right. It's going to be fine. This is Al Jahra. It's the capital. They have taxis. Trust me. Just relax and do what I do." He gave him a quick kiss before heading to the exit.

Jared watched him walk down the aisle. "Okay, time to get on with it." The pit in his stomach seemed to grow. He wondered if anyone would notice him if he stayed on the plane and headed back home. *How could he not figure all this out? This is going to be ugly.*

"Jared." Derek motioned to him. "Let's go!"

The doors opened. The other passengers made their way out of the plane.

Jared hurried to catch up to Derek. The last thing he needed was to lose him in the shuffle.

As they walked through the airport, Jared tried to settle himself. *Calm down. There's no reason to panic.* He looked through the large windows toward the main doors of the airport. A line of taxis waited out front. He sighed his relief.

Derek sounded thrilled as he read each sign aloud to Jared. "Oh, look! Baggage claim." He led them to the escalator.

Jared grabbed his arm. "Hold on. Now that I know where that is, how about I get the bags and you get a cab."

"Good idea. I'll meet you out front." Derek took a few steps then turned back. "Do you remember what I taught you? How to say 'I am American' and 'I don't speak Arabic'?"

Pulse racing, Jared went over the phrases in his mind. He wasn't sure they were right, but he wanted to get out of the airport and get to the hotel. "Yeah, I think so. Go ahead."

#

Bags in hand, Jared pushed through the front doors. He looked around for Derek. The sun felt brighter and hotter than back home. He slipped on his sunglasses.

Derek stood at the end of the row leaning into a taxi. He didn't look happy. The cab pulled away and Derek yelled something. Jared had no idea what it was, but it didn't sound friendly. "What's wrong?"

"Remember when I told you that Kuwait was a friend of ours? I guess I was wrong."

A taxi pulled up, honking at them. Derek ran over to the window and talked to the driver. He looked up at Jared, smiling. "He'll take us."

The driver opened the trunk and piled the bags inside. Jared got in the taxi. He studied their surroundings. He thought he was prepared for the differences between here and home, but he wasn't sure anymore. Some things were recognizable, but the feel of the place was different.

Derek got in the other side and smiled. That comforted Jared. He listened to Derek chat with the driver. They laughed about something. *That's impressive. Thank God he's here with me.*

They pulled up to a hotel. Derek helped the driver get the luggage, then paid him. The door to the taxi slammed shut and it sped down the road, pulling one of the bags Jared was holding and throwing it on to the sidewalk. "Nice knowing you, too."

Derek chuckled as he picked up the bags. "I'll go in and see about our room. I'll be right back." He leaned in to give Jared a kiss.

"Derek, no! We can't!" Jared pushed him away, looking around at who might have seen them.

"Right. I forgot." Derek walked into the hotel.

The bench outside was uncomfortable. Jared shifted, looking into the hotel to see what was happening. The crowd forming on the other side of the street made him uncomfortable.

The door opened and Derek came out. He looked upset, turning and yelling at the guy who'd followed him to the door.

Jared ran to him. "What's the matter?"

Derek threw the bags to the ground. "They won't give us a room."

"We had a reservation? Did you show them the papers?"

"They don't care about our reservation." Derek stared into his eyes, his jaw tense.

"Now what do we do?"

"Start looking for one that will." Picking up the luggage, Derek walked down the sidewalk.

Jared followed, but not too close. Derek seemed to need the space. They'd been to six different hotels by now and all of them said no.

The heat was getting to him. He collapsed onto a bench outside the next hotel, while Derek went in to beg for a room. He put his head back on the bench, trying to relax for a moment and to stop the pounding in his feet.

Derek ran out of the hotel, tripping over one of the bags Jared had put down and landed on the sidewalk.

"Sorry!" Jared helped Derek to his feet. "Let me guess. No room."

"They have one! They're going to let us stay here!" Derek gathered the bags.

"Thank you, God!" Jared pushed himself off of the bench.

"Just a little farther. It's on the second floor!"

They hurried to their room. It was small, without the amenities that even the cheapest hotels back home would provide. After hours of walking the streets of Al Jahra, however, it looked like a room in a palace.

They said little to each other, readying themselves for a good night's rest. Landing in the bed at the same time, their heads knocked together. Derek giggled uncontrollably as Jared stared at him, rubbing his head. "What is wrong with you? It's not funny."

Derek lay out on the floor, trying to stifle the laughter. "Sorry. I think it's the lack of sleep!"

"Could it be any smaller?"

"It's all they had." Derek lifted the blankets to crawl in.

"You looked kind of comfortable on the floor. I'll take the bed." Jared lay in the middle and closed his eyes.

"Scoot over! I'm not sleeping on the floor." Derek snuggled close. He put his arm around Jared.

Jared raised an eye brow, looking at him. "Now behave. I'm exhausted!"

"Fine." Derek turned away in a huff.

The sounds from the streets of Al Jahra filled the room, reminding Jared that they were far from home. He pulled Derek's arm back over him. "Thanks for taking care of everything."

#

Sitting in the corner of the room, Derek looked through some papers and made notes.

Shielding his eyes from the sunlight pouring in, Jared rubbed his face and sat up. "Good morning."

"Morning." Derek mumbled, not looking away from his work. "How'd you sleep?"

Jared was aware of the bitter tone in Derek's voice. "All right, I think, but for some reason I still feel tired."

"I'm not surprised." The note pad Derek was holding slammed onto the table. He walked to the bathroom. "You and Luke must have had a great time. It's all I heard all night." The door slammed behind him.

"Shit." Jared put his head in his hands. He got out of bed and threw on some clothes. He did have dreams about Luke, but it wasn't what Derek was thinking. When Derek came out of the bathroom, he grabbed his arm. "Honey, I'm sorry. I didn't mean to keep you awake." He tried to put his arms around him.

"Let's just get going." Derek pushed him away. He threw his things in his suitcase and headed out the door. "I'll meet you outside."

Jared grabbed his backpack and followed. He found Derek sitting on the bench on the street. "I'm sorry. I did have a dream about him, but it's not the kind you think I had."

Shaking his head, Derek got off the bench.

"Are you going to talk to me?" Jared ran after him.

"What do you want me to say?"

"I don't know! Just something." Jared grabbed his arm, turning him. He tried to pull him close.

"We can't. Remember?" Derek pushed him away. He pulled out a map and read it as he walked. "Let's just find this Mr. Nehme and figure out what we're doing."

Following behind him, Jared thought about the dream. *I can't control what I dream about!* He considered stopping Derek to try again to explain himself, but knew it wasn't a good idea. *I'm trying, Derek, but it's those letters. I can't help wondering what they said.* As they walked, Jared kept trying to get Derek to say something. Finally wearing him down, Derek started talking to him. He even got Derek to laugh once.

Derek stopped. He looked around then motioned to Jared. "This is the place. Act as natural as possible. Just pretend we're taking a break."

People were watching them. Jared's hand shook as he put down his bag. He sat on the ground, took out some paper and pretended to work, keeping a cautious eye out for any sign of trouble.

#

Noticing Derek becoming anxious, Jared looked at his watch. They had been waiting for over an hour. "Are you sure this is the spot?"

"I checked and rechecked. This is it. I don't know why he's not here."

The small group of people a couple buildings down was growing in size. They seemed interested in what he and Derek were doing. "Maybe we should go back to the hotel and figure out what to do."

"Yeah, we probably should."

Jared gathered his things as Derek kept watch. He was about to tell Derek he was ready to go when a small white car pulled up. An older man got out and pushed them aside as he ran to the door of the house right behind where they were standing. He looked around as he unlocked it then rushed inside. He motioned for them to follow.

Derek put himself in front of Jared. "Stay right behind me." He stepped in the house, looked around then pulled Jared in.

Heart racing, Jared took a position near the window where he could watch what was going on outside. He jumped when the old man yelled at him.

Derek pulled Jared further into the room. "He says to get down and stay out of the window." Jared didn't question. He slid to the corner and sat on the floor watching as Derek engaged the man in conversation.

Why didn't I pay more attention when Derek was trying to teach me? I have no idea what is going on around me. This is awful! Peeking out the corner of the window, he watched the driver of the white car. He shifted in his seat, keeping watch ahead of him and in all the mirrors.

The old man shook Derek's hand and ran out the door.

"What's going on?" Jared grabbed Derek's arm.

"Mr. Nehme arranged for us to get into Iraq. We're supposed to wait here until he comes back."

"Seriously? Can we trust him?" Jared searched his eyes, holding onto him.

"Trust me. It'll be fine." Derek pulled him in and gave him a quick kiss. He smiled.

"I trust you." Needing to feel safe, Jared wrapped Derek's arms around him tighter.

#

Jared watched Derek pacing back and forth, sensing he didn't like how long it was taking for Mr. Nehme to come back. Every time there was a strange noise, Derek would run to stand in front of him. He reached out, touching Derek's arm. "We'll be fine."

"I know." Derek gave a reassuring smile.

THE VIEW FROM A RUSTY TRAIN CAR

Deciding he needed to do something to pass the time, Jared opened his backpack and took out his notebook, making notes about everything that had happened so far. "If we live through this, it's going to be a damned good story!" He chuckled to himself. A few more minutes had passed when Jared heard the sound of a vehicle come to a stop outside.

Derek ran to the door and stood to the side. He looked at Jared and motioned for him to stay quiet.

There was a quick knock and the door flew open. Mr. Neheme checked outside then closed it.

After a brief conversation, Derek patted Mr. Nehme on the shoulder. "Time to go!" He motioned for Jared to follow.

Mr. Nehme cracked the door and peered out. Jared stood beside Derek, holding on to the back of his shirt.

"When the door opens, run!" Derek reached around and grabbed his hand. Before Jared could ask what was happening, Mr. Nehme threw the door open. Derek pulled Jared out the door. "Run to the truck and jump in the back as fast as you can. Okay? Go!" He pushed Jared forward.

Glancing over his shoulder, Jared watched as Mr. Nehme and Derek followed. He ran as fast as he could. Approaching the truck, he wanted to look back again to make sure Derek was still there, but he could hear Derek telling him to keep going. At the rear of the truck, someone appeared from the back. He reached down, pulling Jared in. The truck started to move. Looking over the end-gate, he saw Derek and Mr. Nehme say a few words and shake hands again. His heart raced as Derek got further away. "Derek!"

Derek ran after them, waving his arms.

"Stop!" Jared knocked on the back window of the truck cab. "Not yet! Wait!"

The truck slowed and Derek caught up. Jared reached down, trying to pull him up. A couple other men helped to get him inside.

Slamming against the floor of the truck, Derek rolled over, trying to catch his breath.

"Are you all right? Are you hurt?" Jared knelt beside him, checking him over.

"I think so." Derek chuckled, looking into Jared's face.

"You scared the hell out of me!" Jared shoved Derek then turned away. He sat looking out the back of the truck.

"I'm sorry!" Derek sat next to him. "I didn't mean to make you worry. Are you okay? You seem scared."

"Of course I'm scared. I have no idea what's going on. What aren't you telling me?" Jared watched as a hundred thoughts seem to run through Derek's head.

"These guys can get us as far as Basra. After that, we're on our own." Derek looked down at the floor.

"Then what?"

"I don't know. I'll think of something."

Jared moved away from him. His stomach fluttered as he thought of what might lie ahead. *What did Mr. Nehme say to him?* He didn't understand what had been said, but he knew something was wrong. Mr. Nehme didn't seem to want them to go.

Derek dragged a blanket that he'd found and put it over Jared. He reached over and held on to his hand. "Get some sleep. We have a lot to do." He leaned his head back and closed his eyes.

Staring at Derek's face, Jared sighed. "You'll figure it out. I know you will." The urge to sleep was taking over. He couldn't fight it any longer. It had been a long couple of days. He leaned against Derek. Closing his eyes, he listened to the hum of the truck moving down the road until it lulled him to sleep.

LION OF THE DESERT

Derek looked around the back of the truck. Everyone else was asleep. He wished he could sleep as well, but Mr. Nehme's words kept replaying in his mind. "Go home. You don't want to do this. I cannot guarantee your safety."

Jared moaned and twitched in his sleep. Derek put a hand on him, feeling guilty about not telling him or giving him the option to walk away. He was so caught up in the moment that he didn't think about it. The adrenaline had kept him going. Now he potentially was putting both of their lives in peril. *I should've sent you home as soon as I knew what was happening. I'll never forgive myself if something happens to you.*

The truck jerked a few times as it slowed down. Derek braced himself.

Once stopped, Derek watched the others, noticing they looked worried. They said nothing. He pushed Jared's arm to wake him, motioning for him to stay quiet.

There was some yelling that came from somewhere in front of the truck. Jared moved close to Derek.

A loud commanding voice came closer. Derek moved to shield Jared. Men in uniforms with guns drawn stood looking in at them. A large man in a decorated uniform walked to the back of the truck and yelled.

Derek understood. They were being ordered to exit the truck. Turning to Jared, he whispered to him. "I'm so sorry." He gazed into his eyes and caressed his cheek before following the others out.

Jared followed behind him, eyes wide. He stuck close to Derek. Outside the truck, Derek looked at their fellow passengers who were standing in a line with their hands behind their heads.

One of the uniformed men used his rifle to shove him toward the end of the line. He looked back to see the same happening to Jared. He was sickened seeing the horrified look on Jared's face, but he was relieved they wouldn't be separated.

Taking his place in line, he saw the driver's door of the truck was open. A man was lying on the ground with a soldier standing over him, holding a gun to his head.

Jared shook as he looked around. His eyes locked with Derek's, fighting to hold back tears.

Ashamed, Derek looked away. *Please, God. I'll do anything. Don't let them hurt him.* He looked up as the man in charge yelled more orders. Glancing at Jared, he winked and turned to the left as instructed, hoping Jared would follow his lead. One of the soldiers walked up to Derek and screamed in his face. His heart raced, searching for the right words, trying to answer.

The butt of the soldier's rifle hit hard into Derek's stomach. He collapsed onto his knees gasping for breath. Jared was reaching out to him. He yelled. "No! I'm fine." He looked away when a tear fell down Jared's cheek as he got back in line.

Two of the soldiers pulled Derek back to his feet. The man in charge stood in front of Jared. Laughing, he mumbled something to the soldier beside him then pushed Jared backward. "Americans."

The leader yelled more orders. The soldiers pushed the people in the front of the line to start moving toward the trucks that surrounded them.

Derek stared at the back of Jared's head. "If you can hear me, just do what they want you to do. You'll be fine." He got no response. Once at a truck, he watched as they grabbed Jared and turned him. Derek mouthed an 'I love you'. Jared's face disappeared as a hood was thrown over his head. After tying his hands and feet they threw Jared into the truck.

Fists clenched, Derek fought the urge to run to him. *It won't do either of us any good.* He stepped forward then turned around. The sound of a gunshot echoed. "No, God!" He watched as a soldier walked away from the driver's side of the truck they had been in. Behind him laid the man on the ground, now covered in blood. Everything went black. He felt the ropes dig into his wrists then the force of being thrown into the back of the truck. Once he felt they were moving he called out to Jared. "Where are you? Are you all right?" Tears filled his eyes. There was no response. He fought to get the restraints off, but it was no use. There was nothing left to do, but pray for both of them.

DeeJay Arens

THE MAN THAT GOT AWAY

The picture on the TV blinked. Luke was crouched behind it trying to connect the new cable box. He held a knotted jumble of cables.

"Be careful. You're going to electrocute yourself." Megan stood above him holding a flashlight.

"Just hold the light still. I can't see!"

"Sorry." Megan looked at the piles of wires lying around the room. "How many wires does it take to do this?"

"Where the hell is that cable for the VCR? I just had it." Luke slammed his hand against the wall. "Sorry." He'd been at it for an hour. "It's that damned new medication. I can't concentrate on anything!"

"I don't see it."

Luke popped his head up over the back of the TV and looked at the floor. About to crawl out from behind, he raised an eyebrow at Megan.

"What?"

"You don't see it?" Luke grabbed the cable from her hand. "Oops."

"All right! Television will be up and running in moments!"

"Can I be done now?"

Luke sighed. "Fine. Thank you. You've been a lot of help."

"I'm sorry!" Megan put the flashlight on top of the TV. "I'm going to go warm up something for lunch." She kicked a path through the cords and went into the kitchen.

After plugging in the last wire, he crawled out. The screen was blinking on and off. He wiggled a wire and the picture stayed on. "We have lift-off." He pushed the TV against the wall, sat on the couch, and put his feet on the coffee table. Flipping through the channels, he tried to find something both he and Megan would like. He stopped on a station showing 'Star Wars'. *Jed's favorite movie.* He chuckled remembering all the times he was forced to watch it.

The phone rang. "I've got it," Megan called from the kitchen.

Reaching to the magazine rack by the rocking chair, Luke pulled out an issue of *Time*. The dog-eared page opened right to the spot he wanted. He stroked the picture of Jared by his article. Megan was so happy when she brought it home. It was just the thing he needed; Jared was alive and well. He got to see him again. *Damn I miss you.* Touching the photo once more, he closed the magazine and put it on the coffee table.

Luke flipped through more channels, stopping on CNN. He'd catch up on news until Megan came to pick something to watch. The piles of wires seemed to stare at him. He decided to put them back into their storage container.

"Breaking news just in to the CNN News Center." The television blared. "We've just received word that two American journalists have been taken hostage inside Iraq." Luke glanced at the TV as he tried untangling the wires.

"We've learned the two are free-lance journalists who had recently been published in *Time Magazine*. CNN called *Time* for more information. Gerard Campbell, a spokesperson for the magazine, confirms that *Time* had been contacted by a rebel group in Iraq that claims to have helped the two American's get inside the Iraqi border. They told *Time* that the vehicle used in trying to smuggle them into the country had been stopped by the Iraqi military. Those on board have either been killed or taken prisoner.

Luke threw the wires down, shaking his head. "They invented these as torture. I swear!" He sat on the couch and was about to turn the channel.

"*Time* has confirmed the identity of the two journalists as photojournalist Derek Carson and journalist Jared Montgomery."

The remote fell from Luke's hand as Jared's face filled the screen with his name underneath. He had a hard time breathing as he walked to the screen and knelt down. "No. It can't be. He's in Seattle!"

"At this moment, their condition is unknown. The University of Washington has released a statement saying, 'Derek Carson and Jared Montgomery are recent graduates from their journalism program'. They go on to say, 'that the hearts and prayers of all the faculty, staff, and students are with them and their families'. Stay tuned to CNN for updates."

"Megan!" Luke ran to the kitchen and found Megan sitting against the wall with the phone in her hand. She stared at the floor; her eyes swollen and red.

"It's Jared... he's..." She choked on the words.

Luke ran to her and held her in his arms. "I know. It's on the news."

"That was Mom. Their phone is ringing non-stop. Everyone's calling them. They keep waiting for word. Mom's beside herself." Megan tried to stand. "She's hysterical."

"Let's go. We have to get over there, in case they hear anything."

Megan nodded, grabbing his arm. Luke pushed her out the door and to the car. He held her hand as he drove. "He's going to be fine." The car hadn't come to a full stop before she jumped out and ran to the door. Candace met her, throwing her arms around her, crying.

THE VIEW FROM A RUSTY TRAIN CAR

Feeling his chest tighten, Luke leaned against the car trying to fight it. He took deep breaths and massaged his chest. *Not today. I have to be strong. Jed needs me.*

#

Luke sat at Candace and Michael's dining room table, picking at the food on his plate. He looked around the table; everyone else was as disinterested in the food as he was. No one said a word. Two days had passed since they'd heard Jared had been taken hostage. Luke hadn't left their house, waiting for any word that might come.

When the TV changed back to the news, Candace leaned her head to listen, praying for more information.

Mike looked up at Candace, breaking the silence. "You should eat. You need to keep your strength up."

"I'm fine." Candace didn't look at him.

"Can I get you anything?" Mike touched her arm.

"No. Just leave me alone, thank you." She pulled it away, placing it in her lap.

Throwing down his fork, Mike stared at her. "I know you're upset, but there is no reason to take it out on me. I'm worried about him too!"

Candace pushed away from the table "No reason to take it out on you?" She pointed her finger in his face. "I have every reason to be upset with you. You did this! You're the reason he left. You're the reason he won't talk to any of us." She trembled; her voice wavered. "I will never forgive you if anything happens to him. Never!" She stormed out the patio door.

Megan jumped up to follow her, but Luke stopped her. "Let me go. I'll talk to her." He stood beside his mother-in-law, leaned against the railing and looked around the neighborhood.

Candace wrapped her arm around his. "I can still see you and Jared running around in the yard, laughing and playing. He was always so happy when he was with you." A tear rolled down her cheek.

"We had a lot of great times." Luke looked toward the corner of the fence. "I miss him, Mom. I love him, you know."

"I know." Candace touched Luke's face. "I never had to worry about him when you two were together. You took such good care of him."

Luke froze; his words to Jared echoing in his mind. *I'll always take care of you.* He shook, holding her hand. "I shouldn't have let him go... from the wedding... I should've talked to him."

"You can't blame yourself, Luke. It wasn't your fault." She looked over her shoulder into the kitchen. "I was so angry at Mike I could barely speak to him. I know he was upset about what Jared did at the wedding... we all were, but he shouldn't have yelled at him like that. He shouldn't have told him that he wasn't wanted; not after what happened earlier." She grabbed Luke's shoulders. "Why, Luke? Why did he have to go over there? I just don't understand it." Candace held onto him. "No matter what... or who he is, I still love him. He's still my little boy."

Luke rested his chin on her head. "He'll come back to us. I promise. We'll figure something out."

"Are you guys all right?" Megan poked her head out the door.

Candace pulled away, wiping tears from her face. "We're fine. We were just talking about Jared."

"Why don't you go lay down for a while. Get some rest." Luke took Candace's arm, leading her to the door. She gave him a kiss on the cheek then went inside.

Megan reached her arm around Luke. "How are you feeling? It's been a long week."

"Megan, I've got to go." Luke stared in her eyes.

"I'm tired too. I'll get our stuff." She turned toward the door, but Luke stopped her.

"No. I mean I'm going to Iraq. I've got to find him."

THE VIEW FROM A RUSTY TRAIN CAR

Megan chuckled. "Come on. Let's go in."

He grabbed her arms. "Megan, I'm serious. I'm going to call the airlines. I can't just sit around here waiting while they're doing God knows what."

"Luke, be serious! Where are you going to go? No one knows where he is." Megan grabbed his face and held it. "I know this is driving you crazy and you want to do something, but think about this. Even if you knew where he was, what would you do? Just march in there and take him? You couldn't go in your condition, anyway. You can't fly with your heart the way it is. We just have to wait... and pray."

The door to the patio flew open. Candace called out to them. "Luke! Megan! Get in here! There's news about Jared. Hurry!"

Running into the living room, Luke saw Mike sitting in his chair staring at the television. "What's going on? What is it?"

Megan sat beside her mother, holding her hands.

"There's word about Jared." Mike grabbed the remote, turning up the volume as the commercial ended.

"We have new information on the missing American journalists being held hostage in Iraq."

Luke shifted in his seat, finding it hard to breathe. He couldn't take his eyes off the TV.

The news anchor continued, "CNN has just received a video from the group claiming responsibility for the kidnapping."

Video of Jared and Derek appeared on TV. They knelt with their hands tied behind their backs. Two men with masks held guns to their heads. The subtitles showed the soldiers questioning them about being American spies.

"Oh, my God. He looks awful!" Candace held a hand to her mouth.

Luke studied Jared, fighting the urge to blink. *Give me a sign, Jed. Let me know you're okay.* He couldn't help the smile that formed on his face, watching Jared stare forward, refusing to answer their questions.

"He must be so scared!" Megan held onto her mom, staring at the video.

"He has to be, but look at him... he's not showing it to them." A tear ran down Luke's face. "That's my boy," he whispered.

Candace screamed out, watching Jared being forcibly dragged into another room.

"No, no, no!" Luke ran to the TV as Jared disappeared from view. A scream could be heard off camera as the video ended.

Luke looked away, shaking at the pain in Jared's voice. "Why?" He kicked the chair, knocking the table over. Looking around the room, he tried to say something, but all he wanted to do was scream. He ran out the front door, began pacing in the driveway. *No, no. He's all right. He has to be. I need him.* Shaking his head, he walked down the road. The video replayed in his mind. *Why did you do this, Jed! What the hell is wrong with you, putting yourself in that situation?*

Something nagged at him about the video. He went back into the house to see it again, sure it was replaying ad nauseum. Mike hadn't moved since the video came on. He remained in the same spot, staring at the television.

The video repeated, Luke studying every moment. His eye was drawn to the other guy, Derek, watching his reaction as Jared was being dragged off. Derek reached to Jared, mouthing something. Moving closer to the TV, he watched his lips. This time he understood it.

"I love you."

What? Luke felt his fists clench. *No wonder they're there together.* He took a deep breath. *Come on, Luke. This is about Jared.* His mind turned back to the video and Jared being dragged off, imagining the horrible things he must've gone through to make him scream like that. *He's dead.* A sob threatened. He shook his head. *No! He's tough. He'll survive. We just have to get him home.* Tears burned the corner of his eyes. *Before it's too late.*

THE VIEW FROM A RUSTY TRAIN CAR

STONE PILLOW

Jared awoke with a pounding headache. The open sores on his face burned and the bruises all over his body made him cringe when he moved. He opened his eyes, but couldn't focus. The room was dark, damp and cold. He tried to sit up but fell backwards; his feet were still bound. He rolled onto his side and saw the shadowy figure of a person laying a little way from him. "Derek? Is that you?" The figure jerked then rolled to him.

"Oh, Baby! You're alive! Oh, thank God. I was so scared." Derek leaned over him, struggling to touch him, arms and legs still tied. He gazed at Jared's face then turned away, crying.

"Derek? Where did you go?"

"I'm here." Derek's voice broke. "This is my fault. What they did to you... I... I dragged you into this."

"What are you talking about? I knew what I was getting into. I knew there could be trouble." Jared tried to move closer to him.

"This didn't have to happen. I didn't tell you everything. I didn't give you a choice."

"Stop! Just stop! We don't have time for this right now. We have to figure out what to do."

Through his pain, Jared crawled to the front of the cell then leaned his back against the bars. He wrapped his fingers around them, shaking the door.

"It's no use. I've tried everything."

"How long was I out?"

"For hours." Derek slid over to him, voice breaking. "I thought they took you away to kill you. You have no idea how happy I was to see you lying there, but when I couldn't get you to respond, I..."

"Now I remember. They took me to a room. The first couple hits hurt, but then I went numb. I remember feeling a horrible pain on the back of my head before everything went black."

Derek leaned against him, snuggling his head into his neck. "I'm so sorry! I wish it would've been me." He sobbed. "They just made me sit and listen to it. I wanted to die hearing you scream. I tried, but I couldn't get to you."

Jared rested his head on Derek's. "It's all right. I'm okay." He chuckled. "Hey! At least I got some good sleep for once."

Voices came from outside, getting closer. They struggled to the back of the cell. Derek positioned himself in front of Jared. Five uniformed men approached.

"Americans."

The cell door opened and the leader walked up to them. Jared stared at the floor. The leader pointed at Derek. Two guards ran to either side of him, grabbing his arms. Pushing Jared against the floor, they lifted Derek to his feet and dragged him to the front of the cell.

The jagged edge of the floor dug into Jared's cheek. He looked up, watching as Derek was questioned.

Derek tried to answer, tripping over his words. They laughed and mocked him. The leader mumbled something to the soldiers on his left.

"Jared! Turn your head away. Don't watch!" Fear sparked in Derek's words.

THE VIEW FROM A RUSTY TRAIN CAR

One of them hit Derek in the stomach with the butt of his gun. Jared looked away as he fell to the ground. Derek coughed, struggling to catch his breath then screamed in pain.

"Stop it! Leave him alone!" Closing his eyes, Jared buried his face, muffling the sound of Derek's cries.

All went quiet. Smirks on their face, the soldiers stared at Jared. He wriggled over, throwing his body over Derek. Laying his head on Derek's chest, he closed his eyes. His body tensed, preparing for them to start in on him.

"Faggots." The men laughed, taunting them.

A chill ran through Jared. *We're not going to make it out of this.* He looked at Derek's face. There was no response. His attention turned to the soldiers, hearing footsteps coming close to them. *Come on, Jared. If you're going to die, go out with a fight.* Jared prepared to lunge at the closest one.

Sounds of gun fire and explosions echoed through the cell. The soldiers ran as frantic voices called out from their radios.

Once the voices disappeared, Jared tried to rouse Derek. Turning him onto his side, a pool of blood trickled toward Jared. He whispered in Derek's ear. "Come on. You can do it. Wake up! Don't do this to me. Please, wake up."

The noises outside escalated, followed by another large explosion. Jared lay across Derek's body as the building shook. He made his way to the small window, watching flashes of gunfire coming from all directions. The street was filled with smoke. People were running to take cover from the shelling.

A thundering sound in the sky made Jared look up. A helicopter stamped with USMC appeared through the smoke, landing a few blocks from them. "They've come for us!"

Derek's body twitched. He tried to speak.

Forgetting about the ropes around his arms and legs, Jared tried to run to him, but fell to the floor. The bruises still fresh, he shook as pains radiated throughout his body. He reached up to massage his throbbing arm. The frayed rope that had been around his wrists was lying on the floor. He untied his feet and ran to Derek, freeing his legs. Derek's eyes opened. He tried to sit up, but Jared pushed him back down. "Just relax. Lay down. Are you okay to roll onto your side?" Derek nodded, trying to turn himself over. Once he saw Derek's hands, he untied them. He helped roll him onto his back again. "We're going to be all right. Help is here."

Derek blinked, grabbing the back of his head. Looking at the blood on his hands, he chuckled. "That's going to leave a mark."

"Do you think you can get up and walk? We have to get outside. There's an American helicopter out there. I think it's looking for us." Jared grabbed his face, looking him in the eyes.

"Well, let's get the hell out of here." Derek struggled to get to his feet; he fell to his side.

Jared caught him, wrapping Derek's arm around his neck. "Just lean on me. We'll make it." The pressure of Derek's body against him intensified his own pain.

"Wait. How are we going to get out of the cell?"

A small push with Jared's foot opened the door. "They were in a hurry." He helped Derek down the hall and through the main door. Peeking around every corner, Jared was sure they'd run into some trouble, but the place seemed deserted.

They were at the stairs. Jared leaned Derek against the railing, needing to take the pressure off his own injuries. Limping, he went on ahead, checking if the coast was clear. The building shook again; the explosions were getting closer.

Jared helped Derek down the last set of stairs. He made Derek sit as he went to the front door. Opening it, he stuck his head outside. The gunfire and explosions were deafening. "Where the hell are we going?" He ran to Derek. Sitting beside him, Jared held his hand. "I don't know what to do next."

"I don't either."

Jared found a small room on the back side of the building. It had a couple chairs and a window. "We should be safe here for a minute." He ran his hand through his hair, looked around. "I have to take a minute. We need to figure out what to do."

He ran back to Derek, helped him to stand. Together they hurried around the stairs and down the small hallway. "We just have to go a little farther. Okay? I need to sit and think." There was another explosion, throwing Jared across the room. Pieces of building fell around them, dust swirling. He lifted his head, looking around for Derek. There was loud crashing sound above them as a beam fell from the ceiling, landing on top of Jared. Smoke and dust swirled, filling their lungs.

"Jared, no!"

Jared turned towards the voice to see Derek attempt to push himself up, choking, coughing, shielding himself from the rubble that continued to fall.

The building shook again. Jared felt a sharp blow to his head. He looked to Derek, getting one last glimpse through the haze, before the building fell down around them.

FREE YOURSELF

The rubble weighed down, pushing against Derek's chest. His legs were pinned under a large chunk of cement. *How long have I been here?* The pain was intense. He'd spent all his energy trying to free his legs. Mouth parched, his voice was sore from calling out to Jared. He never responded. *If he's dead, God, please take me too. I won't be able to live with myself.* Head back, he closed his eyes, trying to relax into death. His eyes popped open, hearing a large rumble. It vibrated through his chest. "Whatever it is, it has to be close." The sound stopped. Frustrated and worn out, he closed his eyes. A distant voice called out. Someone was calling his name and he spoke in English. Dust fell from above.

"Is anyone there?"

The sound of footsteps grew louder, stopping above him. "We are United States soldiers. If you can, please identify yourself."

Derek yelled with all of the strength he had left. "My name's Derek Carson. I'm an American journalist."

"We've been looking for you, Mr. Carson. We'll get you out of there! Are you all right?"

"Thank you." The sound of friendly voices caused his voice to break. "I'll be fine, but what about Jared? Have you found him?"

"No. Was he near you when the building collapsed?"

"Yes!" Derek tried to clear his head. "He was right by me, but the explosion threw him. I think about twenty feet or so away from me!"

The sounds grew intense above him. "We'll find him. Don't worry. Just save your strength. It'll be a while before we get to you."

Exhausted, Derek closed his eyes, but the pictures of Jared being buried under the rubble wouldn't leave him.

#

A light shined in Derek's eyes, waking him. As his eyes adjusted, he saw a hole above him getting wider then a face looking down at him with a smile.

"Mr. Carson, I presume?"

A canteen was lowered down. Parched, he took several long swallows, draining it in seconds.

Once the hole was large enough, a medic crawled down, giving Derek a quick exam. He put the equipment back into his bag and gave a thumbs up to the others watching from above. Another soldier was lowered down. They worked to remove the cement lying across Derek.

As it was lifted from his legs, Derek clenched his jaw to muffle a scream as the feeling came back. He took some deep breaths and the pain lessened.

The soldiers tied rope to a board then helped Derek onto it. It slowly moved toward the surface.

Sunlight hit his eyes, causing Derek to blink. When they adjusted, he looked around at what used to be a building, but was now leveled. Noticing another hole in the rubble about twenty feet away, he grabbed the medic's arm and pointed. "Jared? You found him?"

"Yes, we found him."

"Is he all right? Where is he?" Derek sat up, anxious to see Jared's face.

"He's with the medical team outside." The medic turned Derek's head. "By the looks of this gash, we'd better get you out there as well!"

The medics took Derek into the street. Soldiers were stationed down it and on the tops of buildings. One of them waved down to the medics as a helicopter came from over the building. It landed near another one on the road. The medics rushed Derek to it.

The men at the other helicopter were hunched over, frantically working. One of them jumped out, running toward Derek.

Jared's lifeless body lay on a stretcher; machines and tubes ran from every part of his body.

They strapped Derek's stretcher down, preparing for flight. He clutched the sleeve of the medic who'd come from Jared. "How is he? Is he all right?"

The medic looked down at Derek, shaking his head. "They're doing their best, but he's critical. I'm sorry. It doesn't look good." He ran to the back, strapping himself in.

The helicopter lifted off. Derek watched as Jared's helicopter disappeared over the horizon. Tears welled up in his eyes. *Jared... I am so sorry! God, forgive me!*

WALKING ON BROKEN GLASS

The house was silent. Megan and Candace sat at the dining room table. They took turns looking at the phone, waiting for some word on Jared. It had been hours since someone from the State Department called, saying to expect some news.

Megan patted her mother's hand before going into the living room. She stared at Luke who lay asleep on the couch. Picking up a blanket, she placed it over him. She brushed the hair from his forehead. "Don't give up, Luke. Just hold on. You've got to keep fighting."

"I don't mean to bother you." Candace tiptoed into the room, taking a seat by Megan. She put her arms around her.

"Not at all. It's fine." Megan wiped tears away. "What is it? Have you heard anything? I didn't hear the phone ring."

"Nothing yet." Taking her arm, Candace took her back to the dining room, seating her at the table. "How is he? Has he said anything?"

"No, nothing, but I know he's not well. His eyes are dark and he's white as a sheet. I don't know what to do. He refuses to go to the doctor."

"Sweetie, he's worried. Once we hear Jared's safe, I know he'll feel better. We all will."

"I hope you're right." Megan stared out the patio door. She wiped away another tear. "I hate to say this, but if anything happens to Jared, he won't last long. I know that."

"We aren't going to think like that. Your brother is going to be fine and he'll be coming home." Candace held her. "Then Luke will be able to concentrate on getting better."

"God, I hope so. I can't lose both of them." Megan laid her head on Candace's shoulder. "If I knew then what I know now, I would've done things differently."

Candace pulled away, looking into her eyes. "What do you mean?"

"I don't know. I just wish things hadn't happened with Jared like they did. Luke hasn't been the same since he left." Megan looked at Luke asleep on the couch. "He should've been here. He should've been part of our lives."

"That's not your fault."

"I'm not so sure about that." Megan looked down at the floor, shaking her head. "I could have tried harder to find him. The truth is part of me didn't want to. I was scared."

Candace was about to say something as Mike ran into the room. "A car just pulled up and a guy in uniform just got out." She and Mike ran to the door. Megan followed and stood at the top of the stairs.

A man appeared at the window. Candace threw the door open. "Can we help you?"

"Yes, Ma'am. My name is Commander Johnston. I'm looking for Mr. and Mrs. Montgomery."

"That's us. Come in, Commander. Please." Candace walked him to the dining room. "Can I get you anything?"

"Coffee if you have some ready."

"Of course." She disappeared into the kitchen. "Megan, shouldn't you wake Luke?"

"I think I'll let him sleep." If it was bad news, she wanted to tell him her way. She looked back at the couch to see Luke sitting up.

"Is someone here? What's going on?" Luke struggled to stand.

"I was just coming to get you." Offering her hand, Megan helped him stand. "A Commander Johnston is here. He just sat down."

"Have they found him? Where is he?"

"He hasn't said anything yet." Megan struggled to keep him standing as he rushed as much as he was able. She got him to the dining room and into a chair. "My name is Megan. I'm Jared's sister. This is my husband, Luke."

"It's nice to meet you". The commander took a sip of coffee then sat back in his chair. He looked each of them in the eyes.

"So what's going on? Did you find him?" Luke stared at him. "Say something!"

"I'm sorry, Sir. We're all just beyond worried." Megan put her arm around Luke, caressing his arm.

"I completely understand. I'm sorry." Commander Johnston placed the cup on the table. "We received intelligence suggesting Mr. Montgomery and Mr. Carson were being held by a rogue Iraqi militant group in a small town just over the boarder of Kuwait. We devised a plan to send a special operations force in to confirm their whereabouts. They were to rescue them if at all possible."

Luke's face turned red. Megan could feel Luke's pulse race as he shifted in the chair.

"A member of the group was captured. He confirmed the hostages were being held in a building in town. With that information, we sent in backup and attempted to find them."

"What do you mean attempted?" Luke stood and slammed his hands on the table. "Did you find him or not?"

"Honey, calm down." Megan put her hand on his shoulder.

"I'm sorry." Luke took a deep breath, taking his seat. "Please, go ahead."

"We found the building and encountered some small arms fire. As we approached the building we saw it start to crumble."

Candace gasped, grabbing Mike's arm.

"They must have set explosives and detonated them as they ran. The Special Forces immediately searched the area and found Mr. Carson first. He told them where he'd last seen your son and they searched that area."

"I can't take this." Mike swallowed hard, looking down at the table. "Please tell us that you found him and that he's all right."

"We did find him. He and Mr. Carson were flown to our medical center in Germany."

"He's all right!" Candace cried, hugging Michael. "They found him. Oh thank you, God!"

"Did you hear that? He's fine. He'll be coming home." Megan held Luke's hand.

"Wait." Commander Johnston put up his hand. "We did find him, but I have to tell you that he is in very bad shape. Between the beatings from his captors, the explosion, and being buried under that building, he went through a lot. Believe me, they're doing everything they can, but I'm afraid it doesn't look very promising."

"Are you saying he's not going to make it?" A tear rolled down Mike's cheek.

"Like I said, they're doing everything they can. I'm sorry I can't give you better news." Commander Johnston stood. "I have to get back. I just wanted to tell you in person. I'll keep in touch with you. The hospital also has your phone number."

"Thank you for everything." Mike shook his hand, leading him to the stairs.

"Wait!" Candace stopped him. "What about Mr. Carson? How is he?"

"He's been treated for his injuries and he's expected to make a complete recovery. He's been through quite an ordeal as well. They were treated badly by their captors."

"That's wonderful. His parents must be so relieved." Candace sat, staring out the window.

"That's it." Luke pushed himself to his feet. "I'm going. We can't let him go through this alone. He needs me."

"You can't!" Megan grabbed his arm. "You know that."

"I'm going! He's not going to be alone!"

"Luke, Candace and I will get things in order and we'll go." Mike walked to the hallway.

"Mr. Montgomery, wait." Commander Johnston turned to him. "That is, of course, your decision. However, I will tell you that you may want to consider waiting to hear more. If he stabilizes enough, they may move him to the States."

"But that could take weeks, right?" Luke looked at Candace and Mike. "He'll be all alone for that entire time?"

"Actually, Mr. Carson is refusing to leave him. He insists that he won't leave until Jared leaves with him." The commander looked back at Candace and Mike. "Apparently, he and your son are... a couple?"

"We weren't aware of that." Candace looked at Megan.

Luke sat at the table staring off, his face revealing nothing.

"Thank you again. We should let you get going." Mike led the commander out of the room.

The phone rang. Candace ran to answer it. "Hello... Yes, this is Candace. Who is this?" She put her hand to her mouth, crying. "Derek. It's so good to hear your voice. How is he? How's Jared?"

Megan turned to talk to Luke, but he'd left the room. She found him in the living room putting on his shoes. "What are you doing? You going somewhere?"

"I'm going home. I need to take care of some things." Calling over his shoulder, Luke leaned against the railing. "Call me when you want to come home and I'll come get you."

"Wait. I'll come with you." Megan grabbed her purse.

"No. You stay with your parents. They need you." Luke kissed her before opening the door. "I just need some time alone."

Megan watched until the car pulled away, thinking about Luke's reaction to the news. *Well, there's no question now. You are in love with Jared.* She shook her head. *I thought finding out he was alive would help, but now you know he has someone. Just one more reason for you to give up, isn't it?* She sat on the couch, rested her head in her hands. *If Jared gets back in time, I'm going to make sure he comes home. He has to.* Megan wiped her tears as she lay down on the couch. *It might be Luke's only chance.*

THE VIEW FROM A RUSTY TRAIN CAR

ANOTHER MAN'S POISON

November 1999

Derek's footsteps echoed as he walked down the hall of the hospital in Germany. The weeks had been long as he sat at Jared's bedside hoping he'd wake up.

Derek grabbed a coffee and waved to the nurses. "Has the doctor been in to see him yet?"

One of them smiled. "Not yet."

"Good. I was hoping to catch him." The walk to Jared's room was the longest part of the day. "Come on, Jared. Please be awake." Derek looked down at him. No change. He dropped his bag on a chair, walked over to the window and opened the blinds.

"What in the...?" Jared's bag was on the night table with a note attached.

Mr. Montgomery,

We found this in the rubble of your 'hotel' and thought you might want it back. Please know that all of us are thinking of you and hoping for a full and speedy recovery.

Your friends,
#####Classified####

Amazed, Derek opened the bag and pulled out Jared's writing journal. He flipped through the pages, reading some of the entries. The last one was Jared writing about how terrified he was waiting for Mr. Nehme in the abandoned house.

Derek shook his head as his heart raced. The guilt often overwhelmed him. He opened the bag to put things away. He stopped when he saw a white envelope lying at the bottom under some other papers. Turning it over, he stopped breathing when he looked at the name on the return address. *Luke Morrison.* "Oh, my God. He didn't send it back." He inspected the letter; it was still unopened. He was startled when someone called his name. Throwing everything back in the bag, Derek looked to the door, but no one was there. His eyes moved to the bed. Jared's arm moved.

Opening his eyes, Jared looked up at him. "Hey." His voice was weak. "Can we go home now?"

"I can't believe it. I thought I'd lost you." Derek picked up his hand and kissed it. Tears ran down his cheeks as he stroked Jared's hair. "Can I get you anything? Wait! I'm going to get a nurse and tell them you're awake!"

"They know." Jared reached out to him. "They've been in to do tests, and poke and prod. Trust me; they know."

"How do you feel?" Derek pulled a chair to his bed.

Jared thought for a moment. "I feel like a building fell on me." He chuckled then winced. "My leg feels like it's in a million pieces." He clenched his teeth and closed his eyes.

Derek grabbed a pillow, trying to make him more comfortable. "I'm going to see if they can give you something." He turned to leave, but met a nurse at the door.

"How's everything in here?"

"He seems to be in quite a bit of pain. Can you give him anything?" Derek held his hand, unable to take his eyes off him.

"The doctor ordered something. We should be getting it soon." She checked the readouts on the machines, and recorded them. "The doctor will be in to see you soon. He's going to talk about getting you back home. He talked to your family and they're pretty anxious to see you."

"I don't want to see them. Keep them away." Jared clung to Derek's arm, a look of panic on his face.

"I'm sure they're worried sick. They just want to make sure you're all right."

"I don't care." Jared looked at the nurse. "Where are they sending me?"

"That's what the doctor wanted to talk to you about." The nurse put her hand on his arm. "Your parents want to move you close to home, but it's your decision." She smiled as she left the room.

"I'm not going back to them! I've got nothing to say to them. I want to go back to Seattle! " Jared squeezed Derek's hand. The heart monitor started to bounce up and down.

"Shh." Derek held him. "It's okay. They said it's your choice. Just relax. You don't have to do anything you don't want to."

Jared seemed to calm. His face showed that a million things were running through his mind.

Derek leaned in to him. "Jared? I think I better head home and get things ready. I'm sure Kelly and Chris are getting sick of watching our place." Derek caressed his arm. "It's going to be nice to be home, isn't it?"

Jared nodded. He squeezed Derek's hand. "I can't wait."

"I'm going to let you rest before the doctor comes in, okay?" Derek leaned down, kissing him on the forehead. "I'll be back in a little bit."

"Thank you for staying with me and taking care of me." A tear ran down Jared's cheek.

"I wouldn't leave you. I love you." Derek gave him one more kiss then grabbed his bag.

"Before you go can you do me a favor?"

"Of course. What is it?"

"I noticed my backpack sitting over there. I can't believe they found it! Could you bring it to me? I should make some more notes. We should have quite a story out of this."

"Sure." Derek clenched his teeth, thinking about the letter. *Maybe I can hide it. He'll think it got lost.* Holding the bag in his hand, he peered into it. The letter lay on top. He shook his head. *No. I can't do that to him. I just have to hope his not wanting to see his family also means Luke.* He handed it to Jared. "Don't work too hard. You need to relax and get better."

Taking one more look back, he watched as Jared went through the bag; the letter lay on his lap. "I love you."

Jared smiled, continuing to look in the bag.

Derek walked down the hall, making a mental checklist of everything he needed to get done so he could go home and get things ready for Jared's arrival. It was hard to think, knowing that letter was in Jared's hands. *You'll just have to deal with it as it comes. It's all up to him now.*

#

Mount Rainier stood tall in the distance. Jared took a deep breath, enjoying the familiar sights as they approached the apartment.

Derek jumped out of the car, opened the trunk, and ran up the stairs to the apartment.

A cold sweat formed on Jared's brow as he looked up the first flight of stairs. The permanent limp from the damage to his leg was a sure sign of what they'd been through.

"Give me your arm." Derek raced down the stairs.

"I'm not an invalid. I can do it!" Jared pushed his hand away. He held onto the railing, pulling his body. "Thank you. I'll be fine. It'll make me stronger." He touched Derek's cheek. "Go ahead and get the rest of the stuff from the car." He watched as Derek gathered their things. *You have to stop blaming him. You chose to go. You knew there would be risks.*

THE VIEW FROM A RUSTY TRAIN CAR

The letter from Luke lay folded in his pocket. *Why did I read it?* He shook his head, continuing to climb the stairs, unable to stop worrying about the tone of the letter. *What wrong choices is he talking about and why did he sound so depressed. Something's wrong. I know it.*

Derek caught up to Jared at the top of the stairs. Seeing how taxing the climb was becoming for Jared, he took his arm. Jared didn't fight him this time. He chuckled when the door opened and he saw a banner hanging from the ceiling. *Welcome Home.*

"It wasn't me. That was Chris and Kelly's idea." Derek disappeared into the bedroom with the luggage.

Jared struggled to the couch, collapsing onto it. Walking wasn't an issue. He was used to the limp. Stairs, however, were still a challenge. He looked around the room. A pile of mail lay on the coffee table. He picked it up.

"That's all yours. I'm still looking through mine. I'll help you if you want. I just didn't want to do anything with yours until you saw it all." Derek rushed around the apartment putting things away.

Jared raised an eyebrow, giving him a knowing look. He returned to the stack in his hand. There was familiar writing on one of the envelopes: *Mrs. Megan Morrison.* The postmark was from a week ago. *I have to know what's going on. I have to read it.* Looking over his shoulder, he quietly opened the letter. His heart raced as he read it. The letter fell to the table.

"Are you okay?" Derek put a hand on his shoulder.

"I've got to go." Jared pushed himself up. He looked at Derek. "Something's come up."

"No, you need to rest. I'll take care of it. What is it?"

Staring out the window, Jared straightened. "I'm going home. They need me."

Derek stopped him in the hallway. "Fine. I'm coming with you."

"No. I'm going alone."

"What? What's wrong?" Derek held his arm, but Jared pushed his way into the bedroom. Opening his suitcase, he dumped out the clothes. He grabbed an armful of fresh ones to replace them. His mind raced. There were even more questions now. He looked at Derek sitting on the couch staring at the envelope.

"Are you freakin' kidding me?" Derek threw it down. "You're just going to run to him after all this time? Forget about me. I'll understand, right?"

"I don't expect you to understand." Jared put his bags by the door.

Derek stood in front of him, finger pointed in his face. "You know what? Fine! Go. Just don't expect me to be here when you get back."

"I have to do this. There's something terribly wrong. They need me!" Jared touched his arm.

"You mean, 'he' needs you." Derek pulled his arm away.

"Yes! Maybe! So what? Does that make me a terrible person? He was my best-friend. Shouldn't that mean something?"

"Oh, I know exactly what it means." Derek chuckled. A sneer formed on his lips. "You show up, he breaks your heart and you come running back to Seattle." He walked away. "I've spent too much time picking up the pieces. I can't do it anymore. You know what you're getting yourself into. It's the same old shit... just another day. It's what Jared wants. The rest of us just have to deal with it."

"I need to do this! I'm sorry you don't get it. Things are different now!"

Derek sat on the couch, staring at the floor. "I do get it. I don't mean a damn thing to you." He shook his head. "I knew this would happen. He's sick so you have to run to the rescue."

"That's not it!" Jared stared at him. "Wait! How did you know he was sick? I never said anything about him being sick."

"Shit." Derek put his head in his hand and leaned against his knee. "Your mom told me. I called them while you were in the hospital."

"You had no right to do that!"

"They deserved to know what was going on."

Jared shook as anger coursed through him. "And you didn't think I'd want to know about Luke? I can't believe you!" He grabbed his bags and opened the door then stopped to slam his fist against it. He turned slowly toward Derek. "You know what? You're right. This is it. Pack up your things and get the hell out. Don't be here when I come back." Slamming the door, he heard Derek scream at him and start to sob. He fought the urge to run back in. *No. It's over. Just let go.* He struggled with his luggage down the hall. *This is the right thing to do. You need to know.*

DeeJay Arens

REFLECTIONS

The ticking of the clock was the only noise in Luke's room. He lay in bed, staring at the wall, thinking about what needed to be done before the next surgery. *I don't even know why I'm doing it. It never works.* He looked at Megan's picture. *You're doing it for her. She won't let you quit.* He wiped a tear away. *She'd be better off if I wasn't here.* His thoughts turned to Jared's smile as they ran to the train car. *Well, Jed. I don't have much time left. I'm getting tired. I'm glad you don't have to watch me go through this, but I'd give anything to see you one more time.*

"Hi, you. How are you feeling?" Megan placed a tray of food on the stand next to him. She sat on the bed, looking into his face.

"You know... the same old story." Luke forced a smile. "Thanks for the food, but I'm really not hungry."

"Okay. Can I get you anything?"

Luke shook his head. "No. You do enough. I'm fine."

"Luke, listen." Megan held his hand. "I know we agreed to leave Jared alone, but I wrote him again. This time I told him some things and asked if he would come home. He probably won't read it anyway, but I had to try." She smiled as tears ran down her face. "I know how much you want to see him."

Luke was unable to hold back his tears. "I do."

"I didn't want to tell you because I didn't want to get your hopes up. I guess I just wanted you to know that... I know you love him."

"Thank you. I promise... I won't get my hopes up." Luke grabbed her hand. "Thank you for trying. You are an amazing woman. I do love you, for whatever it's worth."

Megan kissed him on the cheek. "I know you do. I love you too." At the door, she turned back to him. "I wish I could fix everything. You deserve a much happier life. I'm sorry."

"Stop it. I'm the one who should apologize. You shouldn't have to go through this."

Megan smiled, leaning her head against the door frame. "Promise me, if you can, that you'll keep fighting. I know you're tired and worn out. I can see that, but I promise you, when you're better, we'll figure things out. You can still be happy." The phone rang. Megan left to answer it.

Stunned, Luke couldn't speak. *What did she mean?* Hearing Megan pick-up the phone, his stomach tensed into a knot, assuming it was the doctor calling to give final instructions.

"Hello!" He heard Megan gasp, tears filling her voice. "Jared? Oh, God. It's so good to hear your voice."

Luke's heart raced. *It can't be. Is he coming home?* Wiping the tears from his face, he started to cry. *It's too much to hope for.*

DeeJay Arens

I DON'T WANT TO SAY GOODBYE

Luke was hooked up to monitors and IV's. He checked the clock. It had been hours since they thought Jared might show up. *He's not coming. I should've known better.*

Megan appeared in the doorway, watching as the medical team finished up. She walked to Luke and kissed him on the forehead. "How are you feeling?"

"Fine."

"Is there anything I can get you?"

"Stop worrying."

Megan sat on a chair next to his bed. She picked up his hand, stroking it. "I talked to the doctor. He says they're ready for just about anything. There's a good chance this is going to work. Maybe even better than they hoped."

Luke squeezed her. "Is there any word from...?"

"Nothing new. I left a message, but I haven't heard anything. I wish I could tell you he was on his way, but I just don't know."

"I knew he wouldn't come." Luke turned his face away from her, dabbed at his eye quickly. "Where's my bag? Have you seen it?"

Megan got off her chair to help search. She went to the pile of Luke's clothes that were lying in the corner. Moving them aside, she pulled his bag out. "It's right here."

Luke took the bag from her then rummaged inside. He pulled out an envelope and handed it to her. "Whatever happens I want you to get this to Jared. If he gets here, I'll give it to him, but if anything happens to me, promise me that you will get it to him."

"Stop talking like that..."

"Please. Just promise."

"Okay. I promise." Tears streamed down her face as she took the envelope from him.

Taking out another one, Luke put it in her hand. "This is for you. If something happens to me in there, I want you to read it. If not we'll talk about it later. But... just in case."

"I don't need it. You're going to be fine. Now just relax." Megan sat down, looking at the letters in her hands.

A man in scrubs stood in the doorway. "Mr. Morrison, we'll be taking you down to surgery in a few minutes. Are you ready?"

Luke held Megan's hand. "I guess so."

"Don't worry. You're in good hands." The nurse patted his arm. "Mrs. Morrison, maybe you'd like to go to the waiting room at the end of the hall."

"I'll see you soon." Leaning over, Megan kissed him and stroked his cheek.

Luke forced a smile, until Megan was out of sight. As he watched the lights go by overhead, he took a deep breath. "Take care of her."

I WON'T BE THE ONE TO LET GO

"Hi. This is Jared Montgomery. Is my car ready?" Jared waited for the receptionist, hearing fingers type furiously on a keyboard. "A half an hour? Great. I'll see you then." He looked at his phone to see who had tried to call while he was talking. *You have one new message.* He pushed the buttons, checking the caller ID. *Lucas & Megan Morrison.* Taking a deep breath, he dialed his voicemail. The sound of his sister's voice made his heart race.

"Jared. Hi. It's Megan. I really hope you're on your way. He's been asking for you. He's ummm... he's getting prepped for surgery. We were going to hold off for a while, but he took another turn. The doctors told me they're trying to figure out what to do, but they can't promise anything." Her voice trembled. "I hope you can get here." The message paused. "I'm going to go check on him. When you get here, just ask for me. I've told the nurses that you might be coming. God, I hope so. I need you, Jared."

Tears welled up in his eyes. He'd told her that he'd try to get there, but couldn't make any promises.

"Jared, we love you." The message was over.

THE VIEW FROM A RUSTY TRAIN CAR

Jared hung up the phone, leaned back in his seat, dropping the phone into his lap. As he listened to the drone of his surroundings, his eyes closed, thinking of what lay ahead. He'd almost bought a ticket back to Seattle a couple hours ago. *Shit. Maybe Derek's right. I might be heading for trouble.* He did miss them, but after so much time he didn't know what to say. *It's too late. Time to face it.*

He gathered his things then followed the signs to the car rental desk.

#

A voice announced the next flight, waking Jared. He looked at his watch. It was time to pick-up his car. His stomach felt like it was strangling itself. His chest tightened and breathing accelerated. *Jared! Calm down!* He took a deep breath then approached the woman at the desk.

"Can I help you, Sir?"

"Yes." He swallowed the lump in his throat. "My name is Jared Montgomery. There's supposed to be a car ready for me."

"Let me check." She typed on her keyboard then fumbled around on the desk. "Yes. Here you are." She handed him some forms. "I just need you to fill these out for me."

Hands shaking, he tried to hide his nerves from her. He handed them back and got the keys. The car was parked outside the door. He put in his luggage. The sun was starting to set covering everything in red and pink. Hands grasped on the steering wheel, he started his journey home.

Everything looked surreal, as if it was frozen in time. There were small, immeasurable changes, both comforting and terrifying. His mind wandered, driving along the flat, desolate landscape. Autumn was in the air. In this part of the country, it was a beautiful time as leaves turned colors, bringing detail to an otherwise blank canvas.

The beauty of the landscape was often lost on Jared. He'd feel himself fall into depression, seeing everything start to die and knowing that winter was not far off.

Thoughts of Luke flooded his mind. Jared shook his head. His heart pounded, becoming more anxious about the reunion ahead. "It's fine. You'll know what to say when you see them."

He searched through the radio stations, hoping something would help keep his mind focused and, for at least a little while, off Luke. It was to no avail. "Damn it." Even the music seemed a reminder of how complicated his relationship with Luke had been.

Jared wiped the tears from his eyes, straightening up in his seat. His fingers tightened around the steering wheel seeing the sign ahead of him. 'Welcome to Sheldon'. His eyes darted around, soaking in everything he passed. He tried to remember who lived in which house and watched to see if the stores were still in business.

Though small, the hospital was the biggest building in town. Lights shone through the windows like beacons. His fingers tapped against the dash, now aware of how used to traffic and big cities he'd become. His hometown felt lonely. There wasn't the rush of cars or people everywhere he looked.

Jared pulled into a parking space. His hands shook as he reached for the door handle.

A strong smell hit him as he entered the hospital. His stomach felt queasy. The stench was a mix of medicine, antiseptic cleaners, urine, old ladies' perfume, and coffee that had been left too long on the burner. He cringed remembering his own stint in a hospital.

At the nurse's desk, his heart beat so hard he could feel it in his throat. "Excuse me. I'm looking for Lucas Morrison's room."

A small, broken voice called out from behind him. "Jared?"

His arms reached to Megan. Her face was soaked with tears. He threw his arms around his sister.

Megan cried, clutching to him. "I can't believe you're here. It's been so long." Pulling away, she looked him over then stared into his eyes. "You look great. Are you all right?"

"I'm fine. What about you? What's going on?"

A nurse interrupted them, tapping Megan on the shoulder. "You can wait in the bigger Family Room. It's a little quieter on the other end of the hall. That way you can visit." She swiped her tag, opening the large doors.

"Thanks, Betty." Megan took Jared's arm and followed her. She stopped, looking down at his leg. "Jared? You're limping. What's wrong?"

Jared shook his head, pulling her along. "It's nothing, just a little reminder of my vacation overseas. I'm fine. Don't worry about it."

The nurse motioned to a room.

Taking a seat, Jared watched Megan and the nurse, studying the knowing looks between them.

"Can I get either of you anything?" The nurse looked to them, a warm smile on her face.

"No, thank you. You've all been so great!" Megan gave her a quick hug before she left the room.

Jared pushed himself up and closed the door behind her. "Okay. What's going on? What's wrong?"

Megan poured herself a cup of coffee then sat on the couch. "Luke's in surgery. They had to try something. We're out of options unless they can find a donor. He needs more time."

"I'm not sure what's wrong. What kind of donor are they looking for?" Jared sat next to her, holding her hands. "If it's a kidney, they can check me. I might be what they're waiting for."

"Jared, no. It's..."

"I'm serious. I'm fine! I can get through that. I've been through worse." Jared chuckled. "Get the nurse. Have them test me!" He opened the door.

"It's his heart, Jared." Megan pulled him back to the couch. "The doctors can't even agree on what exactly is wrong. It's just failing."

"What do you mean? How can they not know what's wrong? Have they done all the tests?" Jared sat back on the couch, shaking as his mind soaked in the news. He jumped up and paced around the room. "We need to move him to the university hospital. They'll figure it out."

"Honey, he's been there. He's been to every heart specialist who would see him. They just don't know what's wrong." Megan walked over to him, touching his arm.

"I won't accept that!" Pushing her away, Jared walked to the window and put his hands on the sill. "Wait!" He turned back to her. "Seattle! We have some of the best doctors in the world. We'll take him there. They're good. I can attest to that. I'll take him. I'll take care of him."

"Jared! Listen to me." Megan took his hands and sat him on the couch. "Every specialist in the country has been looking at his charts. He's been tested and retested. He needs a new heart. It's that simple."

"Okay! What about a donor? There's got to be one out there somewhere. People die every day. One of them has to be a heart donor!"

"I pray every day, but, Jared, there's a long waiting list. People wait years. He doesn't have years. They're doing everything they can." Megan turned away to wipe her tears.

"I'm sorry. I'm such an ass." Jared took her in his arms. "I know you've done everything you could. This is just a lot to process."

"We've tried everything they could come up with."

"I know you have, Sweetheart." Jared chewed on his thumbnail, a million unanswered questions swirling in his mind. "How long is the surgery going to be? When do I get to see him?"

"We wanted to wait until you got here before he went in." Megan fumbled around in her pocket for a tissue. "He wanted to see you. He was so excited at the possibility that you were coming, but they said we couldn't wait any longer."

"I'm so sorry... I uhhh... I got tied up a couple times." Jared's face tightened, knowing he'd purposely stalled. Self-hatred consumed his thoughts. "Damn it! I should have gotten here sooner."

Megan leaned against his back, wrapping her arms around his waist. "We knew there was a chance you wouldn't get here before he went into surgery. We just hoped you'd come."

"How long has he been in there?"

"It's been about three hours. They said the surgery could be anywhere from four to eight. They had a basic plan going in, but wouldn't know exactly what they were going to run into once they started. All we can do is wait." She patted the seat beside her. "Maybe pray."

"Pray?" Chuckling, Jared shook his head. "I don't even know if I remember how to do that. Or if anyone up there even listens... or cares."

"You're here, aren't you?" Megan put her arm around him. "One of my prayers was answered. You've been through some unimaginable things. I know you couldn't have done that alone."

"Maybe you're right." Jared laughed.

"That reminds me. How's... it's Derek, right?" Megan put her head on his shoulder.

"He's... fine."

"So he's your boyfriend? Is that what we understand?"

"Well, he was, yes, but we had a fight. It's over. That's kind of the story of my whole love life." Realizing what he said, Jared pulled away. He forced a smile at her.

"I'm sorry."

"You should feel sorry for him." Jared laughed, raising an eyebrow. "He's been trying to put up with me for a few years now. We both know that's not an easy task. Poor bastard."

"Well, I'm sorry for both of you." Megan stared into his eyes. "I'm just glad you're here."

"I shouldn't have stayed away. If I knew what was happening, I swear I would've come home. How long has he been sick?"

"Since the wedding."

"What?"

"It all started the night of the wedding. We went to the hotel and I went to change. I came out and he was lying on the floor. Since then he's spent most of his time in bed or in the hospital."

"I had no idea."

"I tried to tell you. We all did."

"The letters." Jared put his head against the wall. "I'm such an idiot. I should've read them. I should've come home to help you."

"Jared, you're here now. That's all that matters. I still need you. Luke needs you." She gave him a gentle kiss on the cheek. "We'll get through this."

"We will. He's a tough guy. He'll beat this." Jared wondered if he was trying to convince her or himself.

"Yes he will." Megan checked her watch. "It could be a while. Do you need anything? Are you hungry?"

"Oh, God. No! I couldn't eat. Not until he's out of surgery."

Tugging at his loose-fitting sweater, Megan frowned. "You look like you haven't eaten in ages. You need to eat something."

"My stomach couldn't take it right now." He grimaced at the thought of hospital food.

"Well, I need to try to eat something. Do you want to come with me?" Megan grabbed her purse.

"You go ahead. I'm just going to sit here and maybe doze off for a second. It's been a long day. You could bring me a soda when you come back. Anything with a lot of caffeine."

Megan stopped at the door. "Oh! I almost forgot. Answer the phone if it rings. They'll call here with any updates on

Luke." She thought for a second. "Maybe I should wait here, too. I don't want to miss it if they should call."

"Go ahead. You said yourself that it's going to be a while and he's only been in there for a short time."

"But if something should happen, I..."

"I'll come and get you right away. Like you said, there's nothing we can do. I'll nap right beside the phone." Jared pointed to the door. "Now go."

Megan hesitated then smiled. "Fine. I'll be right back."

"See you soon." Jared kissed her on the forehead then pushed her out the door. He listened to her conversation with a nurse, explaining she was taking a break and that her brother was in the waiting room, ready to answer the phone if any news came from surgery. He watched her until she disappeared around the corner. He turned to the phone. "Please don't ring. Not until she gets back."

The room felt warm. He took off his sweater, sitting back on the couch. His leg was twitching. He tried to relax. As he lay down, the couch felt especially comfortable. His balled-up sweater served as a pillow. *Luke will be fine. I'll see him soon.* He thought about what he'd say to Luke when he did get to see him. *What does he look like if he's been sick so long?* Unable to stop the smile that formed on his face, he turned onto his side. *I don't care. I can't wait to see him. I'll help get him through this.* He closed his eyes, falling asleep to memories of Luke and the train car.

WHAT NOW, MY LOVE

The door opened, casting light across Jared's face. He rubbed his eyes as he sat up. "Megan? I'm sorry. I must've fallen asleep."

Without a word, she closed the door, standing with her back to her brother.

"How was supper? I can't imagine there was anything too edible." Jared stared at her, waiting for a response. "Megan? You okay?"

Megan turned to him, her face pale, emotion absent. Locking eyes with him, her face twisted as she gasped. She collapsed into Jared's arms.

"Meg? What is it?"

"He's gone, Jared." She shook, holding onto him. "He didn't make it through the surgery."

"No!" Jared sat her on the couch then paced, shaking. "No. It's not true." He fell against the wall, beating his fists against it. "They've made a mistake!"

Megan grabbed his arms. "No, Jared. It's true."

"No!" He pulled away from her, went to the window. His eyes focused on her reflection. "I want to see him! I won't believe it until I do."

THE VIEW FROM A RUSTY TRAIN CAR

Megan walked to him, wrapped her arms around him from behind. "He had a heart attack during the procedure. They couldn't revive him." She turned him, held his face. "It's over. I'm so sorry!"

Jared wrapped his arms around her, holding her head against his chest as they sobbed. Together they sank to the floor, each holding the other, rocking, seeking some moment of comfort from their agony. "I'm sorry." His voice broke. "I'm so sorry."

"Megan." A voice from behind interrupted them. A nurse put a hand on Megan's shoulder. "Is there anything I can get you or do for you?"

Jared pulled his sister close. His eyes darted up to the nurse. "She's fine. I'll take care of her."

"This is my brother, Jared." Megan nodded as she looked up into her brother's face. "He's Luke's best friend."

"I'm sorry for your loss." The nurse turned at the door to give a sympathetic smile. "There's no rush, but if you would like to spend some time with him before we make the arrangements, you can go in. He's in his room." She closed the door behind her.

Jared stared at the floor, his mind swamped, each emotion twisting into the other.

"Are you ready to see him? Do you still want to?" Megan caressed his hand.

"Yes, but I'm not ready. I can't yet." Sweat formed on his brow. The room felt like it was closing in on him. He felt the urge to throw up. "You go ahead. I need some air."

"I'll go see him then talk to the nurses about what to do next." Megan pulled away. "When you're ready, just ask someone to find us." Hesitating at the door, she looked back at him and shook her head as she left the room.

Jared buried his face in his hands, his body completely numb. He tried to stand. He pulled himself onto chair then shook the tingling out of his legs. Mustering the strength, he jumped up and ran out, paying no attention to the screaming pain in his leg. Once at the car, he dropped onto the hood. Through tear-soaked eyes he saw the moon coming up over the horizon. "This can't be happening." His voice shook as he screamed out. He searched his pockets for the keys to unlock the car, battling to control his composure. Inside, he tuned up the stereo and screamed, slamming his hands against the steering wheel.

The tears seemed to slow. He lay with his head against the steering wheel looking up at the lit rooms of the hospital. "I've got to do it. I have to see him one last time."

#

Jared struggled for breath as he walked through the hallway. He stopped at Luke's door, his feet unwilling to take him inside.

"Can I help you?"

Jared turned to an older nurse. His eyes fixed on her name tag. "Thank you, Sue. I'm looking for a friend's room. Luke Morrison?"

The nurse gripped Jared's hand. "I'm sorry to tell you, but Mr. Morrison passed away."

"I know." Jared couldn't breathe again. He raised his arm, wiping more tears away. "My sister... Megan Morrison... said I could go in to see him."

"Sure. Just let me check." The nurse disappeared into the room then appeared again a moment later. "You can go in." She patted Jared's shoulder as he stepped toward the door. "Just let us know if there's anything you need. Take your time." She pushed the door open.

Jared watched the door close behind him. The room was quiet. Dim light came from the other side of the curtain pulled around a bed. Hand shaking, he reached out, closed his eyes as he pulled the curtain away. Luke's lifeless body lay on the bed. Hand over his mouth, he choked back a scream, forcing himself to resist the urge to run from the room. He moved to the bed, looked down at the man he loved. Eyes wandering over Luke's body, his tentative hand reached out. He touched Luke's face. "You're so cold." The chill coursed through Jared's body. His tears flowed freely, dropping gently into Luke's blond hair. His fingers combed through, chasing the tears away. "I'm here, Luke." He forced a smile, his quavering hand caressing Luke's face. He lingered, longing for Luke's eyes to open. "Goddamn it! It wasn't supposed to be like this!" He slammed his fist into the mattress. Anger momentarily spent, his hand sought Luke's, clutched it, lifted it, and held it to his cheek. "I'm so sorry. I'm so sorry. I didn't mean for it to take so long to come home." Sobbing, he caressed Luke's arm. "Please! Come back to me." He kissed his hand then looked away, Luke's hand held to his chest. "You son-of-a-bitch, you can't be gone." His head dropped, snuggling into Luke's chest for the last time. He clutched the bed clothes, knuckles white. "Don't do this to me."

Hearing footsteps enter the room, he looked up at Megan. She locked eyes with him. Wiping tears away, she leaned against the wall. She cried into a clenched fist then looked away.

Jared pulled closer to Luke, stroking his arm with one hand, his hair with the other. *I wish I could die right along with him.*

"Jared, it's time." Megan put her hand on his shoulder.

Jared brushed it away, never taking his eyes off Luke.

"The people from the funeral home are here. They're ready for him."

"I can't." Jared looked up, reaching for her. "I can't let him go."

Megan put her arm around his head and pulled him close. "I know." She wiped tears from her eyes and rocked him. "We have to let him go."

"Just one more minute... okay?" Jared squeezed her hand. "Please?"

Nodding, Megan moved to the other side of the bed. She picked up Luke's hand and kissed it. "I'll wait over here."

Jared crawled out of the bed, hesitant to let go of his hand. He straightened the collar of Luke's gown, put his forehead against Luke's and whispered. "Goodbye, my love." He kissed him, took one last look, one bracing breath then turned to his sister.

Megan took his arm leading him to the elevator. "I put everything from the waiting room in my car." She pushed the down arrow. "I was hoping you'd stay at my house tonight. I don't want to be alone."

"Of course. Thank you." Jared tried to smile at her. "I didn't think about where I was going to stay. I just took off."

"Jared..." Megan looked down at the floor. "I don't know what to do. I didn't think he'd leave us."

"I know." Jared held her. "We'll figure it out."

THE VIEW FROM A RUSTY TRAIN CAR

THE STEEL REMAINS

The house was silent. Reminders of Luke filled the office where Jared unpacked his overnight bag. He tried to avert his eyes from them. The pictures, the mail on Luke's desk, and notes in his handwriting were everywhere. He put the bag on the floor by the nightstand next to the hospital bed. Staring down at the bed, something near the pillow caught his eye. He reached under it and pulled out his senior picture. Wiping a tear, he put it on the nightstand.

"Can I come in?" Megan stood in the doorway, her eyes still red and swollen.

"I was just coming to check on you." Jared put his arm around her and made her sit on the pull-out couch. "How are you? Can I do anything?"

Megan smiled and patted his leg. "No, thank you." She looked around the room. "This is going to sound ridiculous, but part of me thought I'd see him at his desk when I came in. He spent a lot of time in this room."

"That's not ridiculous at all." Jared laid his head on her shoulder.

"This is for you." She handed him a letter. "Luke asked me to give this to you in case he didn't... get to see you."

Jared's hand trembled, staring at his name in Luke's familiar handwriting. He held his breath thinking about what Luke's last words would be. His stomach was in a knot.

"I'll leave you alone. I think I'm going to take a bath and try to relax a bit before I go to bed. I talked to Mom and Dad and told them. They're on their way home. They were helping move Grandma into an apartment. I'm sure they'll be over in the morning." Megan looked at him over her shoulder as she left.

Jared tried to open the letter, but stopped. *I don't know if I'm ready for this.* Grabbing his jacket, he ran outside. The night sky was clear. It was a cold, quiet fall evening. The letter was firmly grasped in his hand. He leaned against the garage. *I have to know.* Before he could talk himself out of it, he ripped the envelope open. Pulling the letter out, he heard something fall to the ground. He picked it up the small brass key to examine it. Curiosity piqued, he opened the letter.

My dearest Jed,

If you're reading this, then I never got to see you again and wasn't able to say this in person. As sad as it makes me having to do it this way, I want you to know that I understand. You have every right to be angry with me and not want to see me again. I wish I could've fixed things before the end.

I made a decision not too long ago that no matter what, I had to explain things to you and make sure you knew how I felt. When I realized that I was most likely not going to survive this illness, I started to think. It's true that as the end nears you begin to think about everything that's happened in your life - the good times, the people you love, the mistakes you've made. You realize that you can't fix things as much as you wished you could. That's not to say that early on I didn't have the desire to make things right. I did, but you accept that the end is coming and it would be useless. Your attention turns to the people you are leaving behind.

I've done what I can to make sure Megan will be all right. I don't have to worry about her. She's a strong, independent woman who didn't deserve being my caretaker for most of our time together. She also didn't deserve a husband who could never fully commit to the role, or a husband who wondered constantly if he'd made the wrong decisions in his life. She deserved a better man, someone I could never be for her even though I tried and thought I could do it. I only hope that in time she can forgive me for using her to try and satisfy my need to be something I wasn't.

This brings me to you, Jed. I realize as I write this, that this letter may be a horrible thing to do to you. You might even think it's mean-spirited, like a final punch in the gut from beyond the grave. Please know that is not my intention at all. I can't go without knowing that you will someday understand how I truly felt about you. I tell myself that I'd rather be telling you in person, but if history is any indication, I would've chickened out and life would continue as it always has. I tried to be what was expected of me so I didn't hurt anyone. All I succeeded in doing was hurting the person I love most in the world - you.

This comes too late, but as I said before, you're able to come to some understanding when you know death is around the corner and there will be no more chances. I need you to know that I always loved you and continued to love you until my last moment. My deepest sadness is realizing my life will be short and I squandered it, allowing the ignorant expectations of people I don't care about dictate my life. In weak moments, I allow myself to think about what it would've been like being able to share my life with you. I remember making plans in the train car, constantly wondering what would've happened if we would've been able to follow through with them. Thoughts of you kept me going.

I have enclosed a key with this letter. Everything that means anything to me is locked away in the garage. I want you to have them. They're only of value to me and no one else would want them or understand what they mean. I only hope that you take them and keep them as reminders of how much I love you.

I find myself torn between wanting you to walk in one last time so I can say all of this in person and a sort of relief that I won't see you. I know now that I wouldn't be able to say good-bye to you face to face. Knowing that I'm leaving you and how much I've failed you would be too painful. So, before I lose my nerve, Good-bye, my love. I hope you find the person who loves you as much as I do, but who is able to show that love to you and give you the happiness you deserve.

All my love forever,
Luke

Jared wiped his face with the sleeve of his shirt, struggling to catch his breath. He reached for the door to steady himself. The door opened; Jared stumbled across the threshold. The key was clutched tightly in his hand. He felt the wall for a switch, turned on the lights then stared, amazed. A collection of hand crafted train cars lined the shelves of Luke's work shop. Jared reached out, touching each one. "You thought about it too." He caressed them, admiring the craftsmanship and love that went into each one. "It was our place, wasn't it?" Wiping away tears, he noticed light reflecting off the lock on the workbench drawer. The metal matched that of the key. Jared slid the key in the lock, his pulse racing as he turned it and slid the drawer open. A note in Luke's handwriting lay on top. 'For Jared Only – Please Read.' Jared unfolded the paper.

Jed, I bought the train car from Mr. Hanson so save it from the scrap yard. I've given him instructions that upon my death, ownership of it is passed to you.

Underneath the note was a stack of letters held together with a rubber band. He removed it and looked through them. The letters were all addressed to him. One letter was leaned

THE VIEW FROM A RUSTY TRAIN CAR

against the back of the drawer. He picked it up, uncovering another train car. It was an exact replica of the one they used to play in except on the side was painted "J & L Railroad".

As he held it, a sharp piece of metal pierced his hand. He flipped the car over. His heart caught in his throat; the piece of wall where Luke had drawn their initials was mounted on the back. He traced them with his finger.

"*L Loves J – Forever*".

Feeling like his heart was being ripped from his chest, he collapsed on the stool behind him, clutching the train car.

IF LOVE WERE ALL

Megan scurried away from the window as Jared turned off the lights and headed toward the house. She sat at the kitchen table, unable to look at him as he entered.

Jared stared at the letter in front of her.

"I got one too." Megan looked at the train car and letters in his hand. "Are you all right?"

Taking a seat across from her, Jared put them on the table. "Am I all right? What about you?" He reached for her hand.

"No!" Megan shook her head, pulling her hand away. "Don't do this. Don't... pity me. I don't know why I'm acting shocked. I found one of yours awhile ago. I wasn't sure what it all meant. I needed to know so I'd read them... all of them. I knew where he kept them." She stood, moving to the kitchen window. "It's not a huge surprise, Jared!" She turned to face him, giving a weak laugh, unable to stop the sneer on her lips. "I've always suspected. I just didn't want to believe it."

"What?"

"I was such a fool. I remember seeing you guys a couple times holding each other. I told myself it was nothing. You were just close friends. Then after you left and he was sick, he was so distant. He was always depressed... lost in thought, you know? Then I found the letters. He never stopped trying to find you." Clenching her jaw, she tried to keep herself from crying. "I knew. I guess I've always known."

"What do you mean you've always known?" Jared's voice was measured, dripping with acid.

Her hand clenched into a fist. She wanted to hurt him as much as she hurt.

"Answer me!"

"No! I don't want to talk about it now!"

Jared stared at her then rushed into the hallway. "No. Wait." He appeared in the doorway. "If you've always known, why did you marry him? You knew how I felt about him!"

"Because I didn't know how he felt! Not then."

"Why didn't you divorce him, let him go when you did find out?"

Megan leaned against the wall. She hung her head, staring at the floor. "I asked him if he wanted a divorce and he said no." She looked up at him. "He never knew that I figured it out and I didn't know what to say to him about it."

"You didn't need him to do it. You could've divorced him!" Jared slammed the door jamb with his hand. "He might have come back to me."

"Why, Jared?" Megan ran to him, standing in his face. "You never answered one of his letters. You never called him."

"I can't believe this! I can't believe you did this to me!" Jared stormed out of the room.

Grabbing his shoulder she turned him, finger pointed in his face. "Don't you dare make me the villain in this! He was my husband, Jared! I loved him. Was I just supposed to push him away? Just let him go? If he wanted to, he could've left!"

"He would've never left you! You know that." Jared pushed her arm down. "You didn't give a damn about him!" He ran to his room.

"Jared, if I knew for sure he wanted to leave, I would have let him go!" She stood in the doorway, watching him pack.

"After he got sick, I had to stay with him. He needed someone to be with him. Do you think it was easy living this last year watching him die and not being able to do a damn thing about it except help him walk or make him food? All the time knowing that I was just a pathetic substitute for you?"

Jared threw his overnight bag onto the bed. "I can't do this! I've got to get out of here!" He closed his suitcase.

"Where are you going?" Megan grabbed his shoulders.

"Leave me alone." Jared pushed his way into the hall.

"You haven't changed at all, have you?" Megan crossed her arms, walking toward him. She yelled as he opened the door. "That's right, just run away like you've done your whole life."

"What is that supposed to mean?" Jared turned, glaring at her.

"Maybe if you'd stayed and fought for him, things would've turned out differently. You ever thought about that?" Shaking her head, she chuckled. "He disappears, so you run off to Seattle. You find out he's getting married, you run off and head across the world. You run at the slightest bit of trouble. You've never taken one bit of responsibility for what happens to you. This is just as much your fault as anyone's."

"Are you kidding me?" The luggage dropped to the floor. Jared marched up to her. "I tried to stop you from getting married. Remember?"

"You told me I shouldn't marry him! That's it. No explanation. Nothing."

"No one would let me talk to you!"

"Fine." Megan chuckled, leaning against the wall. "What do you want from me? I'm sorry? Okay. I'm sorry. I thought it would all work out... somehow. We talked about you before we got married. When I asked him about how he felt knowing you were in love with him, he said he loved you in some way and he wished he could be that person for you, but he couldn't. I believed him. He talked about having a family and I let myself believe he didn't feel for you like you did for him." She put her head in her hands. "When I found out how he really felt, I thought if I stayed married to him, you'd be able to see each other. He'd get better, you'd come home once in a while and you'd both be happy to see each other. You could stay close friends and everything would be fine. Why do you think I tried so hard to get hold of you? I wanted you in each other's lives."

"Are you kidding me? How Meg? How was it supposed to work out? What exactly did you imagine? We'd all get together for Christmas and New Year's. You'd look the other way while Luke and I would sneak off for a quick fuck and everyone would live happily ever?"

Rage shot through her. Megan slapped him across the face. "I didn't know about any of that! I loved him and I wanted what was best for him. I never ran away even though I might have had every right to. I was always there for him. That's more than you can say!" Pushing him aside, she walked down the hall. She stopped, turning back to him. "If this is too much for you, go ahead and leave, Jared. I took care of your lover alone; I sure as hell can bury him alone." She turned away, flinching as the door slammed behind her.

As she turned into the kitchen, her eyes fell on the stack of letters on the table. She sat, laid her head on her arm, staring at the train car with Luke and Jared's initials.

#

Another set of headlights flashed though Megan's room. She jumped up, straining to see if Jared was coming back. These lights didn't pass like all the others. She looked at the clock. *2:20 a.m. I have to find him.* She threw on her robe and ran to the door. She jumped, seeing Jared standing on the other side. "You scared me."

"Is it all right if I still stay here?" Jared wiped his eyes. "I'll understand if you say no."

"Of course you can." Megan grabbed his hand, pulling him into the room. "Jared, listen. I'm so sorry for what I said!"

"No! Don't apologize." Jared shook his head. "You're absolutely right. I'm a selfish asshole. I always have been. I'm sorry for what I said. I have no excuse for it."

"I was wrong to talk to you like that." Megan sat beside him, taking his hand.

"Sweetie, it's about time someone did. Someone should have done that years ago. I've lived my life like a spoiled brat."

Megan smirked, raising an eyebrow. "I won't argue with you."

"I don't know why I said some of those things... blaming you for this mess." Jared looked at her, lip quivering. "I'm so sorry."

"There's enough blame to go around." Megan kissed his cheek. "No one was innocent in this. You were right. I could have left him. He could have left. You could have been here. We're just upset and taking it out on each other. The fact is it didn't work out for any of us."

"I did love him."

Megan put her arm around him, rocking. She stroked his hair. "I know, Honey. I know. I did too."

"I know you did, Meg. I was so busy thinking of myself that I didn't think about how you felt. You lost your husband."

"We both lost him." Megan patted his knee then went to the closet. "I'm just glad you came back. I was wrong. I can't do this without you."

"What can I do to help?"

Megan searched through Luke's clothes. "I have a meeting with the funeral home tomorrow morning. I'm supposed to pick out clothes for him."

"Meg?" Jared put his hand on her shoulder. "Can I go with you?"

"I was hoping you would." She wrapped her arms around him. Wiping tears away, she turned back to the closet. "Help me figure out what he should wear?" After looking through a few more, she stopped. "Jared?"

"What is it?"

"While you were gone, I was thinking and it occurred to me – I didn't know him. All of our conversations were about his health and what was the next course of action. We never talked about the little things, like his favorite music or his favorite color. Did you ever talk about things like that with him?"

A smile came to Jared's face as he stared into the closet. "It won't come as much of a surprise to you, but we spent a lot of time talking about me and what I wanted to talk about." He laughed. "But, yeah, we did talk about things like that."

"Will you tell me things about him?"

Jared put an arm around her. "Well, he loved any music that had a strong beat to it. He loved dance music. His favorite color was orange."

"Orange? Seriously?"

"Yeah, I didn't get it either." Jared sat on the edge of the bed. "He loved sports of all kinds. We were complete opposites about that."

"That I did know." Megan rolled her eyes. "He watched anything and everything that came on T.V." Her hands stopped. She looked at Jared, a smile on his face as he stared at the wall. She sat on the bed next to him, wrapping her arm in his. "Was he romantic with you?"

"Not on his own. I did a lot of pouting and hinting, but every once in a while he'd surprise me." Jared laid his head on her shoulder. "How about with you?"

"Not really, but he was always very sweet. He was one of the kindest people I ever met." She noticed a sober expression on his face as he stared into the closet.

Jared went to the closet and pulled out a pair of jeans that were hanging askew. He took them off the hanger and held them to his chest.

"Are you all right?" Megan put her hand on his shoulder.

"Do you think he could still fit these?"

"Those old things! They're worn out." Megan laughed, shaking her head then stared at them. "I tried a hundred times to get rid of those, but they would always end up back in here. I just gave up. He wore them whenever he'd go for his walks or work out in the garage on his projects."

"Can he wear them?"

"What? Why?"

"Please?"

Megan could tell by the look on his face that it was important. "Sure, if that's what you want."

"Thank you!" He folded them and placed them on the bed.

"No one will see them anyway. We'll put this shirt on him." Megan pulled an orange dress shirt from the closet. "I always wondered about it."

Jared laughed, laying it over the jeans. "Perfect."

Megan saw him yawn, his eyes getting heavy. "You better get to bed. We have to be there early... and don't forget Mom and Dad will be coming over right away, I'm sure. I know how much you're looking forward to that."

Jared raised his eyebrow. "That should be fun."

"I forgot to tell you that I got hold of Susie earlier. She's devastated, of course. She's trying to get a flight home as soon as possible. She was so glad to hear that you were with me. She's looking forward to seeing you." Megan led him to the door.

"I was going to ask about her. It'll be great to see her." Jared kissed Megan on the cheek. "You get some sleep too. It's going to be a long couple of days."

Megan looked down at the jeans then back to Jared. "They were yours, weren't they?"

"What?"

"The jeans... you gave them to him, didn't you?"

"Yeah, I did."

"I thought so." She hugged him. "See you in the morning. Love you."

"Love you too. Good night." Jared closed the door behind him.

Megan crawled into bed and turned off the light. She stared at the ceiling then started to giggle and rolled over to look at the picture of Luke on her nightstand. "Really, Luke? Orange?" Grabbing his pillow, she snuggled it, brushed a tear away then closed her eyes. "He came back to us, Sweetie. I wish you were here for him."

STRUCK BY LIGHTNING

Jared looked out the window, chewing on a fingernail as he waited for his parents' arrival. His stomach was in knots. *What in the hell am I going to say to them?*

"I'm surprised they're not here yet."

He jumped at the sound of Megan's voice. "What? I was just checking the weather. Nice out, isn't it?"

"It's going to be fine." Megan put her arms around him. "Mom's beside herself knowing you're here. I feel sorry for Dad. I can hear her, 'Drive faster... slow down... drive faster.' He's going to be a wreck when he gets here!"

Jared couldn't help laughing. "No kidding!" He looked out the window at a passing car, relaxing again when it turned out not to be them. "It's going to be so awkward."

"They love you. That's all that matters. You'll figure it out." Megan kissed him on the head then walked away.

Another car came toward the house. This time it was Candace and Michael. He held his breath, seeing his mother jump out of the car and run up the sidewalk. *They've aged. How long was I gone?* He stepped to the side, his mother on a collision course with the door.

It flew open and Candace called out. "Meg?" Her jaw dropped seeing Jared standing in the hallway. Hands to her face, tears rolling down her cheeks, she ran to him, holding him tight. "Oh, my God! I can't believe it! It's you! You're here."

"Hi, Mom." Jared whispered, voice broken. He pulled away, took her hands and looked at her. "You look wonderful!"

"You look thin! Are you all right? Are you sick? How are you?"

He couldn't help chuckling. "Mom, I'm fine. Just a little tired. How are you?"

"We're fine, aren't we Mike?" Getting no response, she looked over her shoulder then out the door.

Mike stood on the sidewalk watching the traffic, smoking his pipe.

Jared stood behind his mother, his hands on her shoulders. "It looks like he's really excited to see me."

"Jared, please? Don't start that. Not now." She shook her head, turning to him. "Where's Megan? How is she?"

"In the kitchen. She's strong. She's going to be fine."

"I'll go find her." About to walk down the hall, Candace stopped, turning back. "Go out and talk to him, Jared. He's not sure where to start." She kissed him on the cheek then went to the kitchen.

Jared watched Mike for a moment, trying to chase away the feeling of wanting to scream at him. The memories of their last few encounters were ever present. *It's for Mom.* He walked outside and stood beside his father. "Hi, Dad. It's good to see you."

"Jared." Mike kept his gaze fixed on the distance.

They stood in silence. Jared looked at him then at the ground. "How are you?"

"Good."

"Fine. Sorry to bother you." Jared shook his head then walked back to the house.

"What do you want me to say, Jared?" Mike finally turned to him. "It's good to see you? You look good? All that shit?"

"Actually, I didn't expect anything from you." Jared's hands and teeth were clenched.

"You haven't talked to us in years. We didn't know if you were alive or dead most of the time. You just vanished." Mike repacked his pipe. "Sorry if I don't feel like making small talk. I'm so damn mad at you that I'm afraid to say anything. I'm not sure how nice it'll be."

Jared walked to his father, hands on hips. "That's funny. I left because that's what you wanted. Remember?"

Finger wagging, Mike stood face to face with his son. "That's not what I wanted and you know it."

"Really? Because that's what I seem to remember you yelling as I lay on the sidewalk outside the church." Jared turned and walked into the house, door slamming behind him.

Mike followed, stopping him in the entryway. "We all tried to get hold of you... your mom, Meg, Luke, but nothing... never a word from you."

"Oh yes, Dad. The messages from you were so warm and cuddly. I could feel the love oozing from your voice! It made me want to call you right back. But you know what? You're right about one thing: I should've talked to someone."

"You're damn right! Now you're back here pretending like you care. You don't have to pretend for me." Mike pushed past him, disappearing into the kitchen.

"Wait one minute!" Jared followed. "I'm not taking the blame for this. You had my address. I sure didn't see you busting down my door. The planes fly in both directions, you know."

"You made it perfectly clear that you wanted nothing to do with us."

"Funny! You did the same to me." Jared looked at Megan. "I'm sorry, Meg. This should've waited, but here it is." He walked to her, took her hand. "You see, Meg, all of my faults that we talked about last night; the running away from things, the not taking responsibility..."

Megan gripped his arm. "Jared, we talked about this. I said I was sorry."

"I know, but you were right." Jared patted her hand, looking at his father. "I learned from the master."

Mike stared at him. "What are you implying?"

"I'm not implying. I'm saying it. I learned it all from you!" Jared turned to Megan. "I take responsibility for my faults and failings. If you want to list them, I'll start it for you, but I assure you we don't have time for all of them."

"Jared, please stop this." Candace sat at the table. She put her head in her hands.

"I can't, Mom." Jared put a hand on her shoulder. "It's about time we had a real discussion. I'm tired of pretending."

Mike slammed his hands against the table. "If you have something to say then say it!"

"I'm saying that yes, I've made mistakes... lots of them... and I take full responsibility. I think it's about time you did too."

Mike turned away, staring out the kitchen window.

"Yes, I stayed away. I'm sure to anyone who would listen to you, it was all my fault. I was a selfish bastard." Jared stood behind him. "Did you happen to tell Megan and Luke what you told me at their wedding? That you didn't care if you ever saw me again?"

Megan looked at Mike. "Dad?"

"I was angry!" Mike dropped his head, leaning over the sink. "I had every reason to be!"

Standing beside Mike, Jared stared at his face, leaning into him. "The truth is you weren't just mad that I crashed the wedding. You were still mad about finding out I was gay, weren't you? You made that clear when you came to see me that last day in treatment... the day you stormed out of the office when I told you I wasn't going to change."

"Treatment? What are you talking about?" Megan sat next to her mother, putting her arm around her. Candace sobbed, unable to look at anyone.

"That wasn't talked about either, was it?" Jared crossed his arms, glanced at Megan. "Your father made sure that I was put into treatment. He got a court order. Now, I'm not saying I didn't need it or that it was a bad thing. It wasn't, but he wanted me there for a different reason. He thought they'd 'fix' me."

"You know very well why you were in there! It was recommended by the doctor! You know that!" Mike's face turned red, his hands grasped the edge of the counter.

"You mean this?" Jared raised his sleeve, pushing his wrist in Mike's face.

Megan rushed to him, holding his arm. She looked into his eyes, tears streaming. "Jared? What is it? You didn't?"

"I bet he never told you about that either." Jared pulled his sleeve back down. "Did you ever wonder what was going through my head when I did that? Whose voice I heard? It was yours, calling me 'sick' and a 'pervert', not caring if you ever saw me again. That played over and over in my head."

"Stop!" Mike yelled, turning away, his face in his hands. "I've heard enough!"

Teeth gritted, Jared stood over his shoulder. "You must've been so disappointed to hear that I'd made it out of Iraq alive."

Mike grabbed Jared by the collar, threw him against the wall. "Yes, I couldn't stand knowing what you were, but it's not what you think. I was scared. I watch the news. I saw what happened to gay people... what happened to that Matthew Shepard. I was terrified thinking someone could do that to you. I was desperate. No father wants to think that could happen to their child." His grip tightened as a sob rose out of him. "I just hoped you knew me better than that. I never stopped loving you. Never! When I heard that you were taken prisoner... I replayed those same words in my head and... I hated myself, knowing I had something to do with you being there."

Candace ran to them, putting a hand on each.

Mike took Jared's face in his hands. "I thought I'd die when I saw that video of you. I saw the terror in Luke's eyes, how frightened your mother and Megan were and I couldn't do anything about it. I was helpless. I'm not supposed to be helpless. I watched the video over and over." The sobbing took over. "I tried to memorize your face, thinking it was the last time I would ever see it." His hands slammed against the wall. He looked into Jared's eyes and threw his arms around him. "I'm so sorry. I didn't mean to make you stay away."

"I thought about all of you the whole time." Jared held his father and cried. "I love you."

"I love you too, Son." Mike patted Jared's back then left the room. Megan followed.

Candace held onto Jared as he slid down the wall to the floor. She lifted his head, wiping the tears from his eyes. "You're not my little boy anymore, are you? You've grown up. I never thought I'd see the day that you'd stand up for yourself, especially to your dad."

"I'm sorry I did that right now, but I'm not sorry it happened. I needed to hear him... of all people... say that to me today." Jared grabbed her hand and leaned against her.

Candace held his head to her chest, rocking him. "I wish you could've seen Luke. You needed that too. So did he. He missed you, you know."

"I should've been here." With the help of the wall, he forced himself back to his feet.

"You didn't know. None of us knew. We thought this surgery would be like the others."

"That's not what I mean. I should've been here sooner. I should've been here in time to see him." Jared shook his head. "I didn't tell Megan, but I sat in the airport for hours. I didn't know what to do. I just sat there. I was afraid to see him, afraid of what he'd say. I was afraid of what to say to all of you, so I sat there. Now I'll never see him again; another in a long list of stupid mistakes." Guilt chewing at him, he collapsed into a chair at the table.

"I'm so sorry." Candace handed him a tissue. She wrapped her arms around him from behind. "This isn't the homecoming I wanted for you."

Jared held her hand, kissed it. "Despite everything... I'm glad I'm here."

NON JE NE REGRETTE RIEN

A smiling picture of Luke sat next to the mirror on the dresser. Jared looked at himself one more time, adjusting the orange tie he'd bought earlier that day for the funeral. "Well, Luke? How do I look?" Seeing the tie at the thrift store, he knew it was right, remembering their bowties and cummerbunds from prom. The front door slammed for the tenth time that morning. "Please don't let them ask so many questions. I don't feel like talking." He took one last deep breath and headed into the living room.

Aunt Grace caught him as soon as he appeared. She threw her arms around him, crying. "I heard you were home. I couldn't believe it until now. God, how we've missed you."

Jared gave in. It was clear she had no intention of letting him go. "I missed you too." He felt a punch in the arm. Looking up, he saw Uncle Rick walk past, smiling. "Good to see you, too, Uncle Rick." It was more of a greeting than he'd ever given him. Each family member took their turn hugging him, thanking him for coming home. His lip trembled. No one asked questions; they just welcomed him home. *I've never given them the credit they deserve. They're good people.*

The doorbell rang. Megan hollered for someone to answer it. Jared excused himself and went to the door. A chill surged through his body as he opened it.

"Well, well, well. Look who it is." Sarcasm dripped from Ellen's lips as she pushed her way in.

Everyone fell silent. They stared at her, shifting nervously in their seats.

"You must feel pretty proud of yourself. You finally succeeded." Ellen filled a glass of punch. "I told Luke that one of them would be his ruin. Either that little pervert would turn him gay and give him AIDS or that whore he married would destroy him."

Candace jumped from the couch. "Ellen, you were invited here because he was your son. If you're going to make trouble, you can leave right now!"

"I have every right to be here." Ellen stood in her face. "I just wanted to see Megan and congratulate her."

"How dare you." Megan screamed, appearing from the kitchen.

"Give us a break. The whole town knows about you... you and Matt. There's no need to play the mourning wife. He couldn't die fast enough for you, could he?"

"That's enough!" Jared grabbed her arm, pulling her away from Megan. "Get the hell out of my sister's house! You're not welcome here."

"This is my son's house, too."

"Your son's?" Megan walked up to her, snickering. "You mean the guy who despised you? The one who wanted nothing to do with you? You have a lot of nerve."

Candace ran to Megan, pulling her back. "Sweetheart, no. It's not worth it."

"Do you have any idea what was wrong with him? Where were you when he needed help? Nowhere...because he couldn't stand the sight of you."

Ellen turned to Jared, pushing a finger into his chest. "I've blamed a lot of people for this, but you're the one who caused all of the problems. You might not have killed him, but you sure as hell ruined him. You had him so brainwashed. He was so confused and angry at himself that he didn't know what to do. You might as well have put a gun to his head."

"That's enough!" Mike boomed from the back door.

"How many people are you going to destroy before you're satisfied? You should all be killed." Ellen slapped Jared.

"Leave him alone." A voice bellowed from behind her. Derek stood in the doorway. Susie watched from over his shoulder.

Ellen whipped around. "Who the hell are you?"

Pushing Ellen away, Derek walked to Jared, putting an arm around him. "The better question is who in the hell are you?"

"Luke's mother."

"Really?" Derek grinned. "Luke's mother? The mother who sent him away? Tormented him? Who wasn't even invited to his wedding? I've heard all about you. Mother is the last thing I would call you. Ignorant, intolerant bitch would top the list."

Ellen lunged at him, striking at whoever was in the way.

Susie ran in, restraining her. "That's enough! Get in the car!" She tossed her mother toward the door.

"You can't speak to me..."

"Mom, shut up. You and I have a few things to discuss." Susie turned to Mike. "If you wouldn't mind escorting her to the car, I'll be there in a second."

Mike and Derek stepped forward. Ellen shot them a warning look. "Don't touch me." She spun around then walked out the door. Mike and Derek followed her into the driveway.

Susie turned to Jared, pointing, eyebrow raised. "And you? We'll talk later. I'll find you after the funeral. I had to learn everything from that guy. Nice guy, by the way. You know how to pick them." She hugged Megan. "Don't worry. I'll come back alone. After I'm through with her, she won't be in any shape to want to be out in public. I'll see you later."

"Stay here. You're more than welcome." Megan reached out to her.

"I may need to take you up on that offer tonight." Susie winked as she left.

Pulling Jared close, Megan pointed out the door. "Derek? I thought you broke up."

Jared shrugged, watching the commotion in the driveway. "Wait a minute. She said Matt? I mean, THE Matt?"

"Don't say it." Megan rolled her eyes. "And take that smirk off your face." She hit him in the arm as she left.

Jared watched as Derek and his father pointed in the distance. *Why is he here? I can't deal with this today.* He went out to the patio, sat at the table, his head in his hands. The door creaked behind him.

"I called him." Candace leaned against the doorway.

"What? How...? I don't understand!"

"We talked a lot when you were in the hospital." Candace sat across from him. "He called a couple times a day."

"He told me."

"Even when you were better and refused to talk to us, he called. It got to where I could hardly wait for his calls." Candace crossed her hands, her face blushing. "When I talked to Megan, she told me how devastated you were. She was worried about you, so I called him. He'd given me his cell phone number." She looked to Jared, a guilty expression on her face.

Jared didn't know what to say.

"I know I should've talked to you first, but I asked him to come. When I told him that Luke had passed away, he told me he was on his way."

Jared looked at her. "Did he tell you anything else?" He glanced over her shoulder, keeping watch for Derek. "That we aren't together anymore?"

"Well, we did talk a bit about that and..."

"Wait. Stop. Just stop." Jared got up from the table. "I don't need this today. I have enough to think about."

"He loves you, Jared. He was horrified when I told him what had happened. He knew how upset you'd be. He started to cry, saying that he should've been here for you."

Jared stood, started to leave through the back.

"Don't do this." Candace reached out, grabbing his arm. "Don't run away again." She wrapped her arms around him. "You were lucky enough to have someone love you as much as Luke, but he's gone. It was never meant to be."

Tears poured from Jared. "Who told you?" He turned to her, his heart pounding in his chest.

"No one." Candace smiled. "They didn't have to. I could see it in his eyes. Every time we'd talk about you, a smile spread across his face. Then realization would set in and he'd look like the world had been taken away from him." She held his face, looking into Jared's eyes. "Derek just wants a chance... a real chance. He loves you so much, Jared. You have to stop pushing people away. You're clinging to a dream. It was never going to happen, Honey."

Jared opened his mouth to speak, but only a cry came out. He ran, taking the path behind the garage that led into the woods.

He stopped. Side aching, he tried to catch his breath. He had no idea how long he'd been running, but his leg was letting him know it was enough. He fell to the ground and reached for the pack of cigarettes he'd put in his pocket. Treatment had taught him to keep them around for times when he felt stressed and wanted a drink. This definitely called for one. He took a long drag on the cigarette, inhaling deeply. He felt his body relax as he exhaled, feeling like he'd just escaped the firing squad.

A bench surrounded by a small garden, sat just off the path. The earth in front of it was well worn from where feet had rested. *Luke.* He sat down, leaning forward against his knees. It was the perfect view of everything that had meant something to the both of them; the baseball diamond, the swings, the weird flying saucer-shaped jungle gym, the trees where the fort had been, and the rusty train car. Jared put a clenched fist against his mouth, blocking the sob that wanted to come out. *Luke, I need your help. I don't know how to get through this. Tell me what to do.* He heard the sound of twigs snap behind him.

"Jared!"

Throwing his cigarette to the ground, he wiped his eyes then turned. "Hi."

"Everyone's worried about you." Derek slipped on the path, but caught himself on a branch. "I know you don't want me here, but I had to come. I couldn't let you go through this alone." He stumbled to the bench. "It kills me that you're hurting. I had no idea this would happen. I didn't know he was that sick."

"Join the club." Jared stood and took a few steps down the path. "Well, nothing says closure like a funeral, huh?"

"I am so sorry. I can only imagine what you must feel."

Jared turned to him, his hands locked behind his head. "Why on earth do you even care?"

"Why do I care?" Derek looked him in the eyes. "I'm sure you don't want to hear this, but... I love you."

"Why is that, Derek? All I've ever done is push you away and hurt you. I'd make promises to you then run back to him. I've treated you like shit!"

"You were in love with someone else. I get that." Derek smiled. "You're right; I'm a glutton for punishment. I have no idea why I kept taking you back."

Jared bristled, hearing the word 'kept'. He looked down at the ground and kicked the leaves.

"I wish I could've met him." Derek sat on the bench, looking into the distance. "He sure was hard to compete with."

"What?" Jared turned, his eyebrows furrowed.

"All the time we were together, whether you knew it or not, you compared me to Luke. Well, not Luke so much as the guy he became in your mind."

"What in the hell does that mean?"

THE VIEW FROM A RUSTY TRAIN CAR

"I did some thinking on my way here. Actually, I did a lot of thinking, then I somehow met Susie at the airport. She was looking for a ride. We talked all the way. She cleared up some questions I had. I think I finally understand." Derek's hands in his pockets, he examined the path under his feet. "You compared me to someone who didn't even exist. The Luke you had in your head wasn't the real Luke. You hadn't talked to him in years. You had no idea what he was doing or who he'd become. You invented him. You made him into the person you wanted him to be. How could I compete with that? Luke himself wouldn't have been able to compete with that."

"I loved him, whoever he was." Jared laughed. "God! How stupid could I be?"

"No, no. Not stupid." Derek put his hands on Jared's shoulders. "Admirable."

"I'm an idiot who's managed to screw up everything that could've been good in his life! You have a twisted idea of admirable. It's pathetic."

"Isn't that what we all wish for? For someone to love us that much?" Derek lifted his chin to look into his eyes. "You couldn't help it any more than I could. Why do you think I tried so damn hard with you? Being rejected by someone time and again is not my idea of fun. As corny as this is going to sound, the heart wants what it wants. It's corny, but true. I love you. There's no rational explanation why. Does there have to be?"

Jared held himself, trembling.

"I know. You want to be alone. I give up. I had to make sure you were all right. I'm still moving my stuff out of the apartment. I'll be out by the time you get back." Derek started to leave, but turned back. "He's gone. I am truly sorry about that, but, it's over. It's been over for a long time. You need to move on, let go of everything. You can't spend your life trying to relive the past. Someday you need to let someone in again, to let them love you. You need to find someone you can love in return." He shook his head. "It's time, Jed."

Jared looked up, his heart racing. "What did you just say to me?"

"I... I said it was time to move on."

"No! What did you call me?" Jared ran to him.

"Jed? Sorry. I called you Jed."

"Why?" Jared held Derek's face. "Why did you call me that?"

"I don't know. It just came out. It's stupid, I know."

"Where did you hear that name?"

"It was my name for you." Derek's face turned red. "When I'd write notes about you or talk about you, I called you Jed. Who cares? It's silly. I'm sorry. I never told you because I knew you would think it was stupid."

"No, no. It's not." Jared pulled their heads together. "I love it."

"I love you." Derek hugged him.

"Thank you." Jared looked up at the sky and winked. "I love you, too." Hands shaking, he held Derek's face, looking into his eyes.

"What?" A concerned look came to Derek's face.

Jared took his hand, leading him up the path. "Can you stay a little longer? I'd rather not face the viewing and the funeral alone."

"If that's what you want, of course."

"When this is all over... can we talk? About us?" Jared stopped, turned to him, hand firmly gripped in his. "I know I have issues. I'm crazy, actually; completely and utterly mentally ill. I can't accept success, or happiness. I'm self-destructive, but you already know that. I've told you more than once that you should run far and fast, but... if you can find it in your heart to try one more time; I promise I'll work hard. Can we give it one last shot? I'll understand if you say no. I will." His head dropped. "I know you have no reason to believe me, but I want you to know that I never meant to hurt you. I do love you. I just..."

"Jed." Derek put his finger to Jared's lips and kissed him on the cheek. "Yes."

"You're amazing." Jared pulled him into a kiss. "You know that? You're crazy, but amazing." He put his head on Derek's shoulder. "I don't want you to move out. That is, unless you want to. I'd understand if you already have a place and want some space away from me."

"Now you can question my mental stability. I lied." Derek caressed his cheeks. "I haven't packed a thing. I was waiting for you to come back. I was going to do my damnedest to get you back. I wasn't ready to let you go."

Jared kissed him, holding him close.

"Truth is, we both might have to move out of the apartment. I almost forgot." Derek reached inside of his coat, pulled out a folded magazine, and handed it to Jared.

Jared unrolled it. "Oh, my God! It's *Time*. That's... that's us. We're on the cover!"

"This is the other reason I came. They called two days ago. They want us back to work. They're special assignment positions, but he said it could become something permanent."

"I can't believe it." The magazine shook as Jared tried to read it. Throwing it down, he threw his arms around Derek.

"They want us to fly out next Tuesday." Derek studied his face. "Is that too soon?"

"Next Tuesday?" Jared's thoughts turned to Megan. "They'll be fine. I say, let's do it!"

Derek put his arms around him, picked him up and took him into a long kiss.

Jared glanced back toward the horizon to take in one more look. About to start up the path, some movement caught his attention. His gaze fixed on the train car. He motioned for Derek to look.

The hatch of the train car opened. A boy of about eleven crawled out, looked around, a smile on his face. He put his hand down the hatch, guiding another little boy to the top. He appeared eyes wide, unsteady on his feet. He lost his footing, but the other boy caught him, helping him get situated on the top then pointed toward the tree line in the west. The other boy laid his head on his shoulder, holding onto him.

Don't worry, Luke. It's going to stay right where it is. Jared grabbed Derek's hand, listening to echoes of their laughter being carried on the wind. He felt a smile form on his face as he watched the boys put an arm around each other, settling in close together. He pulled Derek close, remembering two other little boys who'd come time after time to enjoy the view from a rusty train car.

THE VIEW FROM A RUSTY TRAIN CAR

THIS LONG TRIP TO MYSELF

"Ladies and gentlemen of this senate committee, thank you for your invitation to speak to you today. I know the only reason I was invited was because my story received some attention after being published. Please understand... I want this to be clear... I don't think what I've told you is important because it's my story... it's important because it's one story of thousands that continue to happen throughout the world every single day. The fact that I'm not the only one who's been through this is of no consolation."

The vibe of the room was strange. I couldn't read it. It's not that people weren't listening. I felt the pressure, having one last chance to make an impression and to make the whole experience worthwhile. Looking over my shoulder, I saw Derek smiling. He seemed proud of me. It was exactly what I needed.

"I know this vote seems inconsequential to you on a personal level. You think it doesn't affect you on a daily basis. I suspect most of you will be voting along party lines, but when you vote on asking the people of this country to change the constitution to make sure that the gays and lesbians of this country are never allowed the right to marry, understand that it does matter. We may be a minority... one who won't affect whether you are re-elected or not, but we are citizens of this country who you represent.

"Bear with me. I want to give a history lesson. This will be argued about from here on in, but the truth of the matter is that marriage was invented as a legal institution. It was not invented by religion. Religions adopted it. Living in this land of religious freedom, I want to tell you that I am not, nor have I ever, pushed that religious institutions should be forced to perform marriages between loving gay and lesbian couples if it is against their teachings. It is their right not to, just as it should be their right to do it if they so choose. Those who want to... those who see their God and their beliefs as being inclusive of all forms of love, are denied the right to celebrate and affirm our relationships. Not to mention it is a non-issue for those who don't. We all know that imposing such a directive on religious institutions would be unconstitutional, but it's not about that. It's about our legal rights as citizens, not special rights as some would want you to believe, but the rights of committed, loving couples who've already chosen to share their lives together. For those of you who want to argue that we are already sharing our lives so you don't need to worry about it, you are shamelessly unaware of the legal problems that exist for us. They are issues that our heterosexual counterparts take for granted. They don't have the fear of not knowing if they will be allowed to be with their loved ones when they are dying, or whether or not their loved one will inherit their property. Many tax and government benefits, and medical benefit issues are automatically protected and given after marriage. It's about being treated fairly." I dropped my eyes to the desk, struggling to get in everything I wanted to say, so many things rushing to my mind. I looked at each of the Senators before speaking again. "Your vote isn't inconsequential. There are people... kids... out there listening to you, listening to what you're saying and watching what you're going to do. You will either choose to continue having kids grow up in fear by reaffirming the ignorance and hatred of people around them or you will vote to affirm the dignity and rights of loving couples, giving them the ability to truly share their life together. The constitution was written to protect our rights, not take them away. Voting to approve this would be voting to legalize discrimination. Please consider the consequences of those actions."

Realizing I had nothing more to say, I became aware of the cameras around me. I stared into the closest one. "To those of you listening, I know you. I know your struggles and your fears. You are not alone. You are understood. You are loved. No one... not even the people of this Congress, can take away your dignity. Hold on. It will get better... and it's worth it." I turned and winked at Derek.

I stood and took one last look at the Senators. "Thank you, again, for inviting me to be here. I leave you with one last thought. I know this is a tough decision for some of you. I hope some of you think about what's at stake with your vote. Some of you were on the fence and I hope I got through. For those of you who've made up your minds in support of this constitutional amendment, if you're doing it out of religious reasons, I want you to remember that Jesus never instructed you to hate in his name. It shows up nowhere in the New Testament. Are you really comfortable showing up, as you may believe, at the final judgment telling whoever meets you that you hated in his name? If you can do that, then you should vote for this amendment. If not, I ask you to reconsider what you believe about your faith, to consider, no matter what religion, we were called to love. Thank you for your time."

I turned to see Derek rushing to me. I locked my hand in his, leading him to the huge oak doors that led to freedom. The room behind us erupted into murmurs. A gavel pounded, the speaker calling the room to order.

Derek closed the doors then turned to me. He took me into an embrace. "I'm so proud of you." He held my face in his hands. "Are you all right, Jed?"

Pulling him close, I kissed him then looked into his beautiful eyes. "Yeah, it's worth it."

The sounds of reporters rushing toward us were deafening. I looked up at Derek. "Well, here we go."

Derek winked, wrapping an arm around me, the other held up shielding me from the onslaught. "We've been through worse. Don't worry; I've got you." I gave him a smile, grabbing his hand as we were surrounded, barraged by bright lights and questions. For the first time, I didn't want to run. Derek was standing by my side. It was time to stand up. It was time to fight.

THE END

ABOUT THE AUTHOR

DeeJay Arens resides in north central Minnesota. Besides writing, his creative outlets include theater and filmmaking as part owner of a production company. He also works as a vocational vendor and Member/Owner services manager for a natural food cooperative.